Dog Maiden Moons

Bobbie Groth

DEDICATION

For Jenna, the one I started this for, and for Marena and Ingrid and all the wild girls who grew up at the house on Hawthorne

In memory of Glenmoor's Silver Bairn 1998-2012
Photo: Bobbie Groth

Cover photos: Newgrange: Bobbie Groth and Hrimnir: Peggy Morsch
Chapter Graphics: Mark Wooldrage

CONTENTS

AUTHOR'S NOTE

We owe a great debt to the work of the 19th century collectors who recorded and translated the folk rituals and stories of the tribes of the holarctic before they disappeared forever. I borrow, adapt, and redact from these collections liberally in reconstructing the religious and cultural life of the people of the Trabally, for these works are the last repository of traditions that go back many thousands of years, and appear in different versions in the tales of the varied indigenous peoples in that region. For readers who are interested in this lost lore, especially of the areas where the Celts and Scandinavians lived side by side for millennia, I recommend the works of Alexander Carmichael, whose public domain collections have provided the stories, spells and prayers from the ancient British Isles found here. Other great collectors include Patrick Kennedy, William Larminie, W.B. Yeats, Lady Wilde, and twentieth century collector Sorche Nic Leodhas. Though we know little of the language of the people in the time period in which this novel takes place, I have used a mix of archaic and phonetically spelled Welsh, Irish, and Scots Gaelic words and names to suggest its likely melodic nature, and have provided a glossary for the use of readers.

BOBBIE GROTH

1. PROLOGUE FROM THE OLD SAGA: IN THE HUNGER MOON

When the Hunger Moon came in the dead of winter the first people, the tuaha, were hiding in their stone villages. Covered over by layers of thatch and warmed within by open hearths and the last of the food stores of their summer labors, they lived as if those things would preserve them from the world outside built of cold and ice.

The Hunger Moon brought days of spinning and weaving, carving fish hooks and sacred talismans from wood and stone, and using the single needle to knit the fish nets and the socks for the year to come. It was a time spent around the fire. And it was a time of death.

Aefa, She Who Walks Alone, the Death Crooner of the Trabally on the Large Island, knew this, and knew it well. Death was the reason that the Hunger Moon had no holy days, only long dark hours in the lair. The fire's warmth helped her tell the stories that dulled the pangs of hunger until the early spring's fish harvest began. Stories were the rituals of this moon. They were told and retold each year so that the children would know how the tuaha came to be.

The tales in the Hunger Moon always started with how the tuaha came to the Great Maam Isle, and it was this story Aefa was called to croon on the morning when her youngest daughter was in the travail of birthing. There were maams who took to their knees to catch the bairns as they came into the world. Aefa called these knee-maams to her that morning that she might be released from her daughter's side for the ritual of telling. And these are the words that came from her:

Long, long ago, before our people had the secrets of the standing stone calendars, long ago before we had spinning and weaving, we lived cold in the ice that covered the land. There was only an open fire to warm us in our hide tents. We were cold, oh, we were so cold.

One day as a young maam suckled her bairn beneath her cloak, her feet were stiff with freezing on the snow and she was unhappy. She said to her maam, the woman who gave her birth, "I have heard tell of a warm land where trees grow and sun melts the snow for long parts of the year. I want to take me wee bairn there, that her skin might know the kiss of the sun."

So she packed her tent and belongings onto her sled, and tied it to her reindeer, and called all who might join her to join her. Some came, but those who feared the mighty cold did not.

They traveled across the mountains to the flatlands that were once open ocean. Now the water was hidden by ice so tall it kept the sky from their sight also. She could not cross, though on the other side she knew there lay a land sun-filled and green.

She became frightened, and called upon the birds for help. The black raven answered. It flew up onto the ice, and flew back. "The ice is too high and too wide for tuaha to cross."

"But we must cross," said the young maam, "for the bairns are small and the food is sparse, and we must make it to the land of green before the winter death."

So the raven took wing and threw itself at the ice wall and pecked it, and a thin crack appeared. A wolf was passing, and seeing the raven's pitiful gesture, laughed, "These tiny tuaha cannot get through this ice. I will feast upon their bones."

The raven's mate flew up, and pecked at the ice some more, and cracked it wider. The wolf laughed again, for he was so sure of his meal.

Then the raven and its mate took flight together and both broke the ice. The tuaha took to their heels and raced away from the wolf across the shoals of frozen water to the new land.

By and by as they journeyed, the tuaha grew impatient for their land of green, so they gathered reindeer dung and such wood as they might find, and started a fire.

Soon, it leapt so high and so hot it dug deep into the ice. They became afraid it would bore a hole they would disappear into forever, but when they threw ice upon it to put it out, it licked its lips with a hissing sound and burned that much brighter.

The maam opened her arms to the sky and wailed for the raven to come. Down flew the raven and its mate, and told her of the wise maam who was an ice-conjurer in the far north where the deep cold still reigned. She had power over fire. The maam departed to look for her, and after much travail came to a house of ice. Therein resided a tall gray maam, her hair hanging down to the ground in four long braids.

When the tuaha's request was made, the ice-conjuror began to unbind her hair. When the first braid was loose, she took it up in her left hand and threw it across her right shoulder. With a horrendous cracking noise a rough wind began to bite upon their faces.

She unbound the second braid, and when it was loose, she took it in her right hand and threw it across her left shoulder. A soft sound rumbled in from the distance and gentle rain came upon them.

She unbound the third braid. She took it in her left hand, and when she threw it across her right shoulder, a sharp clatter roared around her and sleet pelted down between the rain drops. It fell hard upon the search party and soaked the outsides of their hairy cloaks.

Finally, she unbound the fourth braid. When she took it in her right hand and threw it across her left shoulder, a thundering of hailstones issued from the ends of her hair, pelting all about her. With that, the ice maam told them to return from whence they had come, and she would follow on the morrow.

The tuaha shambled back to their base camp through the dark and snow and ice. They were huddled forlornly around the pit covered with their meager furs and skins when suddenly there came a wind from the north star. The wind blew the fire into a blaze and though rain pelted down, the fire rose hotter and higher. Then, the ice conjurer roared down from the sky and the rain turned into a heavy downpour, with sleet and hail that pounded the fire into submission, pelting it until it died and hissing steam rose from the glowing cinders.

When the tuaha put their heads out of their coverings they could hear neither storm nor fire. Leaping up, they found a lake where the mighty fire had been. A trickling sound rose as the last of the great ice melted. Thus the tuaha found their green land upon the Great Maam Isle and it became their one true home.

It was the knee-maams who came to Aefa at the end of the Tale of Beginnings, to say that the beautiful Ayveen lay dying in childbirth. As Aefa crooned to her people, her daughter had lapsed into pain so deep she closed her eyes and ceased to speak. One of the knee-maams ran from the birthing chamber to the Great Room and flung herself before her Death Crooner, crying that Ayveen was too narrow for the large bairn she was carrying.

Aefa ran to her daughter's side. She reached deep inside her and could feel a tuft of hair. The bairn was at the gate but its way was blocked from this world by Ayveen's slim young hips. With a deathly cry Ayveen gushed forth blood and the knee-maams screamed. Aefa began the Death Croon for her own daughter.

"Whom have I here upon the pallet? Me utter love, the child of me heart, me treasure, the sap of me heart. She comes to ye, O Great Maam. Ye desire her more powerfully than I. I release her to ye Great Maam of All."

Ayveen faded whiter than the new moon, and the light began to leave her. Aefa shuddered, and called for her blackstone knife. As the spirit left her daughter she grasped her dark knife and opening Ayveen's right side, pulled forth an angry red female child.

Aefa would not keen nor shed a tear but began the birth rune instead—the sacral blessing of the new spirit. The knee-maams recited with her. The Death Crooner took the dew-water from her little clay crock and put the three drops of the Great Maam on the bairn and crooned the blessing of the knee-maams like a death lilt. The wee bairn calmed her bleating and looked into her grandmother's eyes.

"The little drop of the Maam on yer little forehead, beloved one." Aefa's words slid over the call of death like dark water over the rounded stones of some secret brook. "The little drop of the sun on yer little forehead, beloved one. The little drop of the moon on yer forehead, beloved one. To aid ye from the death spirits, to

4

shield ye. The little drop of the nine, to wash ye with the grace of the Great Maam of All."

Then, as is proscribed in the runes of the Great Maam, Aefa passed the child to the knee-maams, and they washed her. Each of the nine put the water of the dew from their palms unto her little head, and with it sang the sweetest music that ever lulled a newborn child.

"The little wavelet for yer form, the little wavelet for yer voice...." The wee bairn turned her head to gaze at them, her strange new eyes, one hazel green and brown, one bright blue, already wide with knowing.

They began to pass the tiny one around again, chanting and runing.

"Nine little palmfuls for yer spirit in the name of the Great Maam of All, the Great Three-Maam." With the blessing of the knee-maams the nameless bairn became their own little Ronnat, the little seal child, the daughter of the sea, a new heart for a lost heart.

And Aefa, Death Crooner of the Trabally, knew even then that the angry red girl child would be the Death Crooner to follow after her.

2. SNOW MOON

Hugging my knees to my chin I crouched in the crevice beneath the rock, peering out into the bright sunlight. The old silver female was making her way zigzag up the ice-riddled strand. She stopped here and there, eating carrion coughed up by the sea, sniffing at the driftwood tossed upon the pebbles, licking at the scrim of snow sticking to the rocks.

I stared hard, recognizing old Tonntaban—The White Cap—who I had called for all my thirteen summers after the silver-white foam that dotted the sea on a brisk day. The old ones said these dogs came to the Great Isle riding ice and howling in the New Moon. They were little more than spirit, their mottled fur mixed and swirling with the gray rages of the sea. These stories frightened the other children. But I was never afraid. I already knew I was to be a Death Crooner.

Tonntaban was ancient now—gaunt and ghostlike even in broad daylight. As scrawny as she was, I could see that her breasts hung full with milk—clearly, she had pups again. My stomach flip-flopped. How I longed for a silver-gray pup of my own.

A mere trickle of a stream spilled out of the darkness of the pine forest behind me and meandered across the beach until it disappeared into the sea. The wild dog raised her head and sniffed, then padded up off the beach, following the stream into the forest.

Swinging myself out of the crevice I stalked the old dog at a distance, muttering the incantation to bring her to me under my breath: *The spell is placed in yer right ear for yer good and not for yer harm. Love of the land that is under yer foot and dislike of the land ye have left will lead ye to me.* I had learned my grandmother's spells well, though they were in language more ancient than the one we spoke to each other.

I was down-wind of the ragged creature and the constancy of sea-wind disguised any noise I might make. This was a good thing, me being impatient, and inclined to shift and squirm. Even so, once the dark of the pine forest closed over my head I moved carefully and breathlessly lest I spook the old dogmaam. She stole warily across roots and ice-crusted mosses that clung beside the trickle of creek as it wound further into the woods. From time to time the old dog stopped and looked backwards, sniffing, testing the air. I froze mid-stride then, carefully lowering my foot to keep my balance. When Tonntaban moved on, I moved too.

The rivulet took a sharp turn around a thicket bordering a snow-covered hillock. There the Tonntaban quickly disappeared from sight. Breathlessly I crept to the thicket and peeped through the crisscross of branches. I could see that on the other side, the hillock became a sandy bank. Spring flooding had carved a cavern beneath it. A silvery white flash caught my eye as she disappeared into a hole underneath the overhang of gnarled tree roots.

Collecting my breath I watched, the thankful prayer on my lips. *Me wish has rest this night: fast bound in me bare hand, a twisted rope has brought ye to me.* The woods were silent save for the creaking of the treetops in the wind. Faint rustlings and mewlings came from inside the den. I marveled that so old a dog could still have a litter of pups without herself perishing in the process.

Settling into a hollow of snow-pack I was well-protected by my oiled skin leggings. Chin resting in my hands, elbows on my crossed legs, I watched. Presently, a tiny nose poked out from the darkness, then a pup lurched out into broad daylight, butted from behind by its mother. The tip of Tonntaban's silvery snout appeared briefly as she slammed it into the puppy's soft backside. The little bairnie yipped and rolled over drunkenly on its fat little tummy. Struggling briefly, it hopped up just as one flurry of silver and white after another burst through the den opening, until four beautiful little ones lolled on the sandy ground.

Tonntaban's whole head appeared then, flat to the earth, her eyes, one hazel green and brown, one blue, burning with the ferocity of white coals. She watched the pups gambol and play, snuffling at the loose snow and sitting abruptly to lick at it. Taking up a piece of frozen sea carrion she dropped it for them to tug and pull until they had worried it to small shreds and swallowed them.

As the clumsy tumble continued, my left foot went numb. Carefully I stretched it out before me, trying to gain a new position, but only succeeded in rattling a few dried leaves still clinging to the thicket. Tonntaban's head flew up. She stared directly at the spot where I crouched. Swiftly the old head dove, shoveling the pups before her into the darkness of the den. A low rumble escaped her throat. She cast one last glance in my direction, then disappeared in a swirl of silver-gray.

Scowling, I blew out my breath in an exasperated hiss. Curses, how I managed to be so clumsy I did not know! Rolling to one side, I shoved first one fur-booted foot, then the other under me to heave myself to my feet. I felt old and stiff and clumsy from sitting so long in the cold.

Tripping and tottering along the streambed I soon found myself out on the strand again. The setting sun streaked orange skyward where the mournful blue was split with glaring brightness. My grandmother, *Granaidh* Aefa, would be stoking the hearth for the late afternoon meal. I groaned. In my imagination I could hear the sharp voices of the village naysayers criticizing me, accusing me of shirking my duties to Aefa to— chase faerie dogs. Anger filled me, but also guilt, as my *granaidh* would indeed need help and here was I, out a-playing like some child.

I sprinted across the strand, leaping shards of ice and small rippling drifts of snow. Reaching the gravel beach, I cut sharply inland and followed an icy rivulet uphill through low junipers, then scrub pines and finally deep forest. By now my breath came in sharp hiccups and the spongey floor of a thousand years of cast-off pine needles echoed deeply with the battering of my feet. Sheltered by the tall pines, only meager bits of snow had drifted down and settled upon the path that ran straight to the forest dwelling Aefa and I were opening up in anticipation of the warming time of year.

"Ee-fah! Gran-ee Eefah!" I called out over and over until my headlong charge plopped me panting on a low stool by the hearth.

"I saw her, *Granaidh*!" I gulped air and coughed, trying to breathe in and out at the same time, "I saw her. Old Tonntaban is still with us and she has pups again! Little silver babies. Please can I bring one home, *Granaidh*, please?"

Aefa shook her head back and forth as she shuffled across the room in her felted wool slippers. She gave the pot a stir, scooping deep into the steamy liquid with her wooden spoon. She churned the whole mass up from the bottom, remixing it with the broth.

"Bring one home?" she chuckled, "They're IN their home! What would we need with another mouth when we barely feed our own?"

I moaned. I knew my *granaidh* was right--some winter days we ate but one meal between us and quelled our hunger with ancient stories instead. In this season, before spring fishing and after the winter stores were almost gone, most every day was spent laboriously in the pursuit of something to fill our stomachs. I knew she was right, but I burned with the passions of my youth.

"But with a silver dog, *Granaidh*, we could keep a small flock—wool and mutton whenever we want! Just think, *Granaidh*!" I clapped my hands together, "Just think, meat through the winter, right through to the time of First Milk!"

Aefa shook her head again, still grinning. "And dear one, how does the wild silver pup learn not to be a wild silver wolf and devour the sheep before our very eyes?"

My childish frustration surged through clenched teeth in a roar.

"No, *Granaidh*, no," I insisted, "It's love. Love in the silver dog's life--it turns a wild spirit to a helpmate. Ye'll see."

Granaidh laughed deep in her bosom and waved her hand behind her as if to push me out from under her skirts. Just what she did when I was wee. I grimaced but held my tongue in respectful agony. This woman was my foster-maam, the woman who was mothering me because my own maam died; she was my beloved grandmother and the revered Death Crooner of my whole people.

I knew there was a time before I came to live with Aefa, but that time was dim in my memory. I knew my own maam died bringing me forth, too young, maybe, to nurture a babe inside her and feed her own growing body. I was born as the dead of winter swung to the earliest spring moon, as were most bairns of the *tuaha*, my people, the first people on the Large Island.

But I was different. In the midst of these small dark folk, I stood out with my long, cedar-red hair. I was one of the brits, the spotted ones—my face, arms, every part of me scattered with freckling. And my eyes, like the silver dogs I so relentlessly pursued: one hazel green-brown, one ice blue. I, too, frightened children and old maams.

Aefa took me when none other would--after all, Aefa was my true *granaidh*. The strange, giant, squalling, red-haired infant that was me could have been left for the waves to swallow, as the village naysayers had been so fond of reminding me all the days of my childhood. No one would have mentioned my birth again if that had been my fate.

But Aefa lifted me from her younger daughter Ayveen's deathbed to her elder daughter Grania's breast. There I nursed alongside Grania's own Fia, who was just enough older than I to already have teeth for bannocks and berries alike, leaving milk for a smaller infant. Aefa bade Grania bring me back to her when weaned from the breast and out of moss swaddling, and then she would raise me.

All that was well before my knowing time. I heard the story much from Aefa's lips, in answer to my endless "why, *Granaidh*, why?" when I was small. I did not remember when I passed from Grania's breast to Aefa's chambers in the stone village, or perhaps to the forest hut where herbs were gathered and dried through the summer. But I remembered Aefa as the one who held me close when I was hurting, and told me stories or rocked me in the firelight.

Before the year I found the silver pup, I only thought of how Aefa taught me everything I knew--the herbs, the sweet flowers, the bannocks and dried meats, the root soups and the sea soups. She taught me the lambing and rooing, the cleansing and carding, the spinning and weaving. She taught me the work of the one needle that fit so easily into a pocket or bag, to be carried everywhere to knit socks and mittens and hats. I had even learned the building of looms and the laying of gardens from Aefa. My *granaidh* was held so dear in my own heart it took my breath away sometimes.

The thirteenth year was the time of life when my people called their children the "owners of shade," for it was in this year that all children suddenly became dissatisfied with those they had loved, and complained of the very tasks they had done since they were bairns. They flopped insolently in the shade of trees while the whole village labored, and complained of the gifts that were theirs in the bounty of the Great Maam and the work of their families.

And so for me, no different in my thirteenth year than any other child, my beloved *granaidh* was slowly becoming the source of some un-nameable misery—a wellspring of suffering and imprisonment. It was this mysterious transformation of my *granaidh* that I held responsible for her resistance to my great desire for one of the silver pups, and I was flooded with resentment.

Bleakly I turned to the fire and filled our bowls. We sat, broke the bannock and supped in silence as the firelight threw shadows onto the deepening night. *Granaidh* Aefa cocked her head and peered at me over her bowl, finally.

"Has the day taken yer tongue, me love? Are ye ill?" The softness of her concern turned my hard heart to her again, and I mumbled and shook my head. But I was released from my childish anger. After I cleared our meal I curled myself at Aefa's feet and stared deep into the molten glories of the hearthfire. This was the moon of the First Milk, the ewe's milk that announced the coming of spring. It would bring the *tuaha* out of starvation and into plenty.

The fire snapped and settled, humming quietly. I felt Aefa gently pat my hair, and heard her murmur, "So bright, ach, the fire cannot outshine yer own glory."

It was times like this, so close to Aefa, my own *granaidh* and foster maam, that I felt love for the Great Maam of All and her daughter, our young goddess Bri, well up in my heart, bringing me somewhere between laughter and tears. I knew I was born to serve the Great Maam, to learn all I could from Aefa, and someday, to fill her shoes as Death Crooner. I wished I felt only the warmth of love, but as seemed to happen now, along with my resentment of Aefa, a pang of pain found its mark in my heart too, as I thought of the many ways I failed my *granaidh*. I disappeared into the woods for hours, I avoided my chores to dangle a twig in the brook, I sat sullen and feeling out of place at the great rituals. How could Aefa really love me when I fell so short of my own destiny?

As if she knew what I was thinking, Aefa lay her hands, then her cheek, against my head. The warmth of them penetrated to my toes at the bottom of my rough-knitted wool socks. I sighed and snuggled even closer into her arms. Yes, that nothing could disturb this peace. That would be my only prayer to the Great Maam of All, and her daughter, our Young Goddess Bri.

****

The Days of First Milk dawn warm with promise that the earth carries the seed of the coming spring within the heat of her womb. The first of the lambs are coming, and the goat-kids with them. Milk drips from the paps of ewe and doe-goat.

Granaidh Aefa and I waked ourselves well before the dawning, and met the other maams outside the door of the village. Oil lamps in our hands, we began our yearly procession through the dark to the meeting place on the high hill, mouthing the whisper-chant:

Fire of the Great Maam Isle in the secret places where tuaha enter. We feed it the sacred hawthorn, yet the ashes never increase. For our goddess Bri, our foster-mother, we keep the household fire alive, and bank it upon the night time for her protection upon us, her children.

As the sacred chant commanded, we had woven the Eyes of Bri, the straw suns of three rays that now hung from our necks. Leading us were the maams new this early spring from childbed. They held their oil lamps aloft to thank Bri for their safe passage through the birthing. They walked slowly, and the other maams of the village followed behind in respect.

Aefa's voice rang with the ritual commands: *And upon The First Milk of the ewes take ye bannocks, milk, dried fruits, and a torch and climb ye the mound of Bri, and there, watch ye for the serpent. For early on this morn of Bri the serpent shall come from the hole, though there might yet be deep snow on the ground.*

Matching my pace with Aefa's, I repeated the words in my own mind, drawing their familiarity from memory. I ducked my head and turned to sweep my eyes over the maams behind me. I meant only to glance, but my eyes were caught by the sharp gaze of old Mae, and froze there. The old maam lifted her lip as if to snarl. I tore my eyes away and fixed them on the ground. *That old besom*, I thought, *why doesn't she ever leave me be?* Mae was one of them who thought I was elfkind—I imagined it was she who enthusiastically advocated putting me upon the strand for the waves to feast on right after I was born.

Around me the other maams took up the chant, no longer whispering, but quietly and of one voice, bringing in the dawn. *I will not harm the serpent nor the serpent harm me. This is the day of Bri; the first of serpents, our foster mother will come from the mound. I will not touch the first of serpents, nor will she touch me.*

I joined them, head upright, eyes straight ahead, that I might not snag myself in Mae's glare again. The loom of our words caught the splendor of the rakish sun and pulled it into the warp of clouds strung across the hills around us like shoals of herring. The light of dawn melted the fear of Mae in me, and in its place, I felt a growing annoyance, and even anger.

Aefa called: *Bri put her finger in the river on the Day of First Milk and away went the sacred maam of the cold.*

The maams answered, *Bri bathed her palms in the river on the Day of First Milk and away went the secret maam of the cold.*

I loved this part of the ritual and nothing in the sting of Mae's bitter old eyes could take it away from me. We were at the end of the Calling for First Milk, at the top of the mound, beneath the sky looking far out towards the sea. As one group we circled in the rising sun and finished our prayers together.

On the feast day of Bri the Great Foster Maam shall be with the maams and the ewes, and the ewes' milk shall flow. The sun shall warm the serpent as it warms the depths of earth that the spring may begin from the heat in her womb.

I knelt to kindle the ritual hearthfire in honor of Bri, the maam of hearth and mothering, as that was my simple task as Aefa's apprentice. The crowd of maams settled themselves beside it, looking for serpents to come from the mound beneath as fire and sun warmed it on this first day of spring. They sat on their woolens, soaking up the light of this day, weaving the Bri's Eyes, and waiting for the night festival as they sang the songs and told the stories of this day.

I sat with the maams all that day, hearing the bairns cry, and watching their maams or foster maams duck them beneath the shawls to stay warm as they suckled. My aunt Grania nodded to us, when she knelt beside me to take food at the height of the sun.

"Thus I once fostered ye Ronnat," she said, "Ye gave me much to be celebrated on this sacred day." I smiled at her, and leaned into her as she fondly stroked my hair. In truth, as Aefa's daughter, Grania could not refuse to give me suck when Aefa asked it of her. But Grania was a merciful and tender-hearted maam who loved children and took the strange bairn that was me into her arms and fed and cradled me alongside her own. It was a thing I was just beginning to understand as a great gift to me.

As the sun sank late that day, the ritual hearthfire was built up until it became a great crackling bonfire. The elderly maams were supported by their children and grandchildren as they brought armloads of wood to it. We celebrated the ending of the wood-gathering of the hag of winter, who with spring was released to sleep until the dark time came again in the late autumn.

As the flames grew higher, the *tuaha* of the villages and hamlets all came to pay homage to the new maams. We brought them gifts of warm woolens in which to clothe their new ones, peering at the new babes wrapped in shawls. We threw the Bri's Eyes into the flames to flare up with good luck. As the fire grew taller and sent showers of sparks into the air, it drew all the villagers to the top of the hill to dance, sing, and encourage the fun and frolic of the lads and lasses who would, one day, hope for bairns of their own.

I was content on this day and its familiarity in our sacred year. But I could not help but think of the little pups beneath the sand bank, and my heart went out to them. Spring was coming, yes, but the nights were still cold, and I wondered how all small things stayed alive in them.

3. SAP MOON

The cold dry winds of the very early spring brought the *tuaha* of my stone village Cloch Graig out to begin the preparation of the ground in their gardens. With the wooden hoes we broke the soil. Children scampered and knelt to crush the huge clods or carry away the stones that sifted to the top, as they did each spring. Cold fingers and toes marked the rough work, and it was this discomfort that always figured heavily in my dislike of the task.

Our garden plot was a short distance from Aefa's forest hut. It was carved out of a meadow that had full sun throughout the short northern summer moontides, but in the early spring lacked protection from fickle blasts of cold air. The winds bounced along the landscape, tossing old leaves and violently combing the trees to release twigs and branches that had snapped in the winter ices.

My eyes burned from the cold assault; my fingers and toes ached from exposure to earth bound tight with ice crystals. If I brushed a hand or forearm across my face to wipe away wind-wrought tears, I left in their place the smart sting of icy dirt and its pungent scent of loam.

Aefa and I worked quickly because of the cold, for we would not get to rest when our own plot was done. Instead, we would shoulder our hoes and trek down to the stone village to lend a hand there, for to preserve from hunger and want was a community affair. Although the village folk might whisper derision about a neighbor who did not throw his or her back into the work whole-heartedly, nevertheless, that neighbor would be fed. The garden plots of Cloch Graig village were small, which made their yield that much more important to our survival.

By nightfall, hands washed and fingernails scraped clean with small bone sewing needles, my hands felt twice their normal size. They ached painfully with the bleeding cracks of chilblains. The only respite this time of year brought was that the constant demands of spinning and knitting were put aside. These tasks were too painful for our over-worked, raw and blistered fingers.

After our evening meal of savory root soup, the lucky meal of the early cold spring, I snuggled back against Aefa as we curled together before the hearth. Like all hearths in the Trabally, the small stone villages on the Large Island connected by traditions and ancestors going back to ancient times, our hearth was in the center of the hut, releasing its smoke lazily to exit through a hole in the roof above it. We massaged Aefa's oils and liniments into our hands as we contemplated the slow fire.

Presently, Aefa began to singsong one of the old tales. I listened rapt, taking in each word, letting it come into my very bones, for one day, I would pass it on to my own grandchild.

A bairn was born and a faerie maam came on a soft day with slyness in her heart and the quietness of fog to cover her footfall. She meant to take the sweet thing through the door at the foot of the mountain so she might have him forever. As she stood transfixed by the bairnie's beautiful slumbering face, she said the praises nine times, as if she would never tire of admiring him. Then, she stretched out her little arms to put them under his to lift him away with her. Aye, she tried, but she could not. He slept blissfully on and she could not so much as raise him enough to take him up in her shawl.

It was a long story about the constant struggle between *tuaha* maams and faerie maams over the beautiful bairns that *tuaha* bore. In this one, the bairn had a birthmark that kept it safe from faerie. But still a *tuaha* maam must always look sharp to keep a faerie maam from getting to her bairn.

I shivered when the story was over, both in delicious terror of it, and in dark dread of how shadowing Aefa through the spring rites would bring me before Mae and her ilk the next day. The naysayers could still make me feel shame, as if my own mother in dying had declared me unlovable. As if my father, mystery that he was, somehow made me unclean—not only unfit to be Death Crooner after Aefa, but worse, unfit to live with the *tuaha* at all. I hunkered down into the bedclothes, drawing them over my head as if that could shut out my drear thoughts.

I heard Aefa stir and bank the ashes with the night blessing. As I drifted off I murmured to myself *Birds, birds,* to invoke the spring.

****

"Nests, nests!" The words came automatically to my lips, bursting aloud as I sat up suddenly at the dawn bird's cry. Aye, I had done it, recited the spell of luck to follow my words of the night before immediately upon waking! Aefa was already risen and gone out. I pulled on wool socks and outer boots by the door.

The woolen cloak pulled tight around my ears and shoulders did little to dim the shock of nippy air on my sleepy nose. Immediately it began to run. I trudged to the byre and stood there blearily for a moment, watching the steady rhythm of Aefa's hands as she milked Rosie, the ewe. Then I sniffed deep and sat on the short one-legged stool. Head pressed against our goat Juniper's pungent side, I began to strip her long teats.

A tune hummed from Aefa, starting low, almost like a mutter from the animal she milked. I joined my hum to hers, and the twining of our two voices comforted the animals, and their milk to was good and rich.

On this day, we gathered the new milk coming into the breasts of the beasts to bless the land with fruitfulness. As soon as we were done with the milking, Aefa and I took up the white frothy liquid, still warm, and walked the boundaries of our little garden, muttering the chants of the Great Maam for a good year and a bountiful harvest, pouring a thin creamy line around the garden edge to keep fertility in and pestilence out.

Our words cut the silence of the surrounding woods like a small scatter of rogue raindrops stepping across a limpid pool. *In the full light of the Sap Moon I will go out to break earth in the name of the Great Maam who sheltered it in winter. I will pour milk to the four winds. I will fence me garden with milk. I will fence in the sunlight for warmth. I will fence out the cold and ice. I will free the dew and the nine waves of plenty.*

Afterwards we knelt and dug down to harvest the tubers that were sweetened by wintering over in the ground. They would be washed and hung up in the rafters to dry. All year we would pull them down for soups and stews and to flavor cereals. *Granaidh* and I did not chatter as we worked, for Aefa's barely audible mutter was the string of spells and chants for this sacred day. I followed the lilt of her voice half-consciously, for though it was low, I echoed each word in my own head, as I would be responsible for their magic one day.

It was mid-morning by the time we unearthed the whole patch. Our baskets and creels were heavy with the bulbous roots. We were about to begin the haul towards the stream to wash them when the sound of laughter and shouting, the clink of clay bells, and the clatter of staffs drifted up the hillside from the stone village.

I let my creel drop.

"The Lifters!" I cried as I peered through the brush that separated our high garden from the track that curled downhill towards Cloch Graig. We left our heavy baskets and ran for the hut.

The Lifters came with a joyful noise. They danced and cavorted with strings of tubers hung round their necks and last year's bird nests worn as caps or pinned atop their shawls and knit jackets. The sun had warmed the day, and winter clothes were open and flapping. Bells rattled and staves clumped the ground in the rhythm of their chant song, punctuated by the trilling of flutes, the deep booming of the drums, pounding feet, and shouts and whistles of delight.

In the midst of the lifters was a litter on which a stool was lashed, and upon it sat the beautiful Spring Maam, my dear breast mother and aunt, Grania, Aefa's daughter. She sat in pure white robes, the flesh of childing prominent on her breasts and belly and in the smile of her face. The crew carried her aloft, singing and jangling until they came to an abrupt halt in the dooryard of our hut. There they lowered her, and gently tilted the litter up at one end, depositing her in a standing position.

Instantly Grania's mummers closed around her, encircling the white robes in a green and brown cloak hung with roots and dried apples, hoes and picks, small baskets of eggs. She held aloft a digging hoe, and sang to us a blessing pronounced upon our little croft. *Everything within yer dwelling or in yer possession, all beasts and crops, all flocks and grain, from the hallowed eve till the serpent's new spring, with goodly progress and gentle blessing. May the tending of the Great Maam follow ye.*

Aefa took her place in the litter chair then, and the group raised her high, with the honor and solemnity befitting her age and the wisdom of her Death Crooning. Grania lead the little procession as they carefully paced the perimeter of our garden, the same path that we had traced with the milk of First Light. I felt someone clutch my arm, and there by my side was my cousin Fia, my breast sister. We kissed excitedly and held each other tight, for the friendship that is forged at the breast of the same mother is tighter than blood.

Arms locked, we followed the procession. The chant rang solemn and wise now, as they carried Aefa around her small domain: *Maam all giving I make me circuit under yer cloak. Maam of the beasts, of the brilliant shining, conqueror of hunger: be ye at me back. Though I should travel ocean and the hard trail over hill, no harm can befall me beneath the shelter of yer cloak.*

Perfectly solemn, the chanters paced our garden, and more solemnly still was Aefa put down when the boundaries were fully traversed. Grania the Spring Maam knelt and presented Aefa with the scepter hoe and took Aefa's blessing upon herself. Aefa was the oldest and wisest maam of Cloch Graig, the Death Crooner, of a long line of Death Crooners going back to the Time of Beginnings. Thus it was that she was revered as the Great Maam in our little village, the Maam of all of us. She intoned her part of the sacred chant: *Be I the sacred Great Maam, aye at peace with me goat and beasts, with me woolly sheep in flocks, with the crops and stones of the field, or the ripening of the sheaf on the grassland. Everything high or low, every furnishing and flock, all belong to the Sacred Three-maam, and to me that is kindness.*

Then suddenly, as if released from tight bonds, a whooping cry went up and revelry, dancing, laughing, and shrieking rent the air as the group gave one last salute to Aefa and the Spring Maam and leapt as one mass at me. I screamed and made a break to escape, but Fia clutched my arm, laughing, betraying, and delivering me to the heavy hand of ritual.

The group of mummers quickly circled us and barred my escape while Fia screamed with mirth. She had been a Spring Maiden last year and joined now in the great fun of capturing me for that honor.

With merriment and shouting and good play the mummers lifted me off my feet and up into the litter chair. They hoisted me aloft as they circled the field once again, this time at a brisk trot, singing wildly the song of the young maiden blessing, the song of young love and young play and wild dancing.

Aefa and Grania looked on and clapped and sang. *On the feast day of the Maam of shepherd and flock, I cut me a handful of the new grain. I dried it gently in the sun. I rubbed it sharply from the husk. With me own palm I ground it in a quern at the dark of moon. I toasted it on a fire of rowan. And I shared it round me people.*

The last words rose in a shout with the litter lifted to its highest. It was dropped suddenly down upon their shoulders, leaving me suspended in midair. I met the litter again with a breathless yelp as I tumbled. With this lively song and its riotous dance of joy, they circled the field and the hut and ended their parade before Aefa and Grania.

Then I was tossed from the litter with a great shout, coming perilously close to falling flat into the dirt before the clutch of musicians. At the last second a strong hand caught me by the upper arm and pulled me to a standing position again. I turned quickly toward my rescuer and found the hand attached to a tall lad, his black curls tossed by the wind and his black eyes deep pools threatening to pull me under. He grinned at me widely, saluted me with the tipper stick of his drum, and whirled to follow the revelers.

My heart beat so fast in my chest I felt it might burst. Then Fia was with me, steadying me, still laughing with her head thrown back and her face full in the sun. While Aefa threw last year's lucky sweetened grain to the crowd, they roared their delight. Handfuls were caught and eaten as they once again enthroned Grania upon her litter, and began their wild trek down to the stone village calling us to join them.

Granaidh and I snatched our shawls to ourselves and

followed. The blessing of the Death Crooner's croft marked the beginning of these sacred days. Now, we joined the revelers in circling the village common gardens, hoisting the stewards of those gardens, and any young lasses of an age like mine, who could qualify for the spring maid blessing. As we performed the rite at each dwelling, the inhabitants fell in with us to move on to the next, until the whole settlement gathered in reverie.

Near dusk the bonfire was lit on the high place, and the villagers danced, leaping the fire by dares and by blessings, holding both bairns and lambs to partake of the sanctity of the new warmth. I joined my cousins. Fia and I held hands and cavorted around the fires lifting Fia's little brother Dahi between us to make him laugh.

Osheen my cousin was the younger son of Aefa's son, my uncle Kriafann, and close to Fia and me in age. He was the boy cousin whom I loved and hated at the same time. He wriggled and flung his arms out in a strange parody of ritual dance in front of us, blocking our way, almost making us fall down. We shrieked with glee and tried to pull his hair and drive him away. He disappeared for a while, then came back again to torment us. Several times I caught sight of the black-haired lad who caught me when I fell, and inexplicably, my cheeks burned bright and hot as the fires when I did.

As night came on a feasting was laid out on blankets. Drinking the sweet fermented spring ale kept the villagers drunken with delight far into the night. One by one they dropped exhausted and crawled off home or wrapped themselves in skins or shawls and fell around the fire to slumber. I settled with Aefa on a pile of skins flung on the ground near enough the dying fire to use its warmth, but far enough away to dodge the sparks.

"And how fare ye, young one, in the blessings of this day?" my grandmother asked me.

"Passing fair, *Granaidh*!" I said, "Passing fair!" She chuckled audibly and murmured a sweet good night.

Peeking past the covers I gazed into the blackness of the night. I fixed my eyes on the pale glow of the huge full moon, now high in the sky and moving in and out of clouds and my field of vision beneath the cloaks. The sustained excitement of the full day's revelry rent me exhausted to the bone, but all my senses soared sharp with spring ale.

The stars reached down then and caught me in their net of sparkling light. I was surging skyward, breathless as my robes fell from me and blew away in the rush of the heavens around me. Suddenly I felt the grip of a strong arm on mine and my flight was arrested. I found myself staring into the face of the black-haired lad. He smiled at me and handed me a small bundle, a bairn with eyes and hair as black as his own. I shook my head no, no—I was too young for a bairn. But when he opened the swaddling it was a small silver pup that he put into my hands.

I felt myself falling then, and lost my breath as I landed hard on the ground. When I opened my eyes I was curled like a child, cuddled to my sleeping *granaidh*. The pup, the black-haired lad, the bairn—they disappeared as did all of my visions, in a swirl of black. I was neither asleep nor awake, but as always after one of my visions, smothered by a languor that leaded my arms and legs with paralysis.

I turned on my side and buried my face into Aefa's back. A soft giggle wafted in from the dark, and a disturbing thought nipped at the fringes of my drowse. It would not be long in the future that I would join the young lovers who crept off to giggle with each other in the shadows of the sacred rites. It had never made sense to me before, but the black-haired lad—I felt something new stir. I pushed the thought away, excitement and fear wedded together in it. Not now, not this year. This year I still dreamed of a small silver pup.

****

Some days after the festival I was spinning one night before the fire when I thought of how, when I was very tiny, I would take a length of yarn and tie it to a rock, mimicking the way the maams spun yarn on their drop spindles. I worked hard at it and went nowhere without my doll in one hand, and my rock and yarn in the other. I played at being a maam, and when I was around the other little lasses, we all sat in a circle and pretended to be maams, spinning and gossiping, and thrusting our little poppets to our flat chests and nursing them.

My little Rua was a hank of practice wool wrapped around a

small stick with another twig tied crosswise for arms. Her head was a scrap of knitted stuff wound around a bundle of raw fleece to make a ball. Her eyes and nose were embroidered on by Aefa with black wool yarn, the mouth and the hair fashioned from a few scraggly wisps of fleece dyed red with the juice of berry and bark.

Some of the other lasses laughed at the red hair, but I thought my poppet was beautiful and called her Rua, for the red color of her hair. I, myself, was called Ronnat Rua in the most formal language of the rituals. Aefa told me this as she helped me make a small blanket for Rua, and I wrapped and unwrapped my little bairn constantly. Copying the other maams and lasses I saw, I rocked Rua singing the little song of the nightbirds going to sleep, kissing her, and nestling her where my breasts would rise one day.

Then there came a day when I had to learn to spin in earnest. I at first thought of it as a game, but unlike the games with my dolly, rock and yarn, my *granaidh* and the other adults were very concerned just how I played this game, and I was not allowed to put it down until I got it right.

It was Aefa who first showed me how to pick the fleece, removing the little bits of leaves and sticks that stuck to the sheep as they grazed. I drew my tiny wisps of picked fleece across the wooden combs evenly, and dropped them into the basket along with my grandmother's.

Aefa then taught me how to grab a thin hank of wool and roll it across my thigh until it pulled tight into a string. These little strings I used as tiny snakes when playing with my dollies. But then Aefa tied one of the strings onto a spindle, and set about teaching me to spin in earnest.

I was young, and could not get the spindle to turn evenly. I became angry, and jerked it into a wobble that bore no yarn. Aefa patiently made me stop and unwind the garbled fluff to start again. I hated it. I became cross, and sometimes even cried when Aefa said it was time to do my spinning.

Once I shouted at my *granaidh* and ran out of the hut door and hid in the trees until hunger drove me back home. Aefa pretended to look at me fiercely, and would not give me any food until I sat and completed my spinning for that day. Though of all the lasses in the village I no doubt had the kindest, most indulgent upbringing in the house of my *granaidh*, there was one rule that was never neglected, and that was that the tasks of survival took precedence over everything else. Even hunger.

When we went down into the village the next time, I saw that all the other little lasses were already spinning lengths of yarn. I grew ashamed of myself. As usual, I went to find Fia. My breast-sister took me beyond the warren of stone huts to hide behind a hay shock in one of the small stone-walled animal pens. Fia was a patient teacher. Soon I forgot we were spinning because Fia had me laughing and chattering on. Magically, the yarn seemed to be spinning itself. Out of sight we worked until I could make a serviceable thread.

From then on I went down to the village almost every day to sit with Fia and the other lasses while we all did our spinning. These early threads would be used to make dollies and other toys, but before the year was out, we would be making carry-bags, or maybe even joining our lengths to those our maams made, and have them knit into clothing and other articles.

Soon, I found myself reaching for the spindle whenever my hands were not otherwise occupied. I didn't even think about it anymore. I wore my spindle on my belt, and in a carry-bag was fleece. As I walked, or sat a few minutes to rest or have a conversation, I pulled it out and began spinning.

All this drifted through my head in a calm reverie until I became suddenly aware of the snapping of the fire. Wakened from my day dream, I asked Aefa, "Who was me maam?"

She dropped her hands to her lap, resting them on the knitting she had to hold so close to her old eyes now. She gazed soberly at me.

"Ye are of an age, now," she said simply, and began.

Yer maam was Ayveen, me youngest, daughter of me heart, me child of the Second Sight who would follow after me to whisper the comforts of death to the stone village. I kept her to me from the time she was born, just as I did ye after ye were weaned. She was a beautiful child, as ye are, but black-haired with the ringed grey eyes that see the secrets of the future.

She had no interest in the other children, for within her dwelt an old soul who saw faerie and tuaha alike. She didn't run or play like other children, but followed me closely, absorbing anything I taught her almost faster than me tongue could tell it. Once was all it took to instruct her, and she would have the knowledge forever.

I did not see her fate coming so I could not charm to avert it. I was used to her spending hours away from me. She did everything she was told, though her one habit from the time she was a very little lass, was to disappear for hours on end. Should we search for her, she would eventually be found, sitting in a cavern, or atop a weathered dolmen, or beside the sea, or a river, just sitting and staring aerie-eyed at the clouds, humming to herself, twisting a bit of grass into a Bri's eye, or a handful of flowers into a crown for herself. Sometimes she danced, singing for herself low deep faerie chants, or lilting such a sweet tune, but a tune with no memory.

I should have paid attention, as she moved into her thirteenth year, but I did not think to, for she was a lass like no other, and I did not imagine the need to instruct her about the ways of lads and men. But then, all the village children know from a very young age how bairns are gotten. It is the village maams who need the ritual coming-of-age-telling to their children in order to accept for themselves that their children have moved into the years when maaming and love-making is a drive and a desire beyond all other.

I have no knowledge of how Ayveen came to be with child, given her secret self, and the fact that she, of her own free will, stayed separate from the village lads and lasses. The villagers chattered about a faerie lover. She herself said her child's father was a seal from the sea, and that she would name ye Ronnat on that accord.

Because she kept her secret from me, I did not know when ye were to be born. Her belly was big, very big, and she began to groan with the twinges of a maam about to deliver, even before her breasts held the capacity to feed an infant. I was confused. I began to think, like the others, that this was to be a strange faerie or troll child.

It was at the new moon when darkest winter turns to spring that ye were born. She held herself aloof for a day or so, and I finally saw her flinch, and thus knew her labors had started, though at first she denied herself the knee-maams. I was called to the telling of the Tale of Beginnings, and when I saw her again, her screams were such that the whole village could hear her throwing herself about in pain.

Transfixed by the sobriety of the telling, I paused in my

spinning with one hand raised and the other barely touching the thread. My spindle lay quietly tipped to the side, hanging from its newly spun tether, shifting almost imperceptibly in the quiet dark. Released by Aefa's silence, I put my arms to rest at my sides and gazed at her. I quelled a sob deep within, so that I might speak.

"*Granaidh*," I said, "That is so sad. Me own maam barely had the years I have now."

"True, love," said Aefa, looking me full in the face. "Some nights I would grieve that I was a terrible maam for not knowing the truths of me child's life. Later, when ye came to me and I began to understand yer gifts for the Crooning, I marveled at the power of the Great Maam to direct matters to their rightful conclusion. I loved me child Ayveen, the radiantly beautiful, with all me heart, and the loss of her still cuts me and renders me bleeding. But me faith in yer future as Death Crooner after me is much greater than any I had in hers."

I averted my eyes, stunned by the weight of such an admission from the *granaidh* I loved so dearly. I thought of Aefa as kindly and protecting, not strong with a stone core of craft that she had just revealed. And Aefa thought that I, Ronnat, was more worthy to be her successor than my mother, whom she had lost in pain and blood and sorrow. I blinked. Aefa was telling me I was *chosen, destined*, not the *only one left* to do it when the chosen one died. No wonder my *granaidh* was not swayed by the naysayers, nor put off by my many failings.

We worked on in silence then, lulled by the soft crackling of the fire, and an occasional thin wail of early spring wind. The firelight warmed our small circle of ancestral love grown thick with the blood of devotion, and strong with the revelation of secrets.

****

That spring, I often stole into the deep woods, heavy with the breathing of the Great Maam suckling new life. Silently I padded down the rooty path to the creek overhang to watch the silver pups from under the new spring ferns. Their first drunken gambols had turned to ferocious battles over twigs, a strip of dried fish, a bone.

Tiny growls were punctuated with pitiful yelps when

enthusiasm landed a sharp milk tooth into another's vulnerable baby fat. The shock of the yip would halt the fighting for a moment, each pup staring bewildered at the other until shortly, neither could remember what had interrupted their game. So they leapt again at each other with comical ferocity.

I could not help but clap my hand over my mouth to stifle an outburst of laughter at their tiny, earnest battles. Once a yelp of mirth escaped me, turning two fluffy heads in startled unison in my direction. Gray puppy eyes searched for the source of the noise.

As the spring warmed, the pups spent most of their time outside the den, and even followed the old Tonntaban off a ways through the woods. Now, I thought, I have to take one now, while it was still puppy enough to be gentled, but grown enough to eat from my hand as I tamed it, and not perish without the Tonntaban's milk.

Aefa had to listen to my begging each night thereafter as I gave voice to my longing again and again. Oh, I had plans for a silver shepherding dog, sleek and fast, intelligent and loyal. A dog would extend our bounty beyond just young Juniper, the doe goat that gave milk, and Rosie, the ewe who provided milk as well, and whose wool gave us warmth. A dog would allow extra animals, and therefore more wool, meat, and cheese.

"We could have more lambs and kids, *Granaidh*, with a good dog to bring them in." My imprecations were a daily scourge for my poor *granaidh*. "We could make more yarn and better blankets and have a kid now and then to roast. Just think!" I felt my longing like a starving person on a feast day. "If only" burst from my heart and traveled to my lips morning and night.

"And what, then, would the work of old Darmid be for?" Darmid was my grandfather, my dear *daideo*, and the father of all of Aefa's children. He made his home on the mountains with the village herds. "What of his sheep and lambs? Wouldn't we just be making more work for ourselves, having even more beasts?"

"But I mean we'd keep more lambs and goats right here, by the croft. We wouldn't have to wait for the rooing--we could have a few for ourselves--we could take the fleece when we needed it, and we could have as much as we wanted when we wanted it. *Daideo* has so many to provide for."

Still, Aefa shook her head, and finally snapped peevishly: "We can barely feed ourselves, much less a pup that might devour the only sheep and goat we have. And think on this: we would have to make more pasture land—we would have to clear trees for them to graze on, have ye thought of that?"

I bent my head to my work and grew silent when I heard this. Without my chatter, the rain outside the hut pounded a steady dance tune upon the thatch, and ran off in a trickle down its sides. My thoughts were with the wee pups under the stream bank, longing for them and grieving what was not to be. But I could not know what the Great Maam had in store for them—and for me.

4. RAIN MOON

In the Rain Moon, before the days of rooing, a ferocious summer storm began amidst days thick with fog off the sea. The air hung so full of water that sounds were muffled and the smell of the sea swam into the village dwellings on sodden air. In the forest hut we fed a constant low fire to keep the moisture at bay so we would not have rivers running down the inside walls, molding the early spring herbs that already hung drying.

The fog floundered, twisted and turned, broke and receded. The slow steady drip of trees became the even steadier rhythm of rain, and that turned to a constant downpour. By the time the thunder giant came crashing through the forest, the rain was a raging torrent and the wind a howling angry thing that tore through the trees, ripping the weakest limbs from their sockets, and pushing the trunks over which by youth or age lacked the strength of root to withstand its force.

Aefa and I huddled in the hut for two days, mending, spinning, and keeping busy with all manner of tasks seldom touched on the warm side of the year. On the morning of the third day of the deluge I woke to birdsong winnowing through the pure air and echoing against the new cleanliness of the washed forest. The rivulets had run dry during the night. With the dawn, even the mosses were beginning to relinquish their silvery saturation to the molten glory of the sun, transforming themselves into a velvety green carpet.

That morning, while Aefa was still at her prayers, I took my basket and headed for the meadows to search for new greens and herbs. Before I could even settle myself to the task of picking, wanting-to-know drew my legs through deep forest to the stream cleft. I could see the wreckage left by the storm that had blasted its way along the waterbed. I began to run.

Rounding the hillock to the thicket blind where the pups were, I let out a cry of alarm. The torrenting stream had gouged its banks so far up that the whole wall of sandy dirt and rock collapsed under the weight of the tree above it. The trunk lay half submerged in the churned-up silt, its branches covered with murk and its roots jutting up into the air.

The pups! My stomach dropped in anguish. I splashed across the streambed, the ache of dread already telling me what must be so. The pups could be no more. Rain no doubt had driven them as deep into the den as they could go, and there they would have been suffocated by sand or water.

Tears stung my eyes. I gulped for breath in my anger and sorrow. A terrible loss, a terrible waste of something I wanted so badly. Old Tonntaban was a familiar friend, it was true, but in my youthful and selfish mind she was an old dog and it was just a matter of time for her to die. But the pups, the young pups! I wanted one so badly, I would have gladly taken all of them before the storm did! A fury at my grandmother rose from my agony and I turned on my heel to stumble sobbing down the streambed towards the sea.

Once out from under the trees the rivulet subdued to an icy-cold silver sheen sliding over the sand towards the saltwater. Sun rippled the bottom like the underbelly of a brook trout. As it went the stream cut a deepening narrow canyon into the beach, finally disappearing where sand met wave.

I stopped, despairing sobs catching in my throat. I sought the ocean in my panic, now sparkling with molten sunlight under a clear blue sky. The waves were calmed, the storm no more. The beauty of it gripped me though my heart staggered under the weight of anguish.

Then I heard it. A soft whine barely wheezed out between heavy breaths. My eyes darted to the source, a bundle of gray and white almost indistinguishable from the streaks of beach rock and sand. The whine rose pitifully to me again and I stumbled towards it. It was the old Tonntaban, lying on her side, her flanks barely lifting with each shudder of breath. Life seeped out of her even as I watched.

She rolled her old eyes towards me, unafraid, the sorrow in them overlaid with the dimness living creatures take on as they take flight from the world of sunlight. She nosed something under one of her paws, and I could see, half buried in silt, a small open pink mouth and grey snout.

I threw myself down by her and dug furiously around the small form, pleading with the Great Maam, thanking Tonntaban for her gift, reassuring the old animal that I would guard her bairn should I ever pull its tiny life back across the veil to me. Bedraggled, wet, limp, was it alive or dead? The little creature felt warm but did not move. A nose pushed my hand towards the pup. I looked down at the old one. Tonntaban's half open eyes were fixed on me, willing me, begging me to take the pup even as her spirit raced away to the sky.

I snatched the wee thing into my arms, holding it close. Shutting my eyes, I breathed a prayer of thanks to the Great Maam. Placing my hand upon Tonntaban's flank, I could feel the last breath go from her, and with it, both hope and agony took wing in me.

I stood and sprinted across the sand. It would be faster to Aefa's croft if I bypassed the forest and bog and ran straight for the Minnow Brook that emptied into the sea farther on. There I turned upstream and splashed up the bank tearing along the rooted path until I felt my heart bursting from my throat.

"*Granaidh, Granaidh*!" My screams came out shrill and panicked, like the cry of a seagull. The door covering was flung aside and Aefa appeared, a formidable bolt of black and gray lightning, hair flying in all directions, curly and rippling like a radiant black and silver sun.

"Ronnat!" she called in alarm, "Ronnat, me bird, me heart!"

I pounded the last few feet across the clearing, the pup held before me like an offering. Aefa's eyes searched my face and person, but saw no blood or dismemberment and took on a puzzled squint. Then they lit on the bundle of silver and gray.

"What is it me heart?" her voice faltered, perplexed.

"It was the storm, *Granaidh*," I sobbed. "The old Tonntaban is dead. The pups are---." The story of the creek bed disaster tumbled from my lips and even as I told it Aefa was taking the pup from me as we went into the croft. There, she sat on a low bench by the fire and lifting it, covered its nose and mouth with her own lips and gently, oh so gently, sucked sand and silt from them. Then, with a bit of woven cloth she began to wipe out its eyes, nose, and mouth. The pup lay limp while Aefa carefully felt it all over.

"Nothing broken--at least not bones. Dear heart, how the bairnie must have struggled to take air!" Now, it lay like a dead thing, and yet, the belly rose and fell slowly and steadily with its breathing.

"We'll keep it warm and dry, and clean it as we can. Then all we can do is wait. If the sea Morrigan has taken it..." she turned it over and peered between its little legs, "....him, if the sea Morrigan has taken him, he will not breathe through to the morning."

I watched somberly as Aefa dried the pup more and shook the loosened sand from the cloth onto the floor. Though I did not think of it as a young and selfish lass of thirteen summers, I should have worshipped the ground my *granaidh* walked upon for using all her Death Crooner skills to save this little one she did not want, and had for so long refused to consider allowing me to have.

At last Aefa wrapped him snugly in a thick wool lap blanket and set me rocking him gently by the hearth. The strength of fear gone from me now, I felt weak and spent.

"Hold him firm, but gently," Aefa murmured, "Rock him and sing life to him, me love. We must bring his spirit back to him."

I already knew enough of Aefa's craft to croon the song for the dying beast. In my panic, it was in truth the only blessing I could think of. Urgently, almost tearfully, every ounce of my despair and hope infused each breathless word. *In peace and in comfort, full of marrow and sap, full of tallow and fat, full of pith and power, full of blood and flesh, may I see ye. Be yer healing on the being who created sea and land, who created tuaha and beast, who created ye and me, ye hide-bound one.*

With little more than two moons growth in him, he was already a braw wee thing, and as his coat dried it sprang up silver gray, soft and fluffy. I barely took time from my nursing to taste the hot root soup or eat the bannock Aefa made. As the night deepened, I began to nod myself, and might have been in danger of dropping the poor thing if Aefa had not taken him from me and laid him in a nest she made of wool cloaks nestled into a ring of firewood.

As usual, my *granaidh* banked the fire in the hearth with the night blessing: *I bless the hearth ash as me maam would do it, as the Great Maam bid us, be her hand on me hearth, on me herd, on me lintel, on me ewes and on me household all.*

Then, she led me into her own bed to comfort me.

"There, there me heart," she whispered, "It is only the Great Maam who wakes the day can wake the hurt things as well."

I began to mutter a protest but was fast asleep before the words could form.

****

In the night I dreamt of being drowned in a rushing tumbling wall of water that bore down on me from some unfathomable place. Twisting and turning I tried to get my breath, but each time, instead, my nose was filled with cold liquid and I choked until I vomited water. Just when my spirit was about to loose its hand from my heart and fling itself skyward, I bumped face down in gritty sand, and rolled over, just enough of one nostril free of the filth to draw in a scant breath. A belt of black squeezed my temples and I embraced it, for I had no more fight to live. Around me lightning flashed and thunder roared, and I struggled to breathe as my vision blurred and faded.

Suddenly the thunder became a yapping. Angry, insistent, and finally mournful it pitched itself into a long high whine. I popped one eye open above the bed cloak, trying to clear myself of sleep and the weight of that horrific dream. The yipping split the air again, this time peevish and insolent before it collapsed pitifully.

I sat up. The pup! He lived! I darted from beneath the bedclothes and huddled by the nest at the hearth. The silver and gray ball of fluff sat bolt upright, boldly peering at me. He shook his head and took a short prance in my direction.

"So! We greet the day!" muttered Aefa huskily from beneath the bedclothes.

"Isn't he such a dear thing, *Granaidh*!" I crowed, and only then did I reach for him. He turned and sunk his needle teeth into my fingers.

"Oh, thanks be to ye!!" I chortled, "I had too many fingers anyway!" The pup stumbled to his feet and dabbed at me with one fat white paw before flopping down on his bottom once more.

"*Granaidh*, what should I feed him?" I asked. Aefa struggled out from under the bedclothes and was winding her shock of black, gray and white hair into a knot, securing it up off her neck with a long carved bone hair stick.

"Well, perhaps some broth to start, and soaked in it some bannock. He is still a bairnie, dearie, he'll eat what bairnies eat." She went out to milk Rosie and Juniper.

I ladled a bit of the broth from the stewpot at the hearth into a bowl. Taking bannock left from the previous night's meal, I soaked little bits in the broth. These I fed him with my own fingers. How he gobbled. His whole body shook with delight.

"Slowly, bairnie!" I laughed. "We'll have to turn ye over to the wild pigs!"

"Ach, Ronnat," added Aefa as she came in with the morning's milk steaming from the wooden bucket. "Ach, he is just a sweet bairnie but ye can see he has the wolf in him too!"

I ignored her remark, putting my annoyance by as I continued to feed him until his little belly looked like it would burst. At last he stopped gobbling, gave a sidelong glance at the bannock crumbs I still held out to him, and collapsed to his side. He heaved one enormous sigh and shut his eyes.

"*Granaidh*, I think I've killed him!" I gasped in horror.

"No heart, he's like any sweet bairnie--he eats until he collapses, he sleeps until he's rested, he plays until he's hungry, and then it starts over again. Come, dear heart, have yer own breakfast while ye can." I closed my eyes and buried my face in silver puppy fluff. It tickled my nose and caressed my cheeks with a heavenly softness. Kissing the hard full little tummy, I murmured my gratitude to the Great Maam of All for bringing me this little one.

"*Granaidh*," I said as I plopped onto the bench and began to devour my own bannock and sweet goat's milk. "*Granaidh*, shall we visit Darmid with the wee thing, and let him tell us how to start training him?" For now, it seemed, the decision of having the pup had been made for us by the Great Maam, and we must follow through on our sacred duty to care for the storm's orphan.

"'Tis indeed time to travel to the shieling for the rooing," Aefa replied. "Darmid must have use of us now." When the standing stones foretold the arrival of spring, all my village folk gathered on the high place when the sun was right, and the morning was right, and the time was right. Then we went as one group to the meadows, where the shepherds had their dogs gather the ewes together for the rooing.

As one sweating mass we held the sheep and plucked the thick winter wool off their backs, curdled for the taking by their shedding. All the singing, laughing lads and lasses were together, stripped to the waist, holding grunting sheep as the thick mats of wool were stripped from them and bagged.

After the sheep of Cloch Graig were thus denuded, Aefa and our small group of family straggled up to Darmid's highlands to help him with his own rooing. Darmid's croft was as important to the well-being of Cloch Graig and the other seaside stone villages as Aefa's forest hut was. He was the anchor for the younger folk, teaching them how to nurse the animals, how to cure a bad hoof, or a broken horn. Under the old man's tutelage the *tuaha* of Cloch Graig learned the herd lore of the sheep. They provided not simply meat and milk, but fleece for cloth, leather for shoes and bone for making tools.

Once Grania told me that for all time Darmid was Aefa's love, and Grania called him father. But Aefa had ever refused Darmid's request to be her husbandman because it would take her to dwell at the high shieling with him, and her work as Death Crooner must always be near the village. But she loved him well enough, and they had remained handfasted lovers for all their lives and brought many children into the world. Of those, only Grania and Kriafann still lived.

I swallowed the warm milk and bannock with pleasure as I thought about the journeying to see Darmid. At his high croft the wind blew constantly, crying eerily, and the stars blinked through wisps of night clouds.

When I was little, I would snuggle in his lap before the glow of peat fire, his prickly beard stirring up my hair like any gorse branch. His raspy voice told long tales of his travels as a young man and the lessons of the shepherding. These Darmid recited in the singsong verse of the sacred tales of the *tuaha*, sonorous and hypnotic, always the same, comforting in their familiarity, soothing in their melodious verse, exciting in their mysteries.

When I had cleaned up our breakfast, I went to seek the basket I had left so suddenly the day before at the discovery of Bairnie. Aefa and I had so naturally fallen to calling him the "wee bairnie," it was now his name.

Scooping him up I carried him with me to the meadow where I set him beside me while I resumed picking spring herbs and greens. He played and gamboled and then after taking milk-soaked bannock from my hand, curled and slept in the grass while I labored on until basket and bag were full. Going to him often, I could not help but sink my face into his downy fluff and feel I might faint away, caught in love woven of soft yaps and softer fur, and the sweet milky breath of him.

****

When Aefa finished packing the herbs and sundries for our rooing trip, she placed a tall pack basket beside the bundle.

"For the wee Bairnie," she said, "Ye can't carry him in yer arms all that way love, and he might not walk it all by himself." He was growing every day, but he was still very small for such a long trip.

I was grateful for Aefa's planning, and excited beyond words to be bringing my pup, and for this covered her with kisses until she batted me away laughing. On this morning I forgot my complaints about her, I forgot my frustration. I had my Bairnie, my dreams were answered.

Once our family started walking, though, the weight of him seemed to grow and grow, and each time we stopped to rest I pulled off the pack basket in relief and dumped the sleepy puppy out of it into the grass. Both Fia and Osheen offered to help me carry him, but I was determined to show Aefa I could do it on my own.

After food and water, and a rest, I bundled him into the basket again, hoisting it up onto my back with enthusiasm. Finding my stride, Bairnie seemed as light as air again. It was not long, though, before I couldn't imagine how such a small thing could hang so heavily on me.

"There's more than his weight will be a burden to ye as he grows," remarked Aefa when she noticed me flagging. "Ye should consider deeply the responsibility. He might be better left with Darmid."

I drew myself up and strode on so as to disguise my weariness. Aefa needed no more reasons to suggest separation from my little treasure.

Caught up by the excited chatter of the family as we made our way, I soon thought little on my burden. The few nights we would spend together on the mountain for the rooing always seemed dreamily long, and were filled with music and laughter. It was more exciting on the mountain, the stories more mysterious, the stars closer to earth than any other nights of the year.

Fia took my arm, and we played our usual game of refusing Osheen's company and shrieking with laughter when he tried to inflict himself on us. The little children ran beside us like little puppies themselves. There were many times they had to be picked up off the ground after falling over a root, have their tears soothed and sore places rubbed, but in spite of their grief at those times, we were a jolly group of travelers.

We slept in the oak grove that marked the midpoint of the journey. Sharing food, we sang when the dark time came on, and quieted for a story whispered by Fia to the little ones. No long stories could be shared around the fire on this trek; we had to be up at dawn to continue our trip.

That night we three cousins lay in our bedrolls near to each other, whispering secrets and stories of faerie, and turning over on our backs to marvel at the night sky above us in the gaps between the trees. In a silent moment Fia suddenly whispered,

"Osheen, when will ye show me yer friend Bran from Clochbeg?" Clochbeg was another stone village, a little way up the beach.

"What do ye mean, cousin?" said Osheen distractedly, "Ye've seen him as many times as I have—for as long as I can remember."

"No, ye oaf," Fia chortled, "I want ye to present me to him in such a way that he might notice me."

Osheen was silent for a moment, then a soft singsong chant arose, "Fia likes Bra-an, Fia likes Bra—argh!" There came the sound of a smart slap on an unprotected head.

"Ow!" Osheen groaned quietly. "Ye're not as nice as ye look. 'Oh Bran,'" he pinched his nose shut to deliver his mocking words, "'Oh Bran, meet me cousin Fia, a pretty one, but not as nice as she is pretty—ouch! Stop it!!" The sound of more slapping sent me into gales of giggling that I swiftly stifled.

"What's so funny, Osheen?" growled Fia, "Even Ronnat is old enough to notice the lads—eh, Ronnat?"

"What?" I squeaked, the vision of the black-haired youth at the spring rites bringing a hot flush to my cheeks. How grateful I was for the cover of darkness.

"Oh, come on, Ronnat!" Osheen's harsh whisper cut in, "I saw ye gazing stupefied at Kerr during the boundary walks! Really! Bran's big brother! Ye lasses want to keep it all in the family I guess—Ronnat, ye'll have Kerr and Fia will have Bran and where will that leave me? Stuck with ye both hounding me for the rest of me life!"

We tried to smother our giggles, both of us swatting at Osheen and telling him to close his mouth and be quiet. In the midst of the play, I turned the name over in my mind. *Kerr, Kerr.* Of course I had known his name from the time I was small, for Bran's family was often in our village, and we in theirs. But his name seemed a new thing now. It was the name they gave the spicy smelling marsh, over-grown with brushwood. It tantalized me.

****

When we reached Darmid's shieling I thought I heard a dog barking. Soon a black form burst from the bushes, wagging and wriggling and yapping. It was Crag, Darmid's shepherd dog, black as the caves under the mountains, with small brown spots above his eyes. Each paw and his haunch feathers were dipped in brown as well. Catching a whiff of puppy, he stopped abruptly and cocked his head, looking incredulously at the pack basket. Wagging his lush tail, Crag whined a bit, smiling, as if to beg me to let him look into it.

"It's a wee bairnie, Crag," I said. Leaning over, I loosed the puppy from his carry pack and held him right in Crag's face. The older dog wagged his tail furiously, licking Bairnie about his little muzzle and eyes. The puppy reared back and wriggled free of me, then bounced about the older dog while Crag sought in vain to hold him down with his front paws and finish the bath.

Bairnie bolted away then and charged back again yapping. For his part, Crag thrust himself down on his front legs, leapt up, and raced off in a wide herding dog's circuit. He was back to the pup, then off again. Each time Crag circled he pounced and yapped in Bairnie's face. Each time the pup returned the greeting, but finally plumped his little back end down, flabbergasted at the whirlwind of older dog.

Darmid followed soon upon the sheepdog's heels, staff in hand, striding out across the high meadows to meet his family. He took Aefa in his arms immediately, and the rest of the family stood back, smiling, in quiet deference to their elders. I, however, was used to their affections, and as a child of their homes had no such restraint.

"*Daideo*," I crowed, "Look, look at wee Bairnie. He's loving Crag. Look *Daideo*, he's to be me own sheepdog."

Darmid paused a bit, and held Aefa away from him slightly, looking deep into her eyes, distracted, softly muttering, "Aye, lassie, and that he'll be." He took time to squeeze Aefa once more before he turned his attention to the puppy.

"Aye, lass, he is a wee monster!" He stooped down on crackling knees, and chucked the little pup under the chin, playfully grasping his snout and pulling it one way and the other. Finally, he patted him firmly on the head. "He's a wee bairnie now, lassie, but he'll outsize Crag by twice before he's grown full. A shepherd it is, ye say? A shepherd! Why, he'll need a fair lot of training for that one."

He stood again and raised his eyebrows quizzically at Aefa. All his body and face asked the question, *how could ye have let this be? Have ye taken leave of yer senses?!*

Aefa rolled her eyes, "'Tis a gift, he was, Darmid, of the Great Maam. Rained on us by the storm." That was all that needed to be said.

Our family ambled on across the meadow. The small children and us young folk ran ahead to find our favorite animals and leap about in the hay lofts. After the evening meal, all were soon quartered in the croft and outbuildings, intent on falling asleep in anticipation of the coming long day of work.

And that work was upon us soon enough with the sun's rise. Darmid's hut was cozied into the mountainside like a small round beetle in the curve of a rock. The back of the hut nestled into cliff and dirt, and the front opened into a vista of splendid pasture curving down to the place where the Large Island highlands dropped abruptly into the sea. On clear days the glint of sun on the waves could be seen. But on many days the sea cliffs were wrapped in mist and fog and all we knew of the sea were the cries of the birds punctuating the deep throb of crashing waves far below.

Dawn spread fair and quiet on this remote hilltop kissed first by the sun as it rose. The Sun-Maam rose majestic, lighting the air, then the clouds, then the water as she flashed fire over the highlands. The constant rush and whistle of the mountain breezes fell off to a whisper. Darmid said the wind waited quietly in the cave of the sun and when the sun rose, its light streamed overhead and out towards the ocean, bringing the wind back with it. Thus it had been since the beginning of time.

I wakened as usual when my grandparents stirred, but lay indolent after they left. Finally I pulled my shawl tight around me as I strode down to the cliffs to join them for their morning prayers. When I reached them I stood between them and slipped my hands into each of theirs, beginning the morning praise with them.

Bless to me, Great Maam of All who nurses me living heart, each thing me eye sees, each sound me ear hears, each fragrance that comes to me, each taste that brushes me lips, each melody that reaches me, each lure that pulls me will. Our words both greeted the sun and pulled her above the shining sea, binding us to her to fly into the day.

By mid-morning my cousins and I, along with our parents, were stripped to loincloths and shifts, and stood by threes and fours in the little stone paddocks. Darmid and Crag herded the mountain ewes to us. We caught them and tied them about the neck, handing the tethers to the smaller children to hold while us rooers stood on either side of them, or sat and pulled the smaller beasts into our laps.

Grasping the fleece high on the neck and yanking it gently

with swiftly moving fingers, we separated it from their skin. Thus the thick winter coats were soon peeled back and pulled off as one piece. Some would be baled with twine and stored in the loft of Darmid's barn; others would be hauled back to the stone village for use there.

While the experienced ewes lay on their sides unmoving, enjoying the tugging and soft touch of the rooers' fingers, the younger ones kicked, bleated, and darted away. At times, four or five of us had to handle a difficult one. One of us held the head, a child grasped its tether, and the rest plucked like mad to make the ordeal as short as possible.

As each ewe was finished, we shouted out the singsong rooing tunes joyfully: *Go shorn and come woolly, bear the spring with ye lamb!* At the final word we leapt backwards, unhanding the ewe as she struggled to stand. In a flash Crag scooped her up and herded her back out of the pen to the pasture, then brought another in.

While the adults and older children worked, the little children ran shrieking and scouring the bushes for tufts of fleece caught there, adding them to the full fleece before it was baled. As the sheep wandered away, naked of their winter wool, soft and thickly shimmering in the meadow sun, the raw wool was already bundled and ready to be stored or hauled to the stone village for the wool-working of winter.

When we could labor no more, either from weariness or the fact that our rooing tasks were complete, out came the satchels of bannocks and cakes, puddings, and ale, fruits and nuts, dried fish and boiled clams. These were spread on clean cloths upon the ground. The feast was rich and filling for a family that hungered and laughed with their work well done.

I loved this time the best. As a child at the village rooing, crouched under the rough-hewn tables of logs hastily erected for the vast picnic, I had been all ears as the stories began and the lads and lasses exchanged saucy winks and roars of mirth. One of the names for the Great Maam was "joy," and I could see and hear her at work on the rooing days. Many a love was made during these times, it was said. Working side by side in the heat and the sweat and the stickiness of the task, young folk got to know each other quite well, for no sweet or sour disposition could be hidden here.

I shoved the rest of my honeycake into my mouth and glanced

around. My family rooing was not at all as raucous as the grand village event. Grania's husbandman, Aidan, a big bear of a man with masses of curly black hair, brought fun into the gathering with his joking and tickling of the small ones who leapt at him like excited puppies. Even Fia, quiet and grownup as she was, laughed and giggled and threw her arms around her father fondly.

As usual, Fia shepherded the younger children. Bradan, her brother, was just under her in age, slender and quiet like his maam. Dahi, next youngest, was wiry and quick. Dag, the baby, was powerful and happy as a big dog, like his father. There were two lasses as well, twins they were, nestled in age between Dahi and Dag. They were dark and lissome things, Kira and Maev, whispering in their own little language, playing together, inseparable.

Kriafann's wife Arda was a quiet maam who seldom spoke. But she could take a full-grown ewe down to the ground and was the fastest rooer of all of us. She and Kriafann had made strong-willed sons, Ohran, on the brink of manhood, and my beloved Osheen, his younger brother, of an age with Fia and me, and as tied to us with fists and kisses as any brother would be.

That evening we lay out under the stars, sated after the resplendent feast, quieted in our fullness. Darmid stoked the fire to bring warmth as the high meadows languished towards the sunset. We wrapped ourselves in cloaks and blankets, and the maams leaned upon their husbandmen. The children snuggled around their parents, with the exception of Ohran, who mindful of being almost fully a man, sat independently, holding Dag in his lap.

Leaning upon Aefa, I encircled Bairnie with my arms. Crag lay at Darmid's feet, and the old man, poking a stick into the fire to turn the logs, settled back in his cloaks and gazed into the flames. I sighed happily. We waited quietly for a few moments, for we all knew what was to come. Darmid, with the seasonal chance at an audience, would not lose the opportunity to tell a story.

"'Twas a simple matter, this," Darmid began.

There was a maam who kept goats who was so poor she had no clothes at all for her son, so when he was a wee lad she set him in the ash-hole near the fire. Putting the warm ashes about him, she kept him cozy. As he grew taller she dug the pit deeper and filled it fuller, until at last she could do no more, and taking an old

44

goatskin, tied it around his waist to cover him. Now this being his
first and only bit of clothing, the lad took the air of a grand one
and walked down the grassy track and over the green amongst
their neighbors, who laughed at the spectacle of him, and the news
of their laughing returned to his maam faster than any news of
praise might.

We all waited while Darmid stoked the fire again. It was a rare
moment to be outside in such early spring and be this warm, but he
was distracted to another world in the telling of the story and built
the fire up even more. Wrapping himself back in his robe he sat
down again and continued. It was a clamorous old tale of giants
and wicked faeries and ferocious wolves. The hero was a clever
lad, who with his intrigues made a farmer's daughter—who swore
against ever being happy—laugh, and so by small steps gained her
for his own so that neither she nor her family ever saw scarcity
again.

Young and old alike giggled or laughed outright at the comical
predicaments of the characters. When Darmid ended there were
murmurs of approval as the family rose to go into bed, for wasn't
that the desire of all good children, to bring their parents to peace
and plenty in their old age?

I turned the tale over in my mind. It seemed unfair that we
were told to work for plenty for our parents, and yet, Aefa and
Darmid clearly disapproved of my way of doing just that. I lifted
Bairnie to my face and hugged him tight until he struggled to get
down. As I placed him on the floor and looked up, I could see that
Fia was already helping Grania with the little children.

My face reddened—I felt like a child myself, all my attention
on a dog, while here was Fia doing the job of a grown maam. I
looked around to see if there was derision on the faces of my
family, for in these days, I was always afraid of how I appeared to
them. But they were too engrossed in moving indoors to spread
their sleeping robes upon the floor and go to sleep. Tomorrow they
would journey back to the village, and not return to the mountain
until they brought the beasts to summer there.

I lay down next to Fia with a heavy heart. My cousin curled up
to me, encircling me with an arm. Fia soon breathed deep and
regularly in sleep. But I lay awake long. A feeling of not being
good enough flooded through me, making me feel unsure of the

love that surrounded me. I squeezed Bairnie closer in my arms. I was among my beloved family, it was true, but the little pup made me feel that I truly had someone—or some thing—of my own to love. With his one blue, one hazel green and brown eye he was the only other being I knew that was truly my own kind.

5. BLOSSOM MOON

I squealed as pain radiated from the sole of my left foot.
Drawing it up, I cursed crossly, and slapped the bottom to clear the
pain, then gingerly put it down again, glaring accusingly at the
offending stone. I had dropped the bundle of sticks I carried. I
reached and pulled down hard on a stubborn alder sapling,
breaking off a sizeable branch and inserting it under the leather
cord that encircled my bundle. I hoisted it to my shoulder.

Fia and the little ones had disappeared through the bushes
ahead of me. I could hear them laughing and squealing, and then a
long wail. That was Dag. Something was once again overpowering
his toddler patience.

We had come down the mountain just in time to gather the
nine sacred trees for the morning bonfires of the coming spring
celebration. As long as I could remember we village children
hunted birch, rowan, ash, hawthorn, willow, oak, holly, hazel, and
alder in the days before the festival. We straggled in from our
forays to every corner of the Trabally giggling and laughing,
poking each other, or grumpy and sweating from our efforts. We
tossed our stick bundles as far up on the bonfire stacks as we
could, until the mounds rose mighty enough for the feast days.

The spring sun was hot and direct, unmediated by clouds or
the thick foliage of full summer. A trace of sweat coursed down
my face, plastering stray red locks to my skin and sending a
stinging salt trickle into my eye. I dropped my load of sticks again
in exasperation and cleared sweat and hair away with both hands.
Loosening the leather thong that held back my waterfall of red

hair, I smoothed the most rebellious strands back together and refastened the thong. Picking up my load yet again, I trudged after the others.

Tough, sharp swamp grasses flayed my bare feet and the clingy alders reached out to grasp at my rough-woven shift as I passed them. Behind me Bairnie struggled with the thicket and occasionally plopped down exhausted. He whined when I continued without him, then leapt up, and gamboled after me.

He was a leggy thing already, his growing bones seeming to lengthen his body and legs visibly each day. He had become a gangly half-grown thing, all stupid and floppy and tripping over his own feet like my cousin Bradan ever since he began to grow wisps of hair upon his face. The endearing tumble of a young puppy was now the awkward clumsiness of the fast-growing young dog. His mouth forever open in a happy grin, his tongue lolled to the side, and his ears drew back with a young dog's pleasure in life. I turned for a moment and bent down to croon to him and stroke his ears. He, of course, rewarded my attention with a vigorous tongue bath.

I giggled and straightened up. It was high time to dump my day's gatherings. I began to hurry. Aefa needed me back at the croft to help with the food preparation, for tomorrow was the eve before the feast day when we would gather on the hillock at dawn for the ritual lighting of the fires. The planting and seeding were done. Now was the time to call blessings upon our work that it might result in good strong wheat corn.

The ground was bumpy with spring turf, the new grass wet and slippery. I struggled, but finally caught up with Fia and the rest.

"Where were ye cousin?" Fia looked at me as she loosened her own bound sticks and tossed them up onto the growing pile.

"Where were ye?" I shot back. "I had to stop because I stepped on a sharp stone and then ye were gone. I heard ye for a while, but I just couldn't catch up."

"I'm sorry, sister," Fia said, her brow furrowed. "Did it bleed?"

"Naww.... It was really nothing," I replied, guilty. I knew I had not hurried after them at all—I enjoyed being alone on the quiet trail to the village high place. Fia smiled then, and turned to

Kira who was tugging at her clothes, asking for help with something. Fia was gone then, as usual, surrounded by her crowd of little ones.

I surveyed the high place. The young lads and lasses were already cutting out two large circles of turf from the ground, spaced just far enough apart that people and beasts could pass through the smoke without being burnt. The two bare dirt fire bowls became the repositories of the enormous mound of brush from the nine sacred trees, each bale of nine thrown upon an understructure of thick oak logs. Once burning, it would roar for the Three Days of Fire. Then the fires would smoke quietly for the full eight days of the spring festival.

Tomorrow Aefa and I would extinguish our own hearthfire and leave our home in the stone village well before dawn to come to the gathering place. Under Aefa's ministrations and sacred words, the bonfires would be lit as the sun came up, and the merry-making begun.

But now I made my way down the hillock, skirted the stone village, then began to climb the rise on the other side to Aefa's hut in the forest. In that year I was young, just an acolyte to the enormous responsibility of death crooning that I would one day assume. Sometimes, my stomach clenched with worry that I would fail at my destiny. As usual, I was rehearsing Aefa's teachings in my mind relentlessly, so that by the time I reached the forest hut and entered through the curtained door, I was calm again in my confidence that I knew them.

"Peace to ye, *Granaidh*," I called, and her reedy voice answered in the traditional way: *"And peace of the Great Maam hold yer heart."* I drank long from the ladle and stopped to let Bairnie drink too before dropping it back in the bucket and joining Aefa at the hearth. My pup curled up and was instantly deep asleep. Aefa had ground the winter oats into a coarse meal and was just beginning to make the bannocks. Together we mounded the meal on the wood mixing board, threw in a bit of this and that, then melted the drawn lard and trickled it into a well in the center of the meal. The kneading began.

"So," ventured Aefa, her voice rising and falling with the effort of forming the dough, "Who's bringing a hen to replace Matty's old bird this year?"

I giggled. Old Matty brought her broody hen for the fire blessing every year. She swore it was the spring bonfires that kept it providing eggs far past the life span of most hens. Matty's eyesight was so poor she couldn't tell one old bird from the next, and thus the village spared her the sorrow of weeping for the one thing that had been family to her all these years. They replaced her old hen with a younger one, after passing it between the bonfires.

"*Granaidh*, why do we do it?" I giggled again. "Surely she could survive the death of one old hen and get a new one on her own."

Aefa pushed back a stray lock, loosed and dangling in front of her eyes by the effort put into kneading the dough.

"Ah child, she was a hardworking lass but her life blood does not run in the village veins, for she never had a child to pass into the village life or care for her in her old age. She was a bonny lass, 'tis true, and many the young lad and grown men sought her favors. But her womb did not rise with child at an age when most lasses begin their maaming. As the other maams' families grew she remained slender and lithe and alone. Though her loves were deep she was not taken to wife." It was accepted by all that lads and lasses who partook of the handfasting were intent upon bringing bairns into their holdings. Thus our little village would thrive.

Aefa's gnarly knuckles clutched and grasped, working the fat into the coarse grain while I stood ready to spill a bit of hot water into the dough so that it stuck together firm, yet could be easily squeezed and molded to shape.

"Matty did not mourn," Aefa continued in the broadened tones of the storyteller. "No, she made a life-time of caring for others' wee ones. She rocked them to sleep with the colic, told them stories when their parents were gone for the rooing—how many times she held ye, love, when I was taken far away on the Death Crooning. Without one child of her own she yet had many children in the village. It was these children who grew up and couldn't bear the thought of sorrow coming to her. When I was yet yer age, one amongst her enormous brood hatched the spring ritual of replacing Matty's old hen. I can't even remember who it was—the habit just seemed to spring up on its own."

I laughed and shook my head. The event, though never spoken of, was just as important as the bonfires themselves. Aefa winked at me and gathered the dough into one piece. I spread the mixing board with a fresh layer of coarse oatmeal. We flattened the dough on the oatmeal and pounded it down until it was no thicker than a skin. Aefa picked up her stone blade and murmuring the sacred words, cut it into sun-shapes.

As she did that, I began the caudle coating. Beating an egg well in the hollow of the clay bowl, I added just a whiff of oatmeal, some rich milk from Rosie, and then thick cow's cream brought to us by grateful villagers. I brushed the caudle onto the bannocks after they were heated and turned once on the hot stone in the fire. Spreading it to the edges, I turned the top side down, and as it cooked, spread the other. Before they were taken off to cool the bannocks would be seared twice on each side.

Beside me, Aefa was busy spreading the tops of the last batch with sweet seeds and wrapping them carefully for the trip to the festival. We gossiped as we worked, moving from Matty's hen to who we'd heard would be jumping through the fire together this spring, and who we thought might never jump unless they found a lad or lass blind since birth to share the occasion.

I laughed at that, and at once felt embarrassed and guilty for indulging in mirth at the expense of some other. My red hair and brown freckles, my strange eyes, my burgeoning height were now giving me cause for alarm—and that pricked my conscience when I jested about others.

Thoughts of love rituals at the bonfires were awakening within me, and with them a critical eye for my own appearance. Thinking of the black-haired boy, my cheeks burned. *Who indeed would ever want to jump through with me?!* I asked this question silently, in horror, and the idea pulled my throat tight shut.

Typical of my youthful temper, in a moment I was also angry. Why did I care whether a lad would jump the fires with me? What did I want of lads? Most of them were worse than Osheen— bothersome with their torments, stupid when they were in love. I was already destined to follow Aefa in Death Whispering, and no husbandman was needed for that. I was, further, fortunate to live alone with Aefa—no smelly obnoxious lads in our household, tumbling over each other like dogs, always teasing and torturing other people, and laughing at their own nasty secrets.

Shaking my head with loathing I glanced behind me at

Bairnie. He had roused with our cackling laughter and come over to thrust his wet nose into the back of my knee. Jump through the fires, indeed. I snorted and freed my hand for one instant to pat Bairnie's head. Indeed.

"Sweet Bairnie!" I crooned down at him, "Me sweet Bairnie! Ye are the most beautiful of babes, aye, ye are! Ye are!"

"Ach, be careful, Ronnat," Aefa laughed. "If ye praise yer Bairnie too much, the faerie will overhear ye, and steal him away!"

"Why whatever do ye mean, *Granaidh*?" My reply was mock innocence; for I loved to hear the old spring tale that I knew Aefa longed to tell again. It would ease the repetitive work of caudling the bannocks.

Oh, aye, and there is danger in taking too much pride in a wee bairn, for wasn't it the case that all the warnings from the village folk never stopped one maam from crooning out loud the beauty of her wee one, and that was to be her undoing.

That poor silly maam, who praised her babe against all the admonishments from her elders, soon had him replaced with a hideous faerie changeling. It was only by listening to the elders that she tricked the faerie into taking back its ugly whelp and returning her sweet fat bairn to his cradle. As the story ended I slid the last bannock onto the pile and Aefa sprinkled the small mound with sweet spiced seeds and then wrapped it and placed it into a basket for the morrow.

"Foo, *Granaidh*," I said to Aefa, "No faerie will bind Bairnie in a swaddle and leave me a brat in his place. He's not a true bairn." We laughed at that thought, and finished putting up the food.

Later I lay in my blankets and thought about the next day. We had a goodly portion to contribute to the feast. The dark before dawn would come very quickly, yet Aefa's story rolled through my head and kept me from sleeping. What if I was a changeling? Some of the village folk thought so. Certainly Mae had muttered it many times as she fixed me in that malevolent stare. I tugged one long curl. Perhaps I was, with my red hair and brown freckles and two-colored eyes. Any one of my strange features would mark me for faerie amongst the villagers.

A question burned deep in my heart, and it rubbed me raw. Not "*who* am I?" for I knew I was Ronnat Rua, Apprentice to

Aefa, She Who Walks Alone, Death Crooner of the Trabally. To this end I was learning my herbs and medicinals and I was to care for Aefa all her life. No, my question was, "*what* am I?"

What was I? The words tumbled over and over in my dimming consciousness, then slowly lost their flame as I faded into sleep.

****

In the dark Aefa stroked my cheek. I sat up even as I opened my eyes, and reached to pull on heavy felted shoes and a shawl against the early morning chill.

The creels of food were packed tight and lashed shut. We slid a long larch pole through the lid handles so we could easily bear the weight of food, blankets, plates, cups, knives, and gifts for Aefa's other grandchildren. With the pole on one shoulder, we would each have a hand free to carry the tethers of Bairnie, Rosie and Juniper.

Later we would decorate the animals with flowers and drive them through the bonfires with prayers, then chase them off to find their own way back up the hill to Aefa's croft. Tiny little sheepwalks crisscrossed the hill around the stone village. All the beasts knew their inherited paths up to pasture and back to the village huts. Generation after generation of sheep and goats had followed their maams and then passed that knowledge to their lambs and kids. On these self-same paths I had spent many a childhood hour tramping the distance between Aefa's croft and the village gathering place.

The predawn air was still, broken only by bird calls echoing sharp and close. I walked silently and single file with my grandmother. The goat and ewe followed with nary a bleat or a clanking clay bell in the gray of early morn. The land was bathed in fog; filmy wisps briefly defined misty curls and disappeared. Here and there a clatter or shout rose from the village below as it wakened. All around birdsong gathered into a swell, and I felt my heart quicken as the joy of the spring celebration gripped me.

Aefa's voice broke our silence.

"It was at the Spring Fires that ye came home to me when ye were just a bairn. Hardly one year old, ye were, but already Grania had ye on the gruel and sweet goat's milk in a little flagon, for ye were not content with just her breast. And even so, for all ye were a feisty wee thing, it seemed I did nothing but feed ye for a whole moontide after ye came to me. I daresay perhaps ye'd been ready to give over the nursing for some time before. Once ye were sated ye were the happiest, most good natured bairn that ever was.

"Little Ronnat ye were named by yer maam for yer father— she gasping it out to me as she lay dying. He was of the ocean, she said, and we all thought he was a selkie. And like a red seal pup ye were, darting here and there, barking from the moment ye woke till yer sleeping. Ye're me child of the Spring Rites, and the blessing follows ye even now."

I treasured these words, for they made me feel spring was my time, and the ocean my father. I turned them over and over in my mind as we walked on, cutting sharply up the hillock where the bonfires were waiting ready to be lit. The early morning moisture bore the fragrance of new grass and the pungence of the wee spring flowers. I wanted to fall to my knees to breathe in the little patches of spicy gill-o-the-ground, but the pole we bore prevented that and I had to content myself with each whiff that rose to me when the stems were brushed or broken by our feet.

By now the whole village was making its way up the hill in small household groups. At the top they set up mats and blankets around creels of food. Maams sat and nursed their bairns as the gathering grew. Later the wee ones would bound like a crop of spring lambs between the family groups, any adult hand providing care, comfort, or discipline when called for.

Suddenly I felt shy. All the other lasses my own age gravitated into a small gaggle of giggling and whispering until their maams shouted for them to come back and tend the little ones. Most hoisted the bairns up on hips, or backs, or grabbed their hands and tugged them along into the knot of lasses as it clotted up again. I saw Fia as she stepped away from the group, frantically gesturing for me to join them. I had no younger brothers or sisters to take care of. I only had Bairnie, and I felt as if the lasses laughed behind their hands at me for that.

Ducking my head, I pretended I did not see my cousin. There was nothing that said I could not join them. But the fears of one as young as I was then are paralyzing. I dreaded that sudden silence that would ensue if I broke into the circle. Their whispering and gossiping would stop, and some of the lasses would stare at me as if I didn't belong. They all knew I was to be Death Crooner after Aefa, and that was a wedge between us that only added distance to my strange and solitary ways.

Aefa said I needed to take courage and push my way in and keep doing it until I was one of them. That it was me, myself, who allowed the separation to grow. I reached for Bairnie and stroked the soft down behind his ears. No, I would wait.

Settling back, I softly rubbed Bairnie's head, watching the crowd grow. Soon, lads began gathering in a group of their own, circling and diving into the group of lasses like hunting hawks. They shrieked and laughed as the lasses yelled at them and kicked them away, or threw clods at them, screaming. The play fighting reached a crescendo that brought parents over to pull the older children back to work, dousing the conflagration of adolescent tension.

For a brief moment I envied their squabbling groups. I envied their silly games, and yet, at the same time felt contempt for them—and a little puzzled. I just didn't understand what they were doing, or why, or why they would want to do it. And I did not even look like any of them—even my cousins.

Averting my eyes from the painful reminder that I was alone in my difference, I began to unpack the creels. I spread out the coverlet and arranged the packets of food and clothing in a neat little nest. Aefa wandered over to greet Grania, who was just coming up the hill with Bradan. I smiled faintly and waved across the meadow to Bradan, who waved back. Finally done with the unpacking, comfortable on our blanket with Bairnie dozing next to me, I leaned back on my arms again and surveyed the holiday camp still getting larger before my eyes.

There was much that came between me and the other children of Cloch Graig. For most of the year I lived a ways from the village in Aefa's hut, or up at the summer shieling with Darmid. I did not fully live and breathe in the village or my age-mates' lives the way they all did in each others'. They shared each other's homes as if they were one. Each had one or two special friends, or even a small group with whom they lived regularly, part of each other's thoughts, loves, hates, families and living space. The children of Cloch Graig had a life of their own running the dark maze of passageways between the stone houses and the sheep-paths, weaving secrets that flowed just under the surface of their parents' world.

I tried to comfort myself, to defend myself from the curse of being an outsider. I had Fia, my breast sister and best friend. I had Osheen, my annoying boy cousin I loved as well as a brother. I had Darmid though he was far away and my time with him infrequent. Above all, I had Aefa, my friend and confidant, my maam and *granaidh* at the same time. No one else came so near to my heart as Aefa.

I turned away from what I saw and declared to myself that I didn't envy the other children in the stone village—their games seemed juvenile and pointless—all the running and screeching and pretense at life dramas. But I wondered what it would feel like to have such a group of friends for myself, and I suddenly felt very vulnerable. Aefa was the extent of my immediate family. Darmid was on the mountain.

I turned my gaze back over to the huddle of lasses, ringed by the children in their care, and saw Fia nodding and smiling and laughing behind her hands with the other girls. Fia and I were inseparable when the families were together, and yet Fia was linked to the other children while I was not.

Fia was so......perfect. Fia was a little maam ever since I could remember. Fia was barely a year older than I, yet she was always guiding me—and all the other children, for that matter. Fia spent her days teaching me, persuading me, pulling me along gently, as if we were years apart and Fia more her own maam's age than mine. And Fia had her own large family.

To be sure, I knew that either my aunt or uncle would take me in if anything happened to Aefa, but it would be cold comfort to me. Grania was strong and loving, and Kriafann, wise and kindly as Darmid, with a mind as sharp as a new flaked blade. But they had braw broods of their own, and I feared that special closeness I had with Aefa would be lost forever if my graniadh left this world.

I shook such dark musings from my head and watched as a new ripple of activity coursed through the crowd. Large baskets of sweet bone cakes were being distributed. I took a cake from the flat basket offered by a young lass from the neighboring village of Clochbeg, and scooped up a handful of ripe redberries to go with it. Slowly I munched the familiar sweetness of honey and the tang the little black seeds gave the cake. The redberries were soft and juicy; I licked the dribbles that went down my arms.

This was the first round of sacred cakes of the holiday. The sweet white honeyed bonecakes speckled with crunchy black seeds melted in my mouth—just like real bones crumbled in the black earth that brought forth the freshness and the sweet newness of spring. It always followed this way: one bite of cake, one of redberries, one bite of gritty earth, one bite of sweetness, until they were all one in the spring rites.

My eyes strayed to a tall youth coming towards me through the crowd. My heart caught in abject terror. The black curls and gentle face were just close enough that I could see it was Kerr. I knew I flushed as red as the juice that trickled from my fingers across my palms and down my forearms. If I was not so paralyzed I would leap to my feet and dart down the hill, crashing like a panicked fawn.

Suddenly Osheen popped up in front of Kerr and grasped his friend's forearms. Osheen began to pull him in the opposite direction. But not before Kerr shot a doleful glance my way and dipped his brow to me just a little. I couldn't help catching my breath, my heart racing before some unknown force. Gritty earth and sweetness. They were all one in the spring rites.

BOBBIE GROTH

6. BERRY MOON

I ran my fingers through the softness of Bairnie's coat. Our matching blue and hazel green and brown eyes were locked together. His were just like the swirl of ocean. Just like mine. That's what we were. Bairnie and me, different from the others, frightening to some: but brother and sister to the ocean. Given a moment of quiet, I fell to musing on my puppy with as much absorption as any besotted youth does in the intensity of first love, or first time maam with her new bairn.

Aefa was seated at the table making fresh batches of medicinals, unguents, poultice bags and cooking herbs to take to the shieling and leave with Darmid. As she finished each I could hear her soft muttering as she tied it up. *Wisdom of the serpent be yers, wisdom of the raven be yers, wisdom of valiant eagle, voice of swan be yers, voice of honey be yers, voice of stars, bounty of the sea be yers, bounty of the land be yers, bounty ....*

The trip to the summer pastures was the promise of almost three whole moontides of pleasure—a lifetime for a lass of thirteen summers. For weeks after the rooing we all climbed to the stone circle and watched the rising sun upon it, moving closer and closer to the stone that marked the day when all would gather the village stock animals and set off on a merry march overland through bogs and across fields, and up the foothills that turned into mountains. Up, ever up we went to the fresh, sweet grass of summer that surrounded Darmid's shieling.

There was a rising tone of excitement in the village in the days before our summer move. We packed baskets of food for *tuaha* and beast alike. Fish bones that had been drying upon the outer east wall of the stone village were scraped down and wrapped to hand-feed the cattle, a treat for them after the long winter of dried hay. On the morning of the departure, the beasts would be bleating and lowing and stamping. It took a strong husbandman to keep them together and orderly, restraining them from stampeding off overland to their beloved high pastures.

One terrible summer just such a thing came to be. I was such a little lass then, but not too little to understand the gravity of the tragedy that struck Cloch Graig. The day before the march was to commence, my uncle Angus, Aefa and Darmid's youngest son, slipped while gathering bird's eggs upon the high cliffs.

One moment he was there, joking and laughing with the other lads as they robbed the nests, the next he disappeared with a curdling scream. Helplessly the lads watched until his body lay sprawled upon the beach cobbles far below. Their own yelling and screaming drew a crowd swiftly from the village. Weeping we carried Angus's crumpled body home.

When a family of our little village lost a beloved one, it was a great mourning that took place. This was worse: this was the mourning for a child of our Death Crooner. Once started, the death ritual must play itself out before any other task could be taken up again.

When the last words of the ritual had been said, Aefa, weak with sorrow for her son, strode silently back from the hill of tombs to Cloch Graig with the rest of the exhausted mourners. To our horror the beasts were gone. They had broken their paddocks in our absence and stampeded away on their own.

And so the din of grief began again. We who had spent so much in tears and weeping for the last three days mustered more, for the animals were as much a part of our lives as our family members. Supplies and things that had been dropped upon the death of young Angus were seized in panic. We left the village in a great haste, following the tracks of the herd. In the end, we reached the shieling right behind the beasts, who knew the way so well that the older ones, in their caution, provided a quieting effect on the younger ones and lead them there unscathed. There they were, all accounted for, placidly grazing on the sweet long grass.

Immediately a murmuring began that there was never a gentler voice with the beasts than that of young Angus. It must have been he who took the beasts to safety before ever he left for the arms of the Great Maam.

I remembered that time so clearly, though I was barely out of moss swaddling when it happened. There was such an intense mixture of the mourning for Angus and the joy that our beasts had arrived unharmed. It opened my young eyes wide to the mysterious bands of love that bound my world so tightly.

Year in and year out, the march to the summer shieling came and went. Some stayed at the shieling for the entire season—some whole families, and the lasses who milked the beasts. The fisher and farmer lads, who returned to the seaside villages after the herding trek, made their way back to the shieling many times over the summer moontides to make music for the lasses and laugh around the fires deep into the night. Each time the lads returned to the stone village to help with the fishing and farming again, without sleep and without a care. The elders shook their heads and sighed, for such was the energy of youth.

I shook the memories from before my eyes and attended more closely to Aefa. The pungent fragrance of the herbs and simples, both fresh and dried, hung in the air. The old maam's fingers were dark purple from the gentian she prepared for the hooves and horns of the sheep. Standing at her elbow, I buried my nose in each small bundle or bag or packet I took from the completed pile of medicines before handing it to my *granaidh*. Aefa fit them tightly together in a large satchel--so tightly they would not rattle or shake or tip.

"Aefa," said I, "How do ye know all this?"

"Know all what, little bird?"

"How do ye know how to make all these things?" I eyed the array of packets. Suddenly, it seemed, for the first time I really looked around the croft. The roof rose sturdily on thick rafters, coming to a point at the very top where the smoke hole revealed blue sky. The walls were built of stone mortared to the squared off tree trunks that held the peaked roof in place. Thickly thatched, it was positively stuffed, floor to ceiling, with drying wildflowers and herbs, with crocks to keep Aefa's potions in, with sacks and bags and wraps and rolls of twine to tie them all up.

"Me heart," said Aefa, "I've been learning every night and

every day of me life for years and years. From the time I was a child toddling after me own maam, when I was a lass, when me own bairns grew inside me and now their bairns are even older than yerself. That's a long, long time. I didn't learn it all in one summer."

"Will I ever know all this?" I felt suddenly defeated by all the tasks that lay before me.

"In yer time," said Aefa absently, counting tiny satchels that she tucked into a larger one.

"But how did this start--how did yer maam know, and hers, and hers before that?"

Aefa put down what she was doing and looked sharply at me, one eyebrow raised. "How ye're hungry for learning today, me love. If that's the way of it, this is how me maam told it to me..." Aefa took a deep breath, and closed her eyes. The sacred lilt issued from her lips, and I drifted far away with its mystery.

In the dawn of days the Great Maam of All lived in a grove of trees by a sacred well. The oak, the yew, the alder, the hazel; each tree of the forest grew in the grove and reached a splendid height and breadth from drinking the waters of the well.

But the tuaha were small and sickly, for the water of the sacred well gave them dreams and visions, but did not slake their hunger. Soon they sang and danced to the Great Maam of All, saying, we're hungry, we're cold, we're alone in the dark.

She heard their cries. Her hazel tree bent down its arms and seven hazelnuts dropped into the sacred well. As they fell, the salmon, the Great Maam's messengers, swam up from the heart of the earth, and swallowed the hazelnuts. As they swallowed them, one by one, the salmon were transformed in bursts of light and magic.

First was the giving of the fire. In it, a salmon leapt from the water a sparkling torch, never to die and always a gift to the tuaha through the fire of storms.

Then was the giving of the bannock. The second salmon leapt out and became the never-ending loaf that fed the tuaha through the cold winter and lived again in spring with the first grains.

Then was the giving of the cloven hooves and horns. The salmon messenger became the horned one that runs with the moon and graces the table.

62

Then was the giving of the herb. This salmon became the rich flowers and tubered roots that cure illness and keep away sadness.

The last three gifts were the most important of all, for they allowed the tuaha to keep ever mindful of the first gifts, and to use them.

Fifth was the joy of the Great Maam of All: the giving of gifts and the celebration of love, of thankfulness, of laughter for all eternity.

The sixth gift was the sadness of want and the desperation of thwarted love and loneliness, the hurt of loss. This was given so the children of the tuaha might remember the time before the Seven Sacred Gifts, and never waste those gifts or keep them from each other.

And finally, the Great Maam of All gave the seventh gift, that of moonsong so that light might become known by dark, and dark known by light. For ever after, it was the keeping of the balance of the two by the weaving of sacred story and song that tied the tuaha to the Great Maam of All, night by night, moon by moon, season by season, year by year, from generation to generation.

So it goes in our village, the turning of the year. Birth and fruitfulness and sleep remind us that we need never return to the days of cold, starvation, and loneliness. The time before the knowing of the seasons, the time before the knowing of the gifts.

Aefa drew a breath then, and tied the top of the satchel, pulling the knot tight, "And so I came to learn of the gifts of kindness and plenty from the mouth of me maam and she from her maam before her, and she from her maam before that, all the way back to the sacred Salmon Well. I know this because me maam knew it, and ye shall know because I know, and so on until ye find another to carry this knowing for the *tuaha*."

I gazed around the stone hut at the clutches of drying plants, taking in the heavy perfume they exuded. This was the secret of why Aefa lived apart: that she might work the Great Turning of the Light between night and day, moons, seasons, life, death, and rebirth. Aefa's task was to look to the Seven Gifts to keep the heart of the *tuaha* grateful, to preserve life and honor death.

I went to the fragrant bundle of lavender hanging in one corner and breathed it in like a prayer. *Great Maam of All,* I willed silently. *Help me to learn.*

****

I tied the lead around Bairnie's neck. I had worked hard to train him every day since Darmid's brief lesson during the days of rooing. My winsome pup could sit and lie down on command, wait for his food, come when called, and no longer fought the lead.

Now he looked at me expectantly and sat wagging his tail while I hoisted my bags to my shoulders. When we at last took our leave, Aefa paused at the lintel post to utter the blessing of journey. *Bless me in all me travels, be ye a smooth way before me. Be ye a guiding star above me. Be ye a keen eye behind me, this day, this night, forever.*

Once outdoors we could hear the general din from the village below. Family groups tied their bundles up for the trip and ambled to the green where the stock were pushed together as a herd, lowing and bleating and scraping their hooves upon the ground.

The stray clank of clay bells cut through the rumble of the beasts and the excited chatter of the villagers. Layered over the firm words of the stock drivers were shrieks of laughter from the young. Excitement gripped me: the loveliness of summer was no longer just a promise.

Aefa and I drew back, moving slowly and allowing the villagers and the herds to surge ahead and trample the way for us. Branches broke or snapped back with the crowd's passing, the din fading until the thunder of hooves diminished into vague thumps. We lagged farther and farther back from the group until silence crept in from the dank forest, broken only by an occasional bird call. Earthen smells kicked up by the passing of so many hooves and feet wafted to us in the quiet.

In front of us Bairnie bounded back and forth grabbing at wisps with his mouth, pouncing upon sticks, and darting suddenly off the trail so that I would have to pull his lead and call him back. I remembered the trip to the rooing with him in the pack basket, and marveled that in so short a time he had become too big to carry. In fact, he pulled me along with his boundless energy.

The shadowy dapple of the woods lay upon us like dreams and soon we stilled our chatter to swim in its languor. The sun was quite high in the sky when we came to the mouth of the forest path and crossed into the vast oak savannah.

I could not help but gasp each time we came to this spot. The sacred groves spread out over the hills in glorious green leaf crownings. The wind ran through the tree tops like the rushing of a rill tumbling softly over rocks on its way downhill. The green and brown masses of trunks and branches rustled in the breeze. Far across the rippling vista the village group was invisible under the spread of the leaf canopy, the faint noises of their movement just audible.

We entered the savannah and walked in comfortable silence until Aefa stopped in the shade of our two favorite trees. I called them the Maam and Da trees—two enormous trunks set against each other so that their bodies leaned and joined together. Above me their vast boughs embraced in a tender lover's knot, their leaves shading and cooling the grass beneath.

It was here that we put down our bundles on every trip to the shieling. Bairnie tugged at his lead, so I slipped it from around his neck. He would not stray. He nipped at the blowing blades, tore one off and shook his head furiously to clear his tongue of the prickly thing. Fixing his eyes on me he carefully squatted and left a puddle right where we had settled. I squealed and we jumped to move our small pile of belongings away from it. Spreading a mat to sit on, we began pulling out our high noon meal while Bairnie lay on his back, snuffling and rolling about in the grass.

When the bannock and cheese were out on the clean white cloth, I said the prayer of thanks aloud. *Give us O Maam the meal of our heart, the seventh bannock, the honey sweet foaming milk, the sap and milk of the fragrant fields, the drink that quenches.*

Aefa smiled, approving of my careful cadence, learned meal after meal, day after day, for my whole young life. We broke the first bannock between us, and I in turn shared a piece with Bairnie.

"He is one of us Aefa, ye'll see." I took my bannock and rubbed it in the sweet goat cheese, holding it out to him. Bairnie fell upon it greedily. Once sated, he bumbled off away from us and continued his rolling and snorting in the tall grass, biting at the roots, then sneezing and spitting the blades from his mouth.

"*Granaidh*, he's so silly!" I giggled as I wolfed my own cheese and bread, hungered by the long walk. Aefa was intent on chewing her meal and closed her eyes while she basked in the breezes and shade. All three of us dozed off when we were done. We startled awake as Aefa stood suddenly and gathered her pack back up upon her back.

"Come, me heart," she rasped, her voice muzzy with drowse, "This is so delightful but it will not help us at the other end of the day trying to find Darmid's hut with only the stars for light."

I sighed sleepily and slipped the lead back around Bairnie's neck. Standing, I took Aefa's arm and we strode through the paths of bent grasses left by the villagers and herds before us. Under the shade of the magnificent oaks, some of last year's acorns crunching softly beneath our feet. The full sun upon the leaves of the oak crowns filtered down in a play of light across the waves of green.

How the afternoon sweetly passed amidst the dapple of sunlight and shade until at last we came upon the seam in the land where bushes began to dot the hillside and breath-taking savannah gave way to hilly scrub.

The trail wound its way upward and on either side of the track yellow chest-high broom flowers grabbed at my rough-woven shift, sticking and pulling and leaving their soft scent upon the home-spun. We walked single file now, with Aefa in the lead and me squinting against the afternoon sun. Behind me Bairnie's gamboling settled to a steady walk.

The bushes and small trees thinned and gave way to moorland bog, thickets, then mosses and low ground-pines and wind-stunted mountain trees. The sun's heat beat upon my hair while the breeze picked up and blew soothing and cool into my face. When dusky shadows began to fall we paused only briefly for Aefa to pull out our shawls. Wrapping them about our shoulders we knotted them tightly across our backs before donning our loads again.

I knew better than to pay attention to my growing hunger. The sun was on its downward journey and we must thrust onward toward Darmid's high meadow to outrace the shadows creeping across the lowlands beneath us. Above, the sky was a bowl of pale blue, fading to white at the horizon. Darkness would come all too soon.

Aefa began humming a soft sprightly dance tune to urge us on our way. I added the words, and soon we were both singing and marching at a brisk pace, laughing at the silly words about a forest hog and a young lad too long in his currach on the sea islands looking for eggs and shellfish, so that indeed, he was smitten by the young sow.

His head was daft from his days on the raft, and her beauty filled his eyes full sore. So he caught the hog, and kissed the hog, and never wanted lassies nae maer!!!

The last two words were shouted out, punctuated by stamping our feet. The pace picked up as we sang and the fullness of giggling overpowered by breathlessness gave me no room to shelter hunger pangs. We soon came upon the trampled trail where the progress of village folk and stock had slowed. All about were battered bushes and flattened grass in places where family groups broke off to wend their way to their own crofts.

With a sharp barking, Darmid's Crag burst upon us with his customary shower of wags and licking kisses. Bairnie's ears perked up when he saw his long-lost friend, and he began to bolt and charge against his lead. Crag ran to him, sniffing and matching the pup's jumps with his own.

"Bairnie! Bairnie! Hep lad!" I pulled his lead up short, squatting down to ruffle Crag's silky black fur. I slipped Bairnie's lead off his neck. In no time he was jumping up on Crag with his front paws and leaping sideways to avoid the older dog's playful nips. Both animals whined and yapped gleefully.

"Come to." Aefa motioned to Crag, who snapped to her side, panting happily and wagging his long lush tail. Bairnie began worrying the older dog's tail and grunting his pleasure.

We clucked and giggled at the silly hounds as we strode our last few steps to Darmid's hut, dark against the lengthening dusk. Cracks of warm yellow light seeped around the edges of the window and door. We ducked through into the full light of a newly stoked fire and dropped our burdens to exchange the kisses and hugs of greetings with Darmid.

The old man was stirring the pot for the evening meal and held the wooden paddle spoon far from him to avoid getting it in our hair during the loving assault. I buried my cheeks in his gorse beard and squeezed him hard and earnestly, finally delivering a huge smacking kiss on his smooth hairless head.

"Ach, lass, go on with ye then," he chortled, wiping his head vigorously with his sleeve. "I'll lose the rest of me hair if ye keep that up." He rose and folded Aefa into his arms. The glowing firelight melted away the years, blurring away the wrinkles, straightening the stooped shoulders, and darkening the gray heads until for a brief moment, I thought I saw young lovers clasped in a happy desperate embrace after separation. I turned my back then, and knelt as Bairnie's soft tongue ran over my bare feet.

"Look, *Daideo*," I said, "Isn't he a braw one now? He's walked here himself, and I've done a bit of training with him." I proceeded to show Darmid how Bairnie could come, sit, lie down, and fetch on command. Bairnie fixed his eyes on me. He loved this game, and he obeyed.

"Aye, lass, he's learning fair quick." Darmid let go of Aefa and moved off to the fire again, bending to stir the stew up from the bottom of the pot. "Come, me hearts," he said, "Ye must be starving."

I pulled three wood bowls down from the shelf and fumbled in our bags for the rest of the bannocks we brought with us. As we ate, Aefa and I entertained Darmid with gossip from Cloch Graig and regaled him with the details of our long walk from the sea beaches on our side of the Large Island to the highlands that dropped off into the sea on the other side; this was the place that Darmid called home.

The old folks continued to murmur and converse long after I snuggled down before the fire on a large fleece, my shawl and blanket over me, Bairnie snuggled in my arms. Crag curled himself up at my back, watching. The fire hissed and fell, orange coals glowing like a sunset and murmuring like circling birds. In the power of its warmth, I fell asleep heavily, before even the night prayers were said, without even begging a tale from Darmid.

****

Coming quietly awake I knew at once that I was alone by the fact that Darmid's prayer upon rising was not the thing that stirred me. I sat up and slipped into my rough-knit sweater. The fire was banked as Darmid always did when he would be out on the mountain. Even Bairnie was nowhere to be found. I grabbed a cold bannock from its covered wooden bowl and slipped out into the pearl pink and gray of the early light.

I heard the stir of the shieling huts below—the clank of a clay bell, the occasional wail of an infant, the bleat of a sheep. The smell of wood smoke chased up the hillside to me. The morning breeze cast its thin allure, sidling through my hair and pulling me farther up on the mountain. Darmid's flocks must be in the high meadow.

My legs pumped hard and I thrust step upon step, grasping the short brush to pull myself up. When the high meadow broke suddenly, wide, sweeping and green, I hauled myself over the hillock's edge and sat puffing and sucking in the sweet mountain air. I could feel the chill of night falling away before the comforts of sun-warmed air.

After a few bites of bannock, I pulled myself to my feet and continued on across the meadow to the flocks on the other side. The bleating of the ewes was now clear and continuous, the clank of the small clay bells distinct, cutting through the morning haze.

Darmid and Aefa were hunched over a spring lamb, less leggy and more solid than the lately born summer lambs. Aefa was cutting away at its thick mat of baby fleece to apply her unguents to a nasty sore up under its foreflank. The lamb kicked and struggled and bleated pitifully as Darmid held it. I ran to its head and knelt down singing the little lamb's song Aefa taught me. My voice rose and fell with the lamb's struggles as I slowly calmed it. Finally it lay contented and still for Aefa's ministrations.

"Ye didn't wake me! Ye left me for lazy!" I muttered between verses, and the old ones chuckled at me.

"If ye're so tired as to lie abed through the dawn, shouldn't we leave ye to the Great Maam's instructions?" asked Darmid.

"No." I scowled and they laughed again. "Where is Bairnie?"

Darmid gestured out toward the herd. I could see the white and silver thistledown bumbling cockeyed about Crag's feathers, trying desperately to shadow his every move, and at the same time planting himself right in Crag's way. The older dog was a black streak, pausing only occasionally to nudge a lamb, then taking off again for the other side, trailing the gangly ball of silver fluff behind him.

"Look Aefa! He's learning!" I declared. "See, he'll be herding before long."

Darmid laughed, "It'll take more than a day to make a fine herd dog, lassie. His interest now is running after Crag. When it turns to the sheep, well then we have a task on our hands to keep him from taking them down."

"Aye," said Aefa, "If it's a sheepdog ye're wanting he'll have to be here with Darmid a good long while past the summer grazing. Think on that, lass."

I turned away from them and gazed across the meadow at the two dogs. Yes, it seemed, Bairnie would need both Darmid's and Crag's guidance and teaching for far longer than the shieling season if he was to be of any use as a shepherding dog. I wondered if Aefa would part with me long enough to stay with him. In truth I couldn't bear the thought of leaving him--even with Darmid, whom I called grandfather. It wasn't because I was afraid Bairnie would come to harm. No, it was because in the short time since I'd rescued the half-dead thing, I, myself, had come to need him with all my heart.

"*Granaidh*," I turned to Aefa again, the sun full in my face and making me squint, "*Granaidh*, couldn't we stay? Couldn't we stay until Bairnie is grown and no longer needs Crag to follow?"

"And what would become of the cures? Who would pick berries and herbs, and medicines, and later crops, and put up crocks for the winter, and dry the herbs and make medicinals for the village and croon the bairns in and the old folks out?"

I screwed my mouth into a grimace. My *granaidh*'s words were true. Plenty went on down in the stone village while the herders were up at the shieling. There was fishing and gardening and gathering of hay. There was no other herb witch for the village save Aefa.

The lamb struggled just then and leapt up at Darmid's release. It tottered stiffly for a few steps then picked up its feet and gamboled away. Crag shot out, a black arrow aimed straight at the lamb, and guided it back towards its maam. Bairnie was left incredulous behind him.

I shielded my eyes and called to him, "Bairnie, come Bairnie." Instead of bounding after Crag, he turned in my direction, ran to me, and sat. I bent and buried my nose in his fur. He licked my face furiously, wriggling with joy and excitement while I giggled at the slimy bath.

Darmid spoke: "He knows he's yours, lass. He knows ye already and wants to please ye. 'Tis time to begin training."

7. ANTLER MOON

I crept beneath the ancient stones in the high pasture. What *tuaha* tomb this once was I knew not, for generations of wind and driving sea storms had stripped its turf mound away, melted its bones, blown its ashes into the ocean, and exposed its giant boulders and the large three-cornered roof stone.

Gone were any of the decorated message stones with their swirls and circles that recorded the names of the dead who had lain here, and the names of their *tuaha* maams, as well as the star calendar of the day the inhabitant's spirit was released. I had been taught all of my life to revere these lonely stones that dotted the lands I lived in. But today this one was simply a welcome respite of shade on a mountain pasture laid bare of trees from generations of grazing sheep.

I squinted out across the glaring sheen of the field. Darmid and Crag attended to the flocks at the far end. In my arms Bairnie whined and struggled to join the older dog. Darmid had bade me keep Bairnie tethered and away from the work of Crag so he would be just that eager to join it when we began his training. I held him fast against me, and presently he stopped, yawned ferociously, nestled his head into my forearm and succumbed to a nap.

I gently stroked the soft hair behind his ears. Like goose down, it was, with a very slight crimp—very like my own on the days when fog rolled in and hung the day heavy with drops of moisture. The two distant figures shimmered and darted above and beyond the undulating light of the sheep as I watched, my precious pup in my arms.

Aefa had left this morning. We talked about it for two days, and Aefa remained firm: a dog had to work if a dog was to be fed, and the only fitting work for a dog was with sheep. Thus, if I wanted Bairnie as my own, he must stay and learn from Crag. I likewise must stay and learn sheep from Darmid. Even *tuaha* bairns took their place in the activity of the village as soon as they could walk and run and speak. I was no bairn, and if my *tuaha* kinfolk and village were to accept my beloved pup, he, as well as I, must be prepared to earn our keep.

"Besides," my *granaidh* said, "I bid ye care for Darmid between the learning times. Ye shall spin his wool and knit another warm hooded sweater to replace the one I made so many years ago. Have ye not noticed how it is tattered and threadbare despite many mendings?"

"Aye, *Granaidh*," I sighed. I felt shame to think I begrudged such simple comforts for my dearest *daideo*. And yet, some part of my young self saw anything that took me away from the training of my silver pup as an imposition.

"And he knows only the simple herbs, birdie," Aefa went on, "So bring some kindness to his cooking pot." Aefa seemed so fierce and strong and yet how her eyes poured tears when she hugged and kissed me goodbye this morning. In all the years I had lived with my grandmother, I had rarely been away from her. I, too, cried into Aefa's gray locks, but at the same time thanked her for relinquishing me to Darmid that I might bring home a young sheepdog of our own.

My eyes brimmed in remembering the morning. I buried my head in Bairnie's side to wipe them. This was not just sadness at being away from Aefa, but also excitement at the prospect of something new--a life on the mountain, learning all that Darmid could teach me, and becoming a strong hand to direct my Bairnie.

I rolled over and sat up, displacing the sleeping dog. He stretched, curled tight by my crossed legs and went back to his slumbers. I pulled the spindle out of my shoulder bag and began to work on the bundle of fleece I brought with me. I knew that in the time my *daideo* had to give me, I wanted to spin up all the wool from the spring rooing that lay in tight-wrapped bundles in the loft of his little croft.

"Aye, lass," he sighed heavily when I told him my goal, "For

72

want of youth, I am a man rich in sheep yet poor in clothing. Me old fingers can spin but clumsily and so I have me fleeces but nothing to spin them with."

When I was very young I was a saucy wee lass who would rather spend her time braiding grasses into faerie crowns than assisting in the ever-present chore of turning raw wool into usable yarn. I couldn't help but grimace when I remembered how many of the carry-bags and utility blankets Aefa and I used demonstrated my childish impulses. My raggy skeins were knotted into ugly, bunched bags and mats. But nothing was wasted in the stone village, so still we used them and so my childishness was not easily forgotten.

Distracted into daydreaming from the earliest, I took to knotting beautiful bits of driftwood, dried flowers, and bright pebbles into my practice weaving. Some hung on the wall of Aefa's hut yet. Old Mae and her ilk clucked and disapproved and thought *Granaidh* Aefa was squandering her wisdom to raise an impulsive, spoiled, dreamer of a lass who would benefit no child as a maam. They even whispered that I made nets for the faerie folk, drawing danger into the village with my silly and fanciful weaves.

But I was a blessed child, for Aefa saw the same beauty in them that I saw. She hung them and complimented my creations before luring me on to make more practical and useful items. Aefa was a wise and tender maam.

Presently my thoughts left their meanders. I began to hum spinning tunes to bathe my arms and hands with a deep calm rhythm that eased and evened the spinning and grew the yarn ball.

I give the sunwise turns, I sang softly, *dependent on the lass, I give the sunwise turn dependent on the maam, I give the sunwise turn dependent on the wise old crone, I give the sunwise turn singing, dancing, all for the thread, all for the cloth, all for the cloak.*

Yes, my *granaidh* Aefa was a wise maam who drank her wisdom from maams who loved her. It made me wonder about my own maam. I knew the stories of faerie and how she ran the meadows and beaches on her own, she, like me, a quiet secretive lass. Though my maam Ayveen was as dark as the other lasses in looks, she was as different from them in every other way as I myself was. Her bairnie only became known to her own maam by the swelling of her belly—that was not just surprising, it was an insult to the tightly knit village that birthed us both.

Young folk lay together in the Spring Rites and every child of every lass's womb was loved alike, even should she later take a handfasted husbandman from another man. The news of a new child was celebrated by all. But my maam Ayveen was a lass who did not talk to others, did not share. And that marked her for suspicion.

The village tongues soon wagged that she would give birth to a seal child for her sea-gazing was her longing for the selkie lover who got her with that child. Selkies were mysterious lovers, seals in the ocean, *tuaha* on land. With the searing warmth of their huge dark eyes they sang deep tremors of wisdom and captured the hearts of their lovers for life.

Despite what the others said I knew my da could never have been one of the seal people, not if he gave me this red hair. Selkie's hair was black as the night. But perhaps my persistent rebelliousness was his. I stopped spinning for an instant and rubbed my eyes and nose and tugged at my red hair. Aye, but if I was no seal changeling, what was I? When my *daideo* Darmid joked about faerie lovers and changelings, *Granaidh* Aefa snapped with annoyance at him for putting such things into my head.

"Ye're a gift, 'tis all," Aefa said. "Whether from the sea or the wood faeries, the seals or the hawks, it doesn't matter. Ye still need to spin and love and be loved. 'Tis nothing for the mysteries but living."

But still I wondered fierce. Some nights I stared at the whiteness of the moon, hoping for a faerie father—an own da for me—to come and claim me for his own and stop my longing.

A sharp whistle cut into my reverie. In a moment Crag pounced on us under our shelter of stone, nosing Bairnie awake and insistently pushing him up from my lap and out into the sunshine.

"Come lad," came my *daideo*'s voice as another series of sharp whistles rang through the air. Crag bounded to his side, herding the younger dog before him just as if Bairnie were a little lamb.

"Hail, lass," called my grandfather. I wound the wool and spindle back into my bag, uncoiled myself and came out into the clear air, standing stiff while I kicked the kinks out of my legs.

"What aye, *Daideo*," I answered.

"Time to work with Bairnie if he is to be useful," said the old man.

"Aye so." This pleased me, for despite being a long way from the willful child who abandoned yarn and spindle in every rock and crevice I came across, I still preferred almost anything else to spinning. Training my dog was the foremost desire of my young mind, perhaps even taking ascendance over my desire to know who I was.

Daideo gave another sharp whistle. Crag herded Bairnie to him, butting the legs out from under the pup so the young dog sat abruptly at my grandfather's feet.

"Here lass," *Daideo* called, "This will be yer own sheepdog, so come and place yerself as master." For the rest of the morning we—Darmid, myself, and Crag—taught the young dog to respond to a whistle that bade him sit, lie down, run, turn and return, or stay upon command. It was a quick learning, but one that would take days or weeks of practice, I knew, before Bairnie could perform without error or question or gambol.

Soon my pup had learned to look equally to Crag and myself for his directions. Close upon that, his youthful rambunctiousness turned its wild impulses to an unrelenting obsession to please and obey my whistle and word. Crag circled Darmid and me. The older dog's obsession to obey my grandfather was key to training Bairnie to join his own infant will likewise to mine.

The weeks flew in this way—hot work out with the sheep, morning drills with the dogs, hours of spinning and singing, the simple warm meals for Darmid, the gathering of herbs and roots for him, and the nights by the fire gazing into its beautiful molten cinders while my grandfather spun his stories from the yarn of the *tuaha*, stretching back older than the mountains that held us.

One night rain and wind battered the thatching as lightning cracked and thunder roared. I could not help myself, I jumped and scowled each time it struck close. Crag paced; Bairnie whined. Darmid's eyes twinkled as he began a story to soothe us all.

Now here's a tale for the telling, and one to make ye thank the Great Maam fer our cozy hut here. A big man from the stone village was out on the hills a hunting of the deer. He got a stag and after praying by it and letting its blood he flung the thing upon his back, for he was a stout man indeed, and thus burdened he went to pass on the dark side of the loch with his load.

A hearin' a squeaking cry, what should the big man see in a deep stone cleft by the waterside but a wee suckling creature. Feeling the natural longings of a da, he lifted the poor thing and tucked it in his cloak, and so it was that he brought a monster's whelp into his croft. He had scarcely the chance to hang his traveling bag upon its hook when the beast who was its maam beat upon the lintel and roared in an angry voice, "Out with me whelp, Big Man!"

Three times the clever and courageous Big Man refused to give the ugly infant to its monstrous mother—until she laid a stone causeway across the loch whereon he could pass with his peat, until she had hauled and stacked the peat herself, and until she had built him a fine new stone croft. I smiled in pleasure when the story was done, winding the finished yarn onto the staff of my spindle. The bulk of yarn there was so high I realized it was time to skein it, so I slid the whole mass off the spindle shaft. Reaching for the half-filled skein winder, I began to twist it on.

"*Daideo*, did ye ever see a monster, just so?" I asked. The old man fixed his eyes on me briefly.

"Aye, lass, in me younger days. I saw just such a monster. Or, I should say, I knew for a fact it was there, though I never saw it by the eyes I have in me head."

"How is that, *Daideo*?" I cocked my head, waiting for his answer.

"Surely ye know 'tis true the eye cannot see all, just as the ear cannot hear all, but the Great All exists just the same."

'Twas a very cold night coming on directly after a thick fog fastened itself upon Cloch Graig for days on end. We saw neither the sun to know when to eat, nor the moon, to know when to sleep. 'Twas a queer, dank fog that muffled the noises and blurred the vision so that ye couldna see yer neighbors and the children were kept in lest they be lost in it and dragged down to the faerie world.

Directly upon the fourteenth day of this fog, in the darkness of night, the wind began to pick up, and within a moment it blew fearsome and rattling so we slid the doors of the village and bolted them, and all hunkered down in our beds with our covers over us hoping to live still in the morning.

In the midst of this, there was a crashing against the outside door so loud it traveled through the passageways to each of our chambers. At first we took it for some stick or rock hurled by the wind, but again the crash came, and finally, yet again, until it built itself up to a fair regular pounding.

The children set to bawling in fear, and no amount of coddling could quiet their din, until me ain brother came to me and said, "Darmid, we might open the door, something or someone needs to come in."

"Aye, yer daft, lad," says I, "for should it be tuaha it couldna make such a racket and if it be monster, we dare not let it in." With that a bellowing joined the thrashing on the door and the cold fist of fear closed around me ain heart and I dove beneath the covers like the rest, shivering and shaking myself into exhausted sleep, praying to the Great Maam to shelter our little village to no harm, or take us quickly so we did not suffer the horror of feeling the teeth of the monster crushing our wee skulls.

Even the children grew quiet, fair exhausted in their fear. Thus the village sank into a horror of silence until the storm quit lashing and the crashing ended and the howling died to a whimper and a sigh and then was silent utterly.

We rose, one by one, still shaken, the weight of fear still upon us. At last I heard the sweetness of dawn's birdcalls and knew I could open the door, which I did. Me eyes were blinded by the bright sparkle of sun on sea and the good clean morning.

We trailed out of the chamber that had sheltered us, and through the dark passage to the outside. The rest of the villagers came out of their own chambers, blinking in confusion. We stood in awe that around us every object that was not battened had disappeared, as if a great broom had swept through, taking all away with it but the very stones of the dwellings and the tightest thatch upon the roofs.

Everything was gone, clean as a whistle--nets, drying racks, traps, pots and baskets. Gardens swept off the earth as if never there—aye, nothing left but the stepping-stones. When we turned back towards the village we saw the outside of the stone door we had opened. On it were the tooth and claw marks of the monster that tried to gain entrance to our dwelling. Great gouges were bitten in chunks from the roof logs and they were scored with the scratches of terrible claws, as the frightened beast had tried to eat its way in among us.

But, ours was the only village thus assaulted: none of the neighboring villages reported the crashing and gnashing and howling upon their doors, and likewise they did not hear what had gone on at ours. They had hunkered down to the sweet winds of the storm and slept the night through like milk-fed bairns.

"Aye, so there lass, was the one time I encountered such a monster and I was not brave enough to open the door and entertain her." *Daideo* drew his blanket around him and in the sudden quiet, the fire snapped softly.

I tied the end of my finished skein, slipped it from the winder and quickly turned my hands in opposite directions to knot it from unwinding. I put it in a bag with the others. The bag was getting quite full, and soon, on a stretch of warm sunny days I would soak and dry the skeins so the knot would keep their winding permanent.

"Grieve not, *Daideo*." I shook my head at the thought of such terror in the night. "I would think had ye let the monster in, ye might never have had the opportunity to be my *daideo* here, telling me this tale."

"Aye so, lass," my dear *daideo* chuckled. "Aye so." We both stared into the dying fire, mesmerized at the wonder of the orange flame and the secrets of worlds unseen and paths not taken.

Presently I banked the ashes and murmured the night blessing for the un-named fear: *Maam before me, behind me, above me, below me. I on the path of the maam. Who is there on the land? Who is there by the door-post? I am here alone. I ask the Great Maam, to aid me.*

My words bound the night to us, as my hands had bound the skeins, and we took those comforting words to our slumbers.

****

The sky was a soft gray, windswept, with a shroud of light clouds moving in wisps across the broad expanse of the mountain meadow. I whispered the flock blessing rapidly under my breath: *The blessing placed by the Maam upon her flock of sheep, against birds, against dogs, against beasts, against disease. On the hillock of yer lying, whole be yer rising.*

As I grasped the leather tie that kept Bairnie tethered to me, he leapt sideways, back and forth trying to shake it from his neck. Finally, thwarted, he plopped down on his haunches with a thin whine. He wanted to be with Crag. I could see Darmid at the far end of the stone paddock, leaning upon his long crook and crooning to the herd.

Crag pulled three ewes out one by one, from the grazing herd. As the other sheep lifted their heads and gazed stupefied at the action, Crag circled each one, cutting her off from her sisters. He haggled her steadily towards the small rock-walled enclosure. Finally, stooping low to the ground he drove her through the entry of the stone paddock to where her shepherd stood.

Darmid was ready, the lashed wicket gate in his hand. As each ewe came through the entryway, he quickly closed off her escape. Crag leapt the gate out into the pasture in one bound, and was off to single out another ewe.

Once, twice, three times the ritual repeated, and when the third ewe was enclosed, my grandfather raised his crook and gave a low whistle. Crag dropped to the ground in a crouch, keeping the three ewes in a tight clutch in one corner.

This was my cue. I grasped Bairnie's tether and clucked him to heel. We quickly crossed the space to the enclosure and I climbed the wall, pulling him over with me. He landed with an ungraceful tumble of legs, bit at his tether, shook his head and sneezed hard before quieting. Gazing intently at Darmid and me, his mouth drew back in a query. *Daideo*'s eyes twinkled.

"Aye, and today is yer last free day, whelp," he chuckled. "Today ye start yer work, sure."

Darmid instructed me to hold the lead, bringing Bairnie swiftly to his feet. At the same time he sent Crag to the other side of the wicket gate. The older sheep dog crouched flat to the ground, his eyes riveted on the cluster of ewes, his face a study of intensity. He quivered, but he did not move. Darmid was his god, and he obeyed. Bairnie jumped up, his attention on the three ewes. They were restive without the pivot point of Crag's eyes upon them.

"Lassie, hold the tether 'til the circle is too large, then drop the

line soft and back away. Hup, hup there Bairnie, come along."
Darmid used his crook to pull at the neck of the largest ewe, and
the others followed her in tight formation. Bairnie followed
behind, his eyes suddenly fixed upon them, interested, alert. The
tether hung slack, and dragged upon the ground, lifting slowly as
he followed the sheep in the gentle and widening circle that
Darmid wove with his crook. When the line pulled tight, I let it fall
from my hands so it dragged behind him.

"See, lassie, we keep him in the circle, ho, hup, lad," Darmid
swiftly moved his crook from the lead ewe's neck and brought it
down in a slicing movement in front of Bairnie's nose, effectively
curtailing his sudden headlong acceleration towards the animal.
Just as swiftly, the crook was back upon the neck of the lead ewe,
keeping the clutch's forward motion in a wide circle so it would
not deteriorate into a panicked crash of legs. Bairnie's
concentration fixed even more, but his gait was smoother, more
disciplined, not the juvenile gambols that I was used to seeing.

"Ye see lassie," said Darmid softly, "Ye must keep the three
sheep together, keep him on their heel, don't let him single one
out. Three sheep together is herding, one sheep alone is chasing,
and this pup being not far from his wolf grandfathers, chasing one
sheep will end in a kill." Darmid's crook came down swiftly again,
slicing off Bairnie's natural instinct to dive into the clutch of ewes
and single one out.

Thus did my grandfather's experienced crook lead the three
sheep and Bairnie in an ever-wider, hypnotically regular circle
until suddenly, by magic, the formation of ewes and dog were
outside his reach. They continued to be held in by the perimeter of
the stone paddock, with Darmid and me at the center of their
circuit.

Four times the little group rounded the pen. Then Darmid
softly bid me track and grasp Bairnie's tether tightly in my hand. I
heard his low sharp whistle, my cue to pull Bairnie back from the
sheep. I jerked the lead swiftly; Bairnie whined and flipped his
snout towards me, as if to loose my restraint, but I held him tight
and gave the whistle that dropped him to a full body crouch.

When Bairnie was down and tethered, Darmid abruptly raised
his crook and gave a sharp high whistle. Crag, as still as a statue on
the other side of the wicket gate for the entire performance,

suddenly leapt straight up over the gate. In a flash he rounded the three ewes up from their chaotic split into a neat clutch, keeping the panting, bleating creatures in tight formation.

When Darmid pulled open the wicket gate, the dog swiftly herded them into the wide pasture. Another sharp signal from him and Crag dropped to the ground as the sheep fled into the anonymity of the herd.

"*Daideo*, he did it!" I exclaimed. "He did it, he can do it!" I pulled Bairnie to me and pounded his back in my joy, ruffling his fur and patting his head vigorously. He snorted and sneezed and shook his head back and forth, happy with me, invigorated by his turn with the sheep. Darmid chuckled at my enthusiasm.

"Aye, he can do it, lass, but we don't yet know if he will do it. Ye have many an afternoon just like this ahead of ye."

I didn't care. I was thrilled at the prospect that Bairnie would be able to earn his keep, a useful tool and companion rather than a drain on the food supply. I had come to *Daideo* to see if a wild dog could be used to herd, and to me, all the proof that was needed had just been laid before my eyes.

"Let's do it again, *Daideo*," I offered.

"Aye no, lass, once today, twice tomorrow with two clutches of sheep, three times the day after with three clutches of sheep, and suchlike. When he knows the signals, and has stopped trying to separate the sheep on his own, then we'll see if he can run with Crag and not be a hindrance. He must be able to take direction without the need of the tether, and that means responding to the whistle alone, without us yelling at him or repeating our commands, and without him having to look at us. It's a ways to go."

"Oh, aye, *Daideo*, 'tis so." I agreed, but I was not daunted. Bairnie's training seemed a foregone conclusion to me. I had the simple confidence of my youth. I pulled Bairnie toward me by the tether and hugged him tightly.

Just as Darmid said, we were out again the next day, morning and evening. In between I held Bairnie by his tether and stayed with Darmid while he put Crag through his paces, singling out a ewe and hauling her in to be inspected for small injuries or mishaps. While Darmid cut away tangled fleece I applied the unguents when necessary. It seemed to me that Bairnie had a new interest in the older dog now. I was sure he stared at Crag's actions as if preserving them all in mind.

"*Daideo*," I said, "If 'one sheep is chasing' then how does Crag know not to do that?"

"'Tis the training' lass. 'Tis a thing that happens, one day, when the practice has been enough, and signals are all remembered and obeyed without hesitation or fault. One day, suddenly, the young dog no longer has an interest in chasing the sheep so much as a desire to obey his shepherd. His sole purpose becomes to please his master, and the way he can do it is with the sheep. 'Tis a far cry from the pup who wants nothing more than to chase the sheep, and the tether and the crook are all that keep him from tearing out their throats."

I thought about that with horror. That night I dreamed that I was petting Bairnie, his long coat softer than eiderdown. Then, suddenly, he was missing, and I was chasing him through the rising shards of fog off the meadow. When I found him, all the sheep were dead in my grandfather's pasture, and Bairnie raised a bloody, smiling snout to me.

I woke suddenly in the dark with a knot in my stomach and a cold hand upon my heart. My dreams were almost never simply dreams and when they frightened me *Granaidh* Aefa said I must always think on them and look for the message that the Great Maam was sending me, the message that defied time and place. I thought on my *Granaidh* Aefa then, and missed her sorely. I remembered how when I was small, I would have crawled in to sleep cuddled up to my grandfather in her absence, and I missed the safety of that feeling.

I suddenly felt as if I might never see my grandmother again, and the tears rolled silently down my cheeks onto my bedclothes. I jammed my fists into my eyes to make them stop, but they would not. Silently I wept, and finally fell back into a sodden sleep. In the morning, I found the blood of my moon courses on my thighs, and I knew then the cause of my dream and my midnight sorrowing.

8. SALMON MOON

The last weeks of summer were coming in. Down in the Trabally on the Large Island, my village would be catching the salmon and drying them upon the racks. Up on the mountain, a long storm had chased the summer warmth away for good. Nights had a chill and mornings a breath of frost already. I found myself up earlier each day to tend the fire, even as the sun rose later. I did not look forward to the encroaching dark, but I knew that soon the villagers would gather to lead the animals away from the shieling, down the mountain to the stone village.

"*Daideo*," I said one day, "What of Bairnie? Is he ready to go down to the village? Is it time for me to go back? They will soon be wanting to bring the beasts back for the winter. What of me and the pup? Do we stay or return?"

Darmid himself had long ago stopped returning to the village and spent his winters in the stone hut, with Crag for company and his few animals indoors to keep warm. He looked up at me and the slight sadness in his eyes made me realize that he was getting older. We regarded each other solemnly.

"Do ye come back to the village this year *Daideo*?" I continued, "Is it time to enjoy the hearth with us again?"

He shook his head and turned away.

"Nay, lass, I be too old to go back among the village. I'm not fit fer living with others anymore. I be too selfish in me ways and private in me prayers."

I let go a little noise of exasperation. This was the excuse he had given year after year ever since I could remember. And yet, my time here had revealed to me just how much Darmid was slowing down.

He rose painfully in the morning, rubbing his hands vigorously over the fire to loosen his joints. His shepherd's crook was not simply a tool for sheep anymore—he used it to get himself up and down from the bed and floor. He sometimes rocked side to side when he walked, painfully stiff in the hips. Though he could still hoist a lamb over his shoulders and subdue a struggling ewe for the rooing, he often winced, and when possible left it to me or one of the lads who beat a constant path to his doorway.

I thought of our conversation as I assembled our morning meal one day. Into wooden bowls I threw some handfuls of the roasted barley grains I had rough-ground in the quern. Letting the sweet warm milk drizzle over them, I did likewise with honey, and sprinkled on a few hazelnuts. Leaving the porridge to soften, I went to fetch Darmid. I swept the door flap aside and stepped out into the early morning moisture. It was cool—cold, really. I knew the frost would be thick on the morning soon.

I began to hum the sunprayer, so natural to me that I did not think of it. *Hail to ye, ye sun of the seasons as ye traversest the skies aloft.* As I came over the threshold my prayer burst full singing from my mouth as I made my way to where the sea spread far below the mountain cliffs in its roiling fullness. *Yer steps are strong on the wing of the heavens. Ye art the glorious Maam of the stars. Ye liest down in the destructive ocean without impairment and without fear.* I inhaled the brisk air and stretched my arms skyward. *Ye rise up on the peaceful wave-crest like a sacred maiden in bloom.*

I treasured my time with Darmid but I missed my *Granaidh* Aefa sorely. I thought I would like to spend the winter high on the headland with my grandfather amidst the howling storms and blown ice crystals, but I had been gone long enough from Aefa and my apprenticeship to her. I feared should Aefa be as stiff as Darmid after her summer labors that she would need me badly. It was time to help with the last drying and gathering for the inevitable needs of sickness in the dark of winter. It was time for the apprentice to help the Death Crooner leave the forest hut for wintering over in the stone village.

Bairnie was close by my side. He sat gazing out over the

expanse of sea with me. When I sighed, he pressed his muzzle into my hand and I felt the moisture of his breath on it.

"Good lad," I said. Squatting down, I patted him, briskly rubbing his ears.

Bairnie opened his mouth. His tongue hung happily as his mismatched eyes fixed on me. Panting just a bit, he whined and gazed at me lovingly.

I couldn't help but smile. What a magnificent creature he was now. Gone was the floppy wee puppy he was when I found him. He had grown into his paws, and the fluff around his ears and hind quarters grew in long soft feathers. He was near to finished dropping his coat in preparation for winter growth. I had gathered it and kept it aside in its own basket—I knew it would spin out beautiful and strong, marbled gray, white, and black. I wanted to spin it all and weave it all by itself into one rare and beautiful garment.

Darmid had never answered my question about me and Bairnie returning to the Trabally with the other shieling folk, but I knew it was time. I ruffled Bairnie's fur again and grasped his head in my two hands, turning his face to my own and speaking directly into his eyes.

"The time has come, wee hound, for us to be going home."

Bairnie flickered his strange eyes, and shot his tongue out, licking the end of my nose. I laughed and wiped away the moisture.

"Come to, lad." He snapped to my side as I strode the path down through the meadow to the far cliffs overlooking the sea. It was there that Darmid was accustomed to taking his morning prayers, but it was time to urge him home for his porridge.

The sun was now high enough to cast aside the mountain shadow. Against the glare of the silver-speckled waves, I could see Darmid's silhouette. He listed to one side, leaning upon his crook. I was sad for his frailty, though in truth, he was not sad for himself. My *granaidh* and *daideo* were the rocks around which my life was tethered, and my soul was bound to them. I did not wish to see them grow older, for older meant someday gone.

Seated beside my grandfather, as still and contemplative as his master, was Crag. The dog turned his head to me and Bairnie as we came up behind. His tail thumped once.

I put my arm through Darmid's, and leaned into his shoulder.
Though I was already nearly Aefa's height, Darmid was yet taller,
and I could still rest my head upon his upper arm, though
truthfully, he slumped with age.

"What ho, *Daideo*?" I said softly. I knew he was done with his
morning recitations, but he was spellbound by the beauty of the
ocean. He stirred and smiled, turning his head so slightly. His eyes
lit up when he saw me in front of him, as they had ever since I
could remember.

"Come, *Daideo*, yer breakfast is ready, and the day waits
after."

We ambled up the long expanse of mountain meadow to the
hut. I stayed on Darmid's arm, a dog on either side of us. Surely
there was nothing more wondrous than a peaceful morning like
this. Soon enough we were in the hut, seated with our porridge. I
sighed, determined to have this conversation I had so long avoided.

"*Daideo*," I began, "The frost will soon be on the morn."

"Aye, so," he remarked, continuing to spoon his breakfast.

"*Daideo*," I pursued, "The folk will be leaving soon, and it is
time for me to return to the village to help *Granaidh* put by for the
winter."

"Aye, so," he said again.

"*Daideo*!" I objected, "I must go, and Bairnie must come with
me! Is he ready, Daideo, is he ready?"

"No, lass," said Darmid matter-of-factly. At last he put down
his wooden spoon and looked up at me. "He has made good
progress, yes, he has the makings of a good sheepdog. But if ye
take him now, he will forget. He needs more time with Crag, he
needs more time on the mountain with the beasts, and with
training. The stew that has been heated must be long simmered
before it is done."

My face fell, for this was the answer I feared.

"I cannot stay, *Daideo*, I have to help *Granaidh*."

He nodded in agreement, his face serious.

"Ye have two tracks before ye, lass. Ye take him with ye, and
training comes to a halt for too long to expect a young dog to retain
what he has so far learned. And that lost time might never be made
up. Or, ye leave him here with me, and with Crag, and he seasons
over for the winter moons, and if ye return after the winter stores

are battened in for *Granaidh*, ye remain here too, and come spring, he will be a full herd dog. That's what ye've been saying ye want. No new training will be happening, but he must have at it for more than one moon, and remember that ye are his master."

Unbidden, mist gathered in my eyes. I felt suspended between the three pillars of my life. *Granaidh* Aefa, back in the Trabally, needed help putting by for winter. True, she had a daughter and a son in that village, and other grandchildren with whom to pass the time of day, but I could not imagine the old maam not needing my simple companionship and my skills in helping with the duties of Death Crooner in the winter moontides. My heart ached to think I would spend that much time away from she who had been maam, da, and *granaidh* to me.

On the other hand, here, on the mountain, were the other two pillars of my life. Bairnie, whom I loved as dearly as an own brother, and Darmid, my precious *daideo*, who now, I could see, was bending under the weight of age. I settled my chin in my hands.

"*Daideo*, I cannot think but with sorrow, of this."

"'Tis true, lass, but 'tis both painful and wonderful."

I glanced at him quizzically.

"Wonderful, *Daideo*? How is that?"

"Ye have wished and wished for the day when you would have a herding dog. It is in these next few moons to bring ye that wish. Ye have been here on the mountain with me and ye have trained yer dog since *Granaidh* Aefa left. Ye miss her sore, lass, I can tell. And she needs ye, at this time of year, she needs ye." He gazed at me and his face softened.

"'Tis only a short time to have everything ye've wished for. Ye go back and help yer *granaidh* put by for the winter. She'll be safe in Cloch Graig with plenty of company for the dark season. And so, if the weather holds, ye pack yer bag again, and come back to the mountain with yer poor *Daideo*, too old a man to stay on the mountain alone!!"

He waggled his eyebrows at me comically, knowing I saw through his play upon my sympathies. Both he and I knew he would fare as many more winters as were left him alone on the mountain, just as he had done up to this point.

"When ye get yer *granaidh* settled and come back here, ye

will take the training of the wee dog to its completion. In the spring, ye can bring him back to the village as a herd dog who will never forget his craft. He'll be ruled by ye, or any other ye tell him to obey."

I contemplated the warmth of his wisdom. My heart felt heavy at the thought of leaving Bairnie, but *Daideo* was right: I had responsibilities to *Granaidh* Aefa, and I could come back to the shieling before the Cold Moon set in.

The challenge of making the long trek to the mountain shieling in winter by myself paled in comparison to my dread of choosing between the ones I loved. Now I look back on that year and wonder how it is that a girl on the cusp of womanhood could both love her grandparents as I did, and bridle against all that was required of me as Death Crooner's apprentice. But so it was.

I rose and leaned over and put my arms around my *daideo*. The old man in turn grasped me to him, his gorse-bristle beard crushed into my face. We squeezed tight, and then I stood up and took our bowls in hand to carry outside to clean.

"There's no help for it, *Daideo*, but living it."

Darmid's chuckle followed me out the door into the dooryard, for weren't those the words that *Granaidh* Aefa was ever spouting when the inevitable must be obeyed. I poured a little water from a bucket and scrubbed the porridge out of our bowls with twigs.

"Lass, ye sound just like yer *granaidh*, just like yer *granaidh*!"

Aye, so I did. *Granaidh* Aefa's voice had begun to come straight out of my own mouth—and I liked that in spite of myself.

****

A quickening of sounds rose from the outlying shieling huts. It was the bustle of packing to leave the high pastures. The animals knew it was time to go and jammed together at the gates, stamping, butting, bleating together and straining to get out. Their excitement fed my own, for though the summer was dying, I always felt deeply the gay excitement of reuniting with the village and its promise of the coziness of winter.

I packed my few personal things—my hair combs, my ritual herb pots, my small Great Maam figurine, my carrying-herbs for everyday needs. All these went into my green handbag. It was a beautiful thing of long coiled slivers of wood bound together with tough bog grasses, then sewn into circles. These were woven together at the sides, with handles of plaited straw, and a small opening left at the top for my hands to move easily in and out.

The rough-woven carry satchel I had brought to the mountain full of warm fall clothing was empty now, for I was layering those things over my summer shift as it grew colder. In the satchel I bundled my spinning tools and the cache of Bairnie wool, along with enough fleece to spin as I moved down the mountain. I had managed to knit *Granaidh* Aefa a new pair of winter socks during the long night when stories were told, and these I wrapped carefully in a length of rough-woven cloth.

I straightened up, casting my eyes around the shieling hut. There was a goodly winter wardrobe laid up for my daideo—a new sweater and new woolen socks. To save his aching fingers I had re-tooled his skin boots with thick, tallowed threads. I patched his leather leggings once again, and knitted him a scarf and a shawl and a pair of thick mittens. I had spun my way through his entire store of fleece in the times between training Bairnie, and I was proud of my output.

Looking over to where my grandfather's herb larder was full to the bursting with my summer gatherings, I breathed in deeply of the air of the small croft, redolent with their fine perfume. I had made a week's bannocks ahead for him, and roasted a goodly supply of barley and stored it away in crocks for him to use as he would.

Over the summer moontides he and I regularly made the descent down the mountain cliffs to the ocean and while Darmid fished, I collected limpets and other shellfish. I had filled his stone tank with fresh seawater and live limpets. That would hold him for the near future. More lay smoked and stored away in clay crocks.

All summer I had cleaned the fish my grandfather caught and dried them on racks outside the hut. These, too, were laid away in cool, dry pots. I felt confident that my *daideo* had enough for himself for the winter moontides. All in all, I felt I had done my love's work for *Daideo* Darmid, and could leave him in good conscience.

Bairnie was another story. When the clank of clay bells hailed the gathering of the herds and villagers for the long journey,

Daideo collared Bairnie and tethered him with a thick rope. He would stay thus restrained for some weeks after I left, for fear that he would follow after me. The dog whined and strained, barking his dismay as the crowd began its descent down the mountain path. I could hear the desperation rise in his yapping as the group moved out of his sight, but not out of his hearing.

My eyes smarted, and much to my horror a sob escaped, just as my cousin Fia caught me up and slipped an arm through my own. Fia squeezed my arm.

"No fear, little sister," she said softly. "He will fare fine, and ye have done him a favor in the end."

I clutched Fia's arm. But soon she was working her little maam's magic upon me, touching my face and hair with her free hand, and praising my handiwork that she had seen on her last visit to our *daideo*'s croft.

Fia's insistent cheer soon cut through my grief. I told her of finishing our *Daideo*'s sweater with a deep blue yarn I dyed using woad from plants I had cultivated outside his hut. I harvested and processed them for the first time all by myself. We chattered on in anticipation of the fall visit from the hill-walker, Hefin, who arrived when the moon stone shadows announced the Harvest Moon.

Hefin was dark as the night from long days spent in the sun going overland with his pack horses. He was a rare and welcome sight to our villagers, and all the others as well. His animals were loaded high with mysterious items from far and wide, items for which the villagers, rich with the harvest and ready for trading, would give much that was of value to them.

Fia and I exclaimed our anticipation of what he might bring, especially the rare dyes and perfumed herbs that spoke of lands afar. In the midst of our chatter we unconciously took our spindles from our carry packs, and lengthened and steadied our gait so we could turn out long, smooth measures of yarn as we walked and talked.

The trip home at the end of the Salmon Moon always seemed so much shorter than the journey up the mountain in the full of early summer in the Berry Moon. Perhaps it was because I was with Fia and the others now, instead of alone with Aefa. Perhaps also because we trod downhill most of the way.

In the noonday sun we stopped to rest, and pulled our foodstuffs from our carrybags. Fia and I joined Grania and Aidan and their crew of young ones, helping to pull food out and distribute it. After eating and drinking our fill, we moved on.

Before long we came to flatter land. The sun was beginning to sink behind the mountains, and long purple shadows made the sunset glories of the sky burn that much brighter.

Fia and I grew quiet at last, each contemplative in our own thoughts, and struggling to keep spinning in the falling shadows. Finally, we gave up our handwork for lack of light, wound up our yarn, and tucked the spindles back in our carry-bags. We trudged on in silence then, wondering how long the adults would march into the darkness before settling.

As if on cue, there was a whistle and a shout from the front. As we came around a long curve the path became a wide field of blowing grasses. Before us the vista revealed the oak savannah that lead to the great forest. That was all that lay between us and the Trabally. Family groups were clotting together and putting down their bags, young people and children running to collect wood. The earliest to arrive were already building and lighting fires.

Fia and I made our way to our family's fire and quickly moved into place beside Grania. Together we tended the little children, unpacked the food, and spread mats on which to make our camp. With Osheen, Ohran, Braden and Dahi all collecting, there was already a formidable pile of wood.

Arda and Grania sent the boys out to offer themselves to neighbor families who had few children and needed the extra help. By the time the boys returned, the younger children had finished eating and Fia and I were trying to get them into the sleeping robes.

It was late, but the storyteller was Ohran, Kriafann and Arda's elder son. The children eagerly crowded up to him, for Ohran already had the reputation as a grand weaver of tales. The black pools he had for eyes flickered in the firelight as he began softly, "This is a tale as was known in the stone villages of the Trabally on the Large Island for as many generations as there have been stars in the skies...."

A hill-walker was traveling the rocky tracks in the autumn of the year with his burdensome pack when he heard the sound of

*flutes and drums from a farmer's great stone house a bit distant
from the trail. Being one to never pass by the sound of the music
and dancing, he turned in at the sight of it and carried himself to
the dooryard. There he saw the man of the house, the good farmer,
and removing a bit of the strong honey-mead from his burden, he
presented it to him with ceremony.*

A stir of delight went through the crowd in anticipation of the
tricks to be played on the poor hill-walker who became instantly so
besotted with the farmer's daughter that he saw his advanced age
as no object to winning her. Snickers of amusement rose and fell as
the sly maam of the house, disgruntled by the crusty old hill-
walker's attention to her young daughter, pressed the unsuspecting
man to assist her in the twisting of some rope, instead of dancing
with the lass.

As he twisted and the rope lengthened, the amorous old fool
backed up to keep it taut, and finally backed all the way over the
threshold into the dooryard, whereupon the lass's maam promptly
barred the door against him. By the time Ohran was done, all were
calling out and brimming tears of mirth at the tragedy that befell
the poor hill-walker.

"More! More!" cried the children.

"Oh, no…" the adults answered, and pulled their little ones
together for bed. Quiet descended quickly, for in truth, everyone
was ready for sleep. Fia and I lay together, but neither of us had the
energy for talk.

"Goodnight, little sister," Fia whispered drowsily, and I
squeezed her hand lightly. Fia held mine, already faintly snoring.

Later, I woke to the glory of the full rising moon, bigger than
the mountain peaks as it broke over the horizon. I willed myself to
watch it as it moved across the sky, trying to catch it growing
imperceptibly smaller as it did so. But in no time I was deep asleep
again.

****

The custom upon the arrival of the fatted stock back in the
Trabally always caught me by surprise and I shrieked loud and
long with the rest of them. As we neared the village, the stock got
restless, bleating and lowing and quickening their pace such that a

bumping and bawling set upon them like a sickness. Before long dust rose above them in a gritty cloud and the herding lads and lasses were forced to lay their staves before the beasts to keep them from running amok.

Suddenly, the village children began to shout as straw-masked figures catapulted from the bushes, and with curdling cries snatched the staves of the herders and drove the stock off the beaten track at the ford and right into the river. Riotous gaming ensued, with splashing and screaming, and the eruption of the herding lads and lasses into chasing, duckings, enthronement upon the largest beasts, and coronations with auras of straw.

The village folk who had stayed back from the shielings soon arrived with baskets of soap and all set about lathering up and scrubbing the summer's dirt and vermin from the beasts. The bellowing that sounded so pitiful during the assault of the hay creatures became satisfied lowing and the splashing of playful hooves in the water.

With the villagers came their Death Crooner. I knew her gait long before I recognized her face. I broke from Fia and the revelers and love sped my weary feet towards the beloved silhouette.

I called to her and Aefa smiled at me, putting down her basket of ritual items and opening her arms wide. I laughed and hugged her tightly. When my *granaidh* groaned, I jumped back.

"Oh sorry, *Granaidh*, sorry!" My voice caught and I lay my head more gently on her shoulder. She returned my affection in kind, and finally, held my face between her two hands.

"Ye're brown as a beetle, lass!" she cried, and I laughed again.

"I've been upon the highlands, *Granaidh*! Tell me, who do ye see coming back from the shieling who is not as brown as a bug?" The long days in the sun on the mountain had increased the number of my freckles until they blended as one. In the tiny spaces between them my light skin, red and burnt though it might be in early summer, had slowly bronzed. My hair blazed with streaks of orange bleached there by the sun.

We fell to chatting about the trip and all that had come to pass upon the mountain. Soon our reveries were interrupted by a calling to order by the farming and fisher-folk who wanted to bestow thanks upon the herding lads and lasses for tending their flocks as they fattened and for leading the beasts down from the summer pastures.

The very first grain of the harvest was already cut, and the farmers' children held the sheaves aloft. Out came the First Loaves made from that first grain harvest—chaff blown away, kernels pounded in a quern, flour mixed with honey and butter and sweet milk into the richest tribute ever imagined.

The flat loaves were hoisted from the baskets and broken and distributed. Out came the cheeses from the carry-bags of the herdfolk, and a goodly number were opened on the spot. The food blessed those who labored to take the stock to the mountain for summer fattening and delivered them home to the seaside safely again. It was always a grand feast, resplendent with fresh, good food, glowing prayers to the Great Maam of the Harvest, and tinkling with the laughter of the young folk.

As we ate the cheese and bread, I looked for Fia in the crowd. Seeing my beloved *granaidh*, I had abandoned my cousin and breast-sister and I suddenly felt disloyal. But I blinked in surprise when my eyes lit upon her. There Fia sat with one of the herd lads, Bran—Kerr's brother! Bran had taken her hand in his. The two of them gazed intently into each other's eyes like twin calm islands amidst the storm of celebration around them.

My brow creased as I fixed the young couple in my stare. When had this happened? Fia was my only companion in summer, and there was plenty of time when the two of us were apart, but.... Fia hadn't mentioned this. Even on the long trek back down the mountain, not a whisper of this.

I turned to *Granaidh* Aefa, and the old maam chuckled at my unhappily furrowed face.

"Fia is a young maam, pet, as ye are becoming as well. Did ye think ye would be children forever?"

I stared at *Granaidh* Aefa, my puzzlement plain to see. Turning back to my cousin I was privy to Bran tenderly grasping a bit of Fia's dark hair and gently putting it behind her ear, all the while never breaking his eyes from hers.

"*Granaidh* Aefa!" I said helplessly, "*Granaidh*, I...." My words broke off and I twisted away into the crowd, running towards the water as if to drown what I did not want to think of.

9. HARVEST MOON

The festival of the First Fruits was only the first of the string of harvest festivals that began in the Salmon Moon, stretched through the Harvest Moon, climaxed in the Hunt Moon and finally began to subside when the Wither Moon brought its killing frosts. Those days in our stone villages were heady days of celebration, for each new crop brought more hope for the winter to come. I was Aefa's constant companion during this time of the year—gathering herbs, helping with the harvest, pulling everything from our own garden patch and accepting gratefully what others brought us from theirs.

My *granaidh* and I spent long hours putting the bounty by for the coming winter. I caught Aefa up on all I had learned and done in the company of Darmid, and raved on about Bairnie's prowess as a herd dog.

After the shock of seeing her with Bran on the night of our return, I avoided Fia, which wasn't hard to do, given that Aefa and I were still trundling back and forth from the stone village to the forest hut as we prepared for the winter. But by and by there we were together, Fia and I, out on the clam flats with the rest of the young folk, bending to the miniature sprays that told us where to find our prey.

I had been working at my task since the earliest moment the tide made a clam hunt possible. My creel was full of the largest creatures, and I was folded in two, scratching away with a long antler fashioned into a clamming fork. A soft voice came suddenly upon me.

"Ronnat, where have ye disappeared to?"

Bent double at the waist, I stood up suddenly to find Fia beside me, her own creel and antler tool in hand, staring at me quizzically. I squinted at her and replied shortly,

"Busy helping *Granaidh* Aefa."

Fia looked at me in silence for a moment. "Did I give offense, little sister? I've seen yer back, but never yer face since we came off the mountain."

I was embarrassed—embarrassed to have hurt my breast sister and cousin, embarrassed that Fia's maturing was embarrassing me.

"I don't know, Fia. Ye're busy too—ye have friends, ye have..." I broke off, horrified by my weak prattle.

"A lover?" Fia asked, "A sweetheart? Ronnat, I have more than fifteen summers upon me."

I lowered my eyes and scowled, "But ye don't need...a pest now."

Fia laughed outright then, her mirth chasing her grave concern away. "I need ye more than ever, now, heart friend. A lover is a lover, but a sister is for life! We're breast sisters! We're cousins— what could replace that?" She threw down her tools and threw her arms about me. I moved right into them, eyes smarting. I hated myself at this moment, but Fia's embrace pulled me back to rights.

"I'm sorry, Fia," was all I could muster in a muffled voice. "I'm sorry."

"Don't be sorry, little sister. Just don't be missing! How will I survive without ye?"

We bent to our task again, then, and chattered animatedly, as if to make up for lost time. Fia broached the subject of Bran gingerly at first, but soon the ice was broken and she began to spill all about her lover: how they noticed each other, where they found places to court upon the highlands, what would happen now that they were back in the village.

When she noticed I had fallen into silence again Fia said, "I don't have a purpose demanded of me like ye do, Ronnat."

She straightened up and stretching backwards to relieve the lower back cramp of clamming. "Ye will be the Death Crooner. Everyone knows that. I have been a little maam for my whole life already. I was made for it, like my maam, our breast maam. I am comfortable with my life. I am ready. I want my own bairns already. Bran will make a good husbandman, for that is his bent as well. He has the farming from his father, he has the herding from Darmid. He loves the children as much as I do. We are of an age, both of us."

I straightened up too, then, so our eyes were more on a level with each other. I squinted at Fia intently. I could feel where this was leading, but it surprised me even more than my initial glimpse of Fia and Bran holding hands.

"What are ye talking about, Fia?" I asked abruptly.

"Handfasting," said Fia. "Bran and I talked about making the handfast. We want to reach through the stone ring to make the Year Handfast at the Equinox, and if it is good for us, to make the sacred marriage next year at this time, to become husbandman and maamwife during the Mid-Year festival."

I continued to stare at Fia. A handfasting? But we were lasses, Fia and Bran were just children.... weren't they? The thought of Fia husbanded and perhaps by next year, with a bairn of her own, startled me further. My only thought was for a dog! And here was Fia, making plans like a grown maam! I shook my head as if to wake myself.

Fia scowled then.

"Ronnat, why are ye so silly! Ye act as if I am a child. Here, look, I think I am already with child." She grabbed my hand and placed the palm over her breasts. Even under layers of shift and sweater, I could feel the firm swellings of the breasts of a maam with child. I pulled my hand back and gasped, but Fia held firm, and guided it low on her belly. That, too, was beginning to firm and swell.

"There, do ye see? What dream have ye been living in, Ronnat? *Granaidh* Aefa knew it the moment she saw me. I am well into the age for handfasting and bairns."

I bent quickly and hacked away at the sand below me. Then I stood again.

"Fia, it's hard for me... to see ye... growing up. I don't know if I'll ever have bairns. I'm meant to be the Death Crooner, I...." I knew I sounded childish—Aefa had many bairns, and she was a revered and gifted Death Crooner. Few maams were denied bairns by the Great Maam. "It's just that I.... I'm afraid."

There, it was out. The tide was now low enough out that the

skim of water on the clam flats was gone. I sat down heavily in the wet sand, my hands in my lap, and from me burst the story of my birth, my maam's death, the cause of that death being me, myself. I grew more and more emotional as I spoke, and Fia, on her knees by my side, was, as usual, softly soothing my fears.

"I know the story, Ronnat," she said. "It is no secret to the village. But listen to me: I know maams die, but I am not afraid. This is the life I choose." We looked deeply into each other's eyes then, and clasped our hands together.

The silent vow was made between us: one of us would be a death crooner with a ritual station, one of us would offer her worship to the Great Maam each and every day through her own hearthwork as a maam. Both of us would live consecrated lives. Both of us. And we needed each other for that.

Later, when I returned to the forest hut, I told Aefa all I had learned from Fia that day, of my hurt, my surprise, and most of all my fears. Aefa regarded me solemnly.

"It is the risk of all maams. At times the Great Maam of All simply takes us back to her, whether or not we are in agreement that it is our time to pass between the worlds. But Ronnat, me love, yer maam died because she was small. Whoever is yer father, man or faerie or selkie, he must be very tall. Ye are very tall. Ye will not lose a bairn in childbirth because the child is too big, unless ye mate with a mountain troll!"

Both of us burst out laughing suddenly, the thought of me husbanded by a giant, stinking mountain troll too funny to bear. The laughing helped me, calmed me, and I no longer felt afraid.

****

The Moon of Harvest stretched before us in a long line of hard work and joyous revels. Trips to the river with offerings were in order, jaunts to the high places for bonfires and dancing were routine.

I had always loved the celebrations upon the ritual hill of Trabally when I was a little lass. But when I became aware that our invocations to the Great Maam were also in the light laughter and soft moaning of the couples spread out on the hilltop in the long grasses, I had begun to stay close to the bonfire, close to Aefa and

Fia.

Ah, but this year Fia herself would undoubtedly disappear
quietly from the stark brightness of the bonfire. A little later, it
would be noticed that Bran, too, was gone. They might later
wander in, blinking, rumpled, full of the knowing smiles of love.
Perhaps they would not come back to sing at the fire at all, but in
the morning all would simply wake to find them wrapped in thick
wool blankets amongst their own family of sleepers, as if they had
never left. Such was the way young people worshipped the Great
Maam of All. Any children born of such unions were gifts. If later
a young maam agreed to handfast with a husbandman, any child of
her womb was a child of his heart, as well.

The high holy season started on the day of first reaping when
we gathered with the rest of the villagers in the fields, brooms of
rowan in our hands, flowers braided into circlets upon our heads,
the long stone sickles at our waists. My uncle Aidan lifted his
sickle in the air and began,

*This day I go forth with me sickle under me arm and I reap,
the cut the first act. I give thanks to the Great Maam for the
growing crops of the ground. She gives food to ourselves and to
the flocks. We will all taste the bannock.*

With that the couples who had made the sacred marriage cast
their head-coverings upon the ground. Taking up their stone
sickles they cut handfuls of the ripe wheatcorn and passed it three
times sunwise around their heads.

The reaping chant began, their deep voices as one, the strength
of stone and earth together. *Great Maam, bless ye thyself our
reaping, each ridge and plain and field, each sickle curved, each
ear and handful in the sheaf.*

The chant was taken up by the rest of us then, voices young
and old joined and mingled. *Bless each lass and lad, each maam
and tender youngling. Safeguard them beneath yer shield of
strength. Encompass each goat, sheep, lamb, cow and horse.
Surround ye the flocks and herds and tend them to a kindly fold,
Great Maam of All.*

After the reaping, the wheatcorns were laid out in the sun
upon a smooth woven cloth by the maams. Aefa and I circled it
sunwise with another blessing: *Ye warmth of sun, burn steady,
gentle, generous, come round about these ripened grains. Fire*

parch fat seed for us yer children in the name of the Great Maam of All who gives us grain and bread and blessing.

Each few hours the kernels were turned and the prayer repeated again. At last Aefa signaled that they were ready, and the dried kernels were gathered into one large close-woven basket-bin. It was now time for the fire of baking, and a grand one would be lit in the meeting place on the knoll over the village. Around it huge boulders had been dragged for the baking. Families gathered, all bringing with them their household tools—the woven rush fans for the holding of the kernels, their sheepskins, and querns for the grinding.

Then came the children with rowan branches, swishing them and singing until the ground was swept clean. The maams spread out sheepskins and placed their querns upon them. The young lads and lasses took turns feeding the querns and collecting the ground grain while their maams turned the stones. Their voices rang out the blessing of the quern in a pretty tune with deep and vibrant harmonies. The gathering place rang with their voices, each singer rapt and joyful.

On the eve of harvest, we shall have flesh, mead, spruce, wine, a feast of sweetness, milk, and honey in abundance. We shall have harp, flute, horn, sweet melodious songs. The gentle Maam of All will be with us, the leafed one of the forest will be with us, the hunger will be from us.

Aefa and I worked along with the others for the ritual baking. Flour was put in large shallow bowls and we made a well in the middle of it. Some warmed milk on the fire, and into it dropped sweet butter and lard until both melted. We used our hands to feel when the mixture had cooled to the warmth of blood, then poured it into the well of flour and pushed it with our fingers until it formed into dough.

Others took up the dough and kneaded it for some time on the flat fan, then covered it to let it rest until it was time for us to knead again, this time mixing in the dried fruits, nuts, and honey. We shaped suncircles bright as open daises, and after letting them rest a bit slammed them onto the hot sides of the boulders near the fire. There they hung and cooked until lightly browned, when we peeled them off the rocks, wrapping each bannock in light cloth.

Now our sacred breads were making their way to the top of

the holy hill in my basket. Aefa and I began our prayers at sunrise, as did each family making the ritual this day. The animals were fed and shut in their paddocks, the necessities were packed. Each family group carried with them the sacred harvest bannocks we had all made the day before, along with food and blankets for the hilltop bonfire that night. So it was every year.

I shifted my creel to my other hip, stretching backwards to relieve the low ache in my back. I looked down the beaten track that stretched behind me from the village. It wended its way through the tough heather, down into the pine forest, and up another hill. At the base of the climb up the ritual hill the one lane branched into six ribbon-thin walking paths. Year after year on the holy days villagers strode side by side for the final climb to the crown of the sacred hill, crested with a tumbled cairn of stones left there by worshippers year after year.

As I walked I stopped often to take in the long view shimmering in the haze of the late summer sun. In the distance beckoned the sacred hunting mountain. The ritual hill was off to my left, and seemed not high at all compared to the sacred mountain, but the weariness in my calves belied that illusion.

At the crossroads I put my creel down, shifted the bundle of bedding off my back, and sat upon one of the large stones. The cross path was a dirt lane that started at the river in one direction and disappeared into heath and forest in the other. Following my own trail's thin ribbon with my eyes, I could see Aefa far ahead of me, stumping along up the hill with her walking stick, surrounded, as she always was on the holy days, with a cortege of family and villagers.

Soon after we left the village, the *tuaha* began to close around my *granaidh*. I had slowed my pace and fell farther and farther behind them until I was quite alone in all directions. I liked my solitude far more than the chatter of the village folk.

Now, from my perch, I heard whoops coming up through the pine forest behind and below me. That would be Bradan and Dahi banging sticks together, with Osheen and Ohran taking up the rear and trying to frighten them with growls and snarls of wild beasts. I laughed. I wondered where Fia was but knew she would be farther back still, helping her maam with the small ones, bringing up the rear with their own parts of the feast and their sleeping gear and all the necessities for a large family to spend a night on the hill.

My mind drifted once again back to Fia and Bran, sad that their courting games would take the place of the companionship Fia and I had shared each holiday up until now. I put a hand down to my side, searching for Bairnie's soft head. Then I shook my hand fiercely as if to cast away a stinging insect. I could not get used to the fact that I had left him behind. It seemed stupid, after all these weeks that I still blindly reached for him.

Hearing the shouting intensify as the lads broke out of the cover of the pine forest below, I saw not four figures, but five, and wondered who the fifth would be. Rising and turning around, I continued my trek up the long slow hill, the harsh shrieking of excited young males coming closer and closer behind me. Finally they were near enough to know I could hear them.

"There she is! Me beautiful cousin the changeling!" I rolled my eyes, though they could not see my face. That would be Osheen—he had always tormented me and made me laugh since I was very small, my imperious elder by little more than a year.

"What is that, then?" I asked the breeze loudly in mock wonder, "Thunder from a sheep's hind end, or is it the grand lies of the little hind himself?" This was the banter I always threw back at Osheen, a play on the meaning of his name, "little deer." But a hind was a female deer, and my barb would recall the fact that he could never aspire to that revered status.

As big and red and fair as I was next to the Trabally folk, Osheen was different too. Small, lithe, slender as a reed, his eyes pierced like those of a hawk. He stood more than a head below most his age and had to scramble to keep his place among them. Thus, his tormenting of me as another outsider got so intense as to sting me into anger as a child. I had one day picked him up, carried him through the passageways of Cloch Graig, and tossed him with all my might into the cold snow.

We were followed by a band of whooping children. Adults, roused by the din, fell in behind. Once outside the passageway entrance, all crowded around laughing uproariously at Osheen's fate at the hands of his younger, bigger cousin. Osheen himself might have been provoked to anger by this, but instead he shrieked with laughter and cavorted and clowned in the snow. Indeed, he had developed an increased fondness and respect for me, his little cousin, over the incident.

Appreciating my jab, the young men behind me on the trail laughed loudly and began to singsong good-humored taunts at Osheen. As they came abreast of me, Osheen prostrated himself at my feet begging for my mercy and promising me his undying devotion should I only let him live.

I turned my nose up in disdain, and caught sight of the fifth youth with them. It was Bran's brother Kerr, the black-haired boy. To my horror I blushed when his eyes—dark as wells of night— turned on me. His smile to me was small and fleeting, he bent his head, his nod acknowledging his respect, but he hung back from his companions and did not address me.

"Ronnat, why are ye so slow? The whole crowd is so much farther ahead. Are ye hurt, sister?" teased Osheen.

I stumbled in my comeback as I ripped my eyes from Kerr's form. "It... it's just that it's such a fine day and my back, strong as it is, has been begging me to rest after all the work of getting ready for the harvest festival."

"Oh then, cousin," said Osheen with gallantry, "Let us be yer servants. Hup lads!" he shouted to his companions. They quickly relieved me of my bundles and creel, adding them to their own loads. When I protested and sought to snatch them back they roared as one, refusing to relinquish them.

We passed the rest of our hike in playful banter, somehow managing to communicate all our hopes and dreams in amongst the joking and laughter. When we came to the summit, the lads delivered me to Aefa's side, then split off with hearty goodbyes and an exaggerated kiss upon my cheek by Osheen.

As they trailed away, their boisterous laughter and shouting drifting back to me, I looked after them just as Kerr turned back in my direction. Our eyes met again. He touched his forehead with the open hand of greeting, then ducked his head to follow his friends.

I stared after him. Something felt new within me. My heart beat faster when I saw him. I turned back to see Aefa looking at me quizzically, but I bent quickly to rummage in the carry-bag for what, I knew not. Aefa, in her infinite wisdom, said nothing.

****

As the sun began to sink and the long shadows were thrown from the high places into the valleys below, I could see the kindling of sharp little lights as those straggling up the hill lit torches. In truth, all would have known their way even in the dark of a new moon. I turned my face back to the bonfire that roared before me, sending sparks up into the night sky as timbers burned and fell. I saw Bradan and Dahi joining the other lads in haste to pile on more logs.

Before the flames grew too high, all the lads and the more boisterous lasses were entertaining themselves by seeing who could leap through in great bravery. Families came one by one and settled in the vast circle of the bonfire's light and warmth.

I was not yet ready for the leaping, and my eyes stole to where the musicians gathered upwind of the fire to begin playing. Out of each family group there was at least one musician—in our family, Osheen, Dahi, Bradan—even I—had all learned to play the shrill little shepherd's pipe. In Bran's family it was Kerr. I ran my eyes over the group looking for him as the stroke of the hand drums sounded echoes as if deep underground in a stone cavern.

There he was, at the far end, his eyes closed, his face relaxed in the grip of the mysteries of the music. Underneath the intricate small drum patterns, the boom of the huge drums, whose breadth required a whole ram's hide to cover them, measured a beat as soulful as time itself. As more musicians trickled in, the clack of the bones and the lyrical patterns of the bone and clay flutes ran from one favorite dance tune to another.

Around me the little ones screamed and chased each other, falling and crying but jumping up again swiftly, not wanting to be left behind by their playmates. The bonfire was entrancing, but the music even more so. Except for the elders, who were settled in comfort upon fleeced sheep skins and under warm woolen shawls, none could sit for long before they were up dancing to the pulsing wall of sound.

The lads leapt high before the lasses, grinning and sweating with their exertions. They performed the ancient mating dance of all creatures, with ever faster steps and higher jumps. Couples grabbed arms and spun together, weaving a large circle around the fire. The dance brought them together, then apart, and moved them on to a new partner.

Try as I might I could not take my eyes away from Kerr, and at last sought my own refuge in dancing. I rose and joined the group, quickly borne away until I, too, was shrieking with mirth.

When the music stopped, we all roared our delight, caught our breath, teased each other, drank long draughts of water or mead, and paced like nervous stock until the next dance began. There were bannocks aplenty, and honey cakes to keep the crowd in good humor and full of energy for the night.

When I was nursing my hurt at Fia, I thought I would hide from the revels. But now there was no beloved Bairnie by my side for companionship. There was no isolating myself from the others while I stroked his soft fur. Instead, Osheen dragged at my arm again and again, and each time I thought I might slink off to pout, I found myself caught up in the dancing. Joining the circle, at times I closed my eyes as I spun, giddy with the danger of it.

That dance ended and I had barely time to catch my breath when the next was shouted out and two circles formed swiftly around the bonfire. Maams and lasses were on the inside, lads and men on the outside. My cousin Fia grabbed me into the line of lasses, but each repetition of the pattern spun me off to a new partner, until I found myself in the grasp of Kerr.

I was grateful for the roar of the fire and music, as they eliminated any possibility of talk. Even so, I felt warm in his arms. Unlike most of the young men of Trabally, he was tall, even taller than I was. When we spun, his strength put a kick in it so fast I was forced to lock eyes tight with him to keep my head from spinning off into the night sky.

All too quickly our round together was gone and I was on to the next dancer, my grizzled Uncle Kriafann, for which I was both relieved and sorry. I had never felt as warm to my Uncle Kriafann as I had to my uncle Aidan. Uncle Kriafann was tall and so stately and aloof that something about him had frightened me a bit as a little lass. But in the revelry of the dance, that childish awe melted away—he looked at me with kindly eyes in the light of the fire, and smiled.

Ducking to speak into my ear so that I might hear him, he said "So, the little red seal is grown now, drawing even the lads from the next village!"

I made a mad face and pretended to slap his arm in mock exasperation as we spun. Uncle Kriafann threw his head back and roared his laughter, even while he passed me on to my next partner.

And so the night went on. When the villagers were too tired or too drunk on strong summer mead to dance any more, the young couples began to creep off into the heather. At last the exhausted children joined the old ones already wrapped in the comfort of cloaks.

The music slowed and the singing started, running through all of the old favorites—the tales of young lads and lasses making their own use of the hay during the harvest time, the sad laments of loss, and finally, as the fire burned down and most had crawled off to sleep, the gentle lullabies and the stories.

The first teller that night was old Davnat from Clochbeg, announcing a tale not often told in Cloch Graig. We signified our approval with grand sighs. I clutched a tankard of warmed mead to me, and bit into a bannock hungrily. Dried fruit leant sweetness to the mead, and soon my head swam just a bit with it, as Davnat began.

There was once a time when bee-keeping was new to the tuaha. At that time, there was a man who loved his bees as bees themselves love flowers. Upon a sunset he sat at his lintel stone, listening to the evening birds and watching them swoop down as it darkened. Of a sudden he heard wild dogs barking and what should burst out of the heather and across his own dooryard but three large hounds chasing a frightened hare. The wee animal leapt into his arms and in one movement he put it under his cloak.

Of course, the kind beekeeper found he had a magical hare—a young lass enchanted by an evil faerie hag—and many hard tasks were required of him to break the spell and release her. The lass became his lover while the evil faerie was stung to death by the loyal bees.

When Davnat bowed his head to indicate he was done, murmurs went around the slowly dying fire expressing the pleasure of the crowd. Someone got up to push another log into the glowing mass. I wrapped myself in the woolen blankets and pulled a flap over my head to keep out the chill. It was time to sleep.

I lay so near Aefa we might have shared one cloak together,

but my old *granaidh* was already fast asleep. I turned on one side, then pulled the covering off my face and stared up into the night sky. In the new moon the night was so dark the stars seemed huge and close enough to touch.

I was in the grasp of a longing I had not experienced before. I felt Kerr's strong grip, though my time encircled by his arms during the dance was fleeting. My heart trembled within me and brought me wide awake. For a moment I began to get a glimpse of what had transpired between Fia and Bran.

The thought brought annoyance to me. I was not, I was quite sure, destined for that kind of love. My life was to be that of the Death Crooner. I felt loneliness was part of the lives of Aefa and Darmid. They were lovers, yes, raising a family between them, but they passed so much time apart, both bound by their respective callings. That kind of loneliness did not appeal to me—but its freedom did.

Ah, yes, its freedom was great, and the thought that I was destined for that kind of freedom comforted me. I would turn my back on love for that kind of freedom.

And so I turned my back on the light and noise of the fire and slept.

10. HUNT MOON

When the Harvest Moon of plants came to an end, the Hunt Moon, the harvest of the meat, began. The moon was still new, and barely bigger than a fingernail when day and night were equal in the wane of the year. The Equinox rituals were at hand.

For three days the *tuaha* from all the little villages like Cloch Graig and Clochbeg were gathering at the Light Mound of the Trabally to witness the sun flood the passageway to the Womb Chamber. As sunrise burst gloriously into the dank darkness, it blazed into the backmost chamber illuminating the whorls carved upon the backstone. They sprang to life, touched by fire. They were the messages from our ancestors, and I was destined to be the messenger, like my *granaidh* Aefa before me.

These were the three days of promised joy and mourning. Joy came to us from the harvest that had brought plenty to ease the winter moontides. Mourning rode in on the knowledge that the light diminished more each day and as it faded, our struggles would increase. After the rituals of Light to Dark in the Hunt Moon, the Wither Moon would set in, followed by the Death, Cold, and Hunger Moons that dragged with them the heaviest travail of winter. We were at the axis of change at this time of year, and so our rituals would bring us both fear and comfort.

Aefa and I began each of the three holy days of the equinox ritual with libations lifted to the dawn and then spread upon the Womb Chamber doorway. With the villagers we cheered and chanted the songs of thanksgiving, our movements and sounds driving back the chill that swirled around us, transforming the heat of our breath into small clouds. The deep drums thumped a steady rhythm while the cold made the mid-sized drums ring eerily under the swift flight of the bone and wood flutes.

The jubilation of our people reached crescendo, then quickly silenced as Aefa and I followed the sun into the Womb Chamber. As Death Crooner and acolyte we pressed our honeyed libations into the outlines carved into the backstone, where they clung—our gifts, our sustenance, our nurture for the threads that wove our lives from birth to death. Golden tones were held in the air by praise-chants, high and echoing within the chamber, as the ancient words passed from Death Crooner to Death Crooner all the way back to the Salmon Well rang with ancient splendor.

When the sun rose high enough that the light left the womb chamber, our sacred chants became mourning cries that trailed after Aefa and me as we followed the sun back to the crowd gathered at the opening. There, as Aefa mumbled the prayers of protection, low, and guttural, in the words of our mothers' mothers, the villagers wailed pleas for the sun to return warmth to them and keep them from a winter grave.

On the first day Aefa and I held high the grain flour mixed with honey brought by each village to signify the first harvest—the garden harvest. On the second day, we would do the same with dried, pounded fruit mixed with honey, to honor the second harvest—the forest harvest. On the third day would come the powdered meat mixed with honey, to praise the third and final harvest—the flesh harvest.

Some years were so shrouded in mist or rain that the sun could barely be seen on one or all of the Three Days of Equal Light. That in itself was reason for mourning. It predicted a hard cold winter. In those years, the grief cries were loud and desperate, and every minor tragedy was blamed on the equinox portent. Those were years of endless toil for the Death Crooner.

Year handfastings were held during our Days of Equal Light. If the couple who had so lovingly fastened their hands at the previous year's Spring or Fall equinox came to grief with each other and sought to undo their oath, the time of equal light opened the portal to natural endings. The handfasting could die a natural death, put to rest with all other things that withered in the autumn and were buried in the sleep of winter. It was a custom that allowed peace to prevail in our families.

This was a good year, for we celebrated on a first day that brought full, bright sunrise that filled the chamber. On the second morning, after the light rituals, we all made pilgrimage from the Womb Chamber out onto the plain of stones where both the Sun Circle and the Moon Circle had stood since the time before the Salmon Well.

I joined this crowd somberly, for this year it was Fia who stood at the oathstone, reaching her hand through to grasp Bran's. They said the ancient words, she gazing into his eyes, and he into hers. The intensity of their locked eyes made my stomach flutter and unbidden, Kerr's face rose in my mind.

The men stood on the side of the stone where stood Fia, and sang their songs of support and warning to Bran of how to treat a lass who made such a trusting promise to him. They chanted that he should praise the ground she walked on.

I took my place with the maams, who stood on the other side, with Bran. We sang our songs to Fia, reminding her of her sacred place with the Great Maam of All in bringing bairns into the world, in preserving them and the knowledge for the good of the *tuaha*. We reminded her that these noble things endured, while young love faded, and she would always have a place beside the strength of the Great Maam.

Unlike many of the other year-rituals, I had no officiant place in this one—I was too young. So my eyes had much time to scan the crowd. Many folks I knew only by sight, as, like Bran's family, they dwelt in Clochbeg or one of the other Large Island villages.

Men from Clochbeg stood with men from Cloch Graig, and maams from Clochbeg stood with maams from Cloch Graig. Their part in the ritual was shared, for the couple that joined benefited both communities. My eyes wandered back to the musicians, and there stood Kerr, his eyes closed, beating upon his drum, completely absorbed in the music.

As I stood anonymous in such a crowd, I used the time to study him. He was a comely lad, yes. Taller than most folk in the Trabally, he was nevertheless the darkest of the dark. His hair was the blackest night of the new moon and curled furiously about his head, the shorter locks on the top in stiff ringlets, the longer locks that hung on his shoulders twisted into tight ropes. All of it shifted and quivered with the movement of his stick upon the drum.

His frame was strong and lean. His skin was tanned deep brown by the sun. The tune he played was full of quick triplets tucked into unexpected places to be heard only by the occasional searching ear. Even in the intensity of the music, his face was unclouded, welcoming.

Suddenly he opened his eyes, and I flinched as if burned. He stared right at me, though he made no acknowledgment. Those black pools that stole my very being at the dance transfixed me and drew me in once again. I dropped my own eyes then, and when I lifted them, I kept them glued to Fia and Bran. Years later all I could remember from this day was the look of fondness on the young couple's faces and the intricate and intense battering of Kerr's drum.

On the third day of the rituals, I rose in the pre-dawn light, saying my prayers to the shadowy mists. The words came easy. I had been Aefa's shadow on these equinox days for as long as I could remember. When I was very small I was carried after her in my breast-maam's arms. It was right and good that the one chosen as the next Death Crooner should be with her at the rituals—even as a wee bairn. I knew the ancient chants by heart, I knew the sequence of the closing of the eyes, the spreading of the libations, the gradual change in the music from joy to mourning.

When we emerged from the passageway of the Womb Chamber on this third day, my eyes were blinded by the raw glare of sunlight. I emerged from a dream, or a cavernous pool of black water into the silver jangle of the village crowd.

As my vision focused I found before me Kerr's face, his dark eyes boring into mine as his right hand flitted across the lower half of his drum, his stick coaxing it in a rapid, penetrating beat. I was jolted out of my trance. Closing my eyes I threw my head back to release a mourning cry that sailed far above the others. I had never before disconnected in the middle of the ritual, and it shocked me. I was afraid, and angry.

My foul mood took me right through the feast of the First Hunt, the final ritual of the Days before the Darkening. I crouched moody, drawing in the fragrance of the roasting full-grown stag, awaiting my share of the sacred meat with every other man, maam and child. When I saw Kerr nearing me I fled, disappearing into the crowd and melding myself to its ebb and flow to stay out of his sight.

Later, Aefa and I returned to the stone village and were carefully laying away the sacred tools of the day in the stone dresser.

"*Granaidh*!" I exclaimed, after pouring out my angry tale of being dragged from my trance by Kerr's face. "*Granaidh* what was that? Why did that happen? Am I not suited to be Death Crooner?"

"Dear heart!" rejoined my *granaidh*. "Why do ye persist in thinking that ye are not like any other lass—that yer head won't be turned by a comely lad? And when it is, why do ye think that somehow makes ye less?"

"It does make me less, *Granaidh*! It has pulled me off the sacred ritual." My thoughts of Kerr were not like those I had of Bairnie, who could be commanded to lie still at my feet during the solemn rites. "What's happening to me, *Granaidh*? What power does that—lad!" I spat the word, as if it were a curse—"that lad have that is stronger than mine?"

Aefa laughed at this, and I was ill-pleased by her lightheartedness.

"Whist, child, do not take so weighty a view! It is not the lad that has power greater than yours, but the Great Maam of All. Ye are coming into yer strength, and that is a call for rejoicing. For it is not a wee child who will be the next Death Crooner, but a full maam. If a young man—and a fine young man at that, a keeper of the flame of music—is drawing yer interest, so much the better. A cause for celebration for yer old *granaidh*! There are wisdoms that come from teaching and learning, and there are wisdoms that only come from joining the flow of life, the flow that ye have no power over. Things like love, and the coupling of lovers, and maaming, and—"

I let out a loud grunt of exasperation and shoved the last of my bundles into the stone dresser. Aefa was standing, and motioned me to her. I obeyed, as I always did. One arm went around me, and she grasped my chin with the other. Black hawk-eyes lanced into my blue and hazel green ones.

"Calm, child, calm. The Great Maam of All will lead ye. If ye pull back and resist, ye are destined for sorrow. Take joy in yer maamhood. It is fast upon ye. Ritual is one way of dedication.

Love is another."

****

Bowstring released, the arrow flew faster than my eyes could track it. Its flight ended quivering, sunk halfway up the hilt behind the buck's front hock. The stone point had found its home in the animal's heart. The beast faltered in place, sinking to the ground, paralyzed by sudden painless loss of blood. In a flash I was beside him, muttering the incantation: *Sleep ye, sleep, ye goest to yer home of winter.*

Noiselessly I drew his chin up with one hand and swiftly slit his throat with the stone knife in the other. I held his head firmly as the last bit of life slipped away, his eyes glazing and half shut, his body relaxing beneath my grasp.

Death without pain, death without fear, death without horror, death without grieving. Go ye to yer winter home and bring me yer spring of life. My prayer slid out amongst the trees like the flick of the serpent's tongue, leading the buck's quivering spirit to freedom in the silence of the woods.

I drew my arm across my forehead, wiping away sweat and letting the hart's head fall from my grasp. As Aefa's mainstay I had long ago learned to use the bow from Kriafann, Aefa, and Darmid—or anyone else, for that matter, who would show me one more skill.

Along with many others my age I was consecrated to the hunt at ten summers. Our heads slippery with Aefa's fragrant oils, the bows our families crafted for us placed in our grasp, we stood with our bare feet upon the dirt, receiving both a blessing and a charge from our elders: *Ye shalt not wound a duck that is swimming, never shalt ye harry her of her young. The white swan of the sweet gurgle, the speckled dun of the brown tuft, ye shalt not cut a feather from their backs. Ye shalt only take that which is needed, be ye thankful for the one, thought nine more be swimming.*

Tuaha killed only what was needed to sustain us, never for the mysterious thrill of power that sometimes came from taking life. No bird upon its nest was to be taken, for that would kill four young birds as well. No sickened beast lying down was fair game, for though it was an easy mark, it might bring illness and death to the village. The murder of a suckling maam animal or sucking brood was a crime, for that would take life from the future. Though there were beasts which might always be taken down along with their young, they were not beasts for the eating, but beasts of prey that threatened village bairns.

This morning I had stood with the others as we consecrated the day to the Hunt Moon and the harvest of meat. We chorused an incantation that each of us would continue by ourselves at the first three streams we found. In each of them we would wash our hands and faces as we called out.

I am bathing mine own hands in the light, in the elements of the sky. I vow I shall not return this day without game, without venison down from the hill, without fat from out of the copse. After the strength of the sun has gone down, void, O void ye to me the hearing of them that I might not loose me arrow foolishly upon those whose sacrifice is not me need.

I completed my own incantations early. I had much woodlore gathered from solitary wanderings in the company of Bairnie that took me quickly to the required three streams of water. From the last rill I went directly to a place my childhood hours in the forest had shown me a stag was likely to pass. So it had, and here it had met with the stone point of my arrow.

The trees stand in a peculiar kind of stillness in the moments after a living thing's spirit passes out of its body and into the womb of the Great Maam of All. And thus, my skills having been proven, I sat quietly now, rubbing my finger back and forth on the top of the young buck's head, regretful, and yet accepting the reality of life which must consume life in order to continue.

Off to my left I heard the sharp snap of a stick breaking, and held my breath. Soon I could hear the breathing of another, and an occasional rustle of leaves as a foot measured its tread. I sat completely still. Though I had not my companion Bairnie to put an intruder on notice with ferocious barking, I was not afraid, only curious about whose path might be crossing my own in these remote parts.

Another crack of a stick, and I could not suppress a giggle. Whoever it was would have to work long and hard to find a deer so deaf it would not hear death stalking it this loudly.

"Who goes?" asked a fierce, deep young voice. I stood up

115

abruptly, scarcely an arm's length from Kerr.

"'Tis me," I said simply. His face registered shock, and then could not hide its delight. This passed immediately to surprise again, as he looked down at the grand young hart at my feet.

"I—I see ye have succeeded this day already," he stammered.

"Aye, 'tis so," I nodded gravely, suddenly shy and overcome with a paralysis for words.

"Might we sit, and enjoy me bannocks in celebration?" His invitation was awkward and formal, yet eager. I nodded, and we moved to two boulders across the small clearing and sat down. Pulling off my bloodied gloves I tossed them in the direction of the hart. Then, taking some dried fruit from my carry-bag, I held them out to Kerr, and we solemnly and with the self-consciousness of the very young, exchanged our food stuffs. Still, no further word had been spoken. Kerr turned to me, finally.

"Have ye no speech? Me sisters cannot keep their mouths closed, but ye are as silent as the dark of a new moon!" He grimaced and took his head in his hands, then stammered, "No, sorry, lass, I meant no offense."

"No offense taken," I said, my words tripping me as well, as I tried to find the ones to make light conversation.

"What is wrong with the two of ye, are ye *in love*?" Osheen emerged from the underbrush, his sarcasm tinged with mirth. "Ye are so—dreamy yer didn't even hear me coming!" He guffawed outright now.

"Go on with ye, Osheen," laughed Kerr, but his face burned scarlet and I felt the heat of my own.

Osheen winked at me. "It's good. Yer secrets are safe with yer beloved cousin. Well, I didn't mean to interrupt the love nest, but since ye're too busy with each other----hey! Can I eat that?" He pointed abruptly to the dried fruits and bannocks we held.

I groaned audibly, for there would be no end to the teasing now that Osheen had seen me blush.

"Osheen, ye are so bothersome, we shouldn't even feed ye."

But he had already flung himself down beside us and was helping himself to the bannocks and fruit. We chewed in silence for a few minutes, stopping only to wash down our meal from the waterskin each of us carried. Osheen's eyes came to rest upon the body of the hart nearby.

"Excellent, Kerr! Excellent hunt!"

"Kerr!?" I shot back in outrage, "That's mine!"

"Owwww!" yelled Osheen, shaking his hand as if he had just burned it, "Owwwww! Watch out for that ferocious one! She doesn't take kindly to the mistakes of a poor weary lad!"

I clutched a handful of dried leaves and shot them at Osheen, which was all that was needed for us to forget our honored status as consecrated hunters and erupt into noisy battle. Hunting for miles around was no doubt destroyed for the duration of our screeching laughter and thrashing as we took up armfuls of leaves and rained them on each other.

Soon, all three of us lay panting on the ground, pulling great draughts of water from our travel skins in between irrepressible bursts of giggling. Slowly our hysterical ardor subsided and we lay winded and quiet, until we sat up abruptly and finished the last of the food.

"So, Ronnat, are ye so powerful that ye can bring the kill back yerself, or would ye deign to accept the brute strength of yer cousin and friend in the endeavor?" Osheen mocked gleefully.

I scowled, but realized he had the advantage of me. Big and strong as I was, there was no way I could hoist the animal by myself. I brought rope with me to lash three sticks together to form the triangle of a travois on which to tie the buck and drag it by myself if I had to. But this buck, though young, was larger and heavier than I thought I could pull by myself. Sheepishly I nodded at Osheen.

"Help me to the Ridge Path," I said, "and I'll wait for ye there until ye've got yer kill." The two lads nodded, and the three of us hoisted the hart clumsily to our shoulders and made our way to the Ridge Path that followed the mountain's crest from the foot hills to the summit. At a good spot, we set the deer down, and I made myself comfortable to await Osheen and Kerr's return.

When the two lads finally got out of earshot with their boasts and their laughter, I put my carry-bag behind my head and lay down. There would be many hunts like this, before the village had sufficient meat to last the winter. The midday autumn warmth filtered through the trees and settled a drowsiness upon me that I could not resist. The browns, golds, and reds of the tree tops swayed with the wind, lulling me into a trance.

Out of my glistening dream came the shining face of a tall young man with long hair somewhere between the color of the burning sun and my own red. His eyes were light blue and penetrating. A blazing smile spread across his face as he drew nearer to me, fixing his eyes on my own. I heard my name as flames crackled around me: *"Ronnat, Ronnat, sister seal, it's me, yer brother!"* and suddenly I was wide awake.

I sat up abruptly, knocking my head into my cousin Bradan's chin as he bent over me. He howled in pain and jumped, only to catch his heels on a log beneath the leaves, pitching him backwards onto the ground with a dull thud.

"Ronnat!" he said in anguish as he sat up. "Owwwwww......!"

I shook my head, trying to clear the vision of the golden lad from before my eyes.

"Bradan?" I said slowly.

"Who else, are ye blind?" He answered grumpily, still rubbing his chin.

"Sorry, Bradan, sorry. Ye startled me—I was.... sleeping?" I shook my head again, trying to tie my thoughts to the present. Poor Bradan paid dearly for attempting to allow me to slumber. But who was the young man in my dream? I would never forget those eyes, bright ice blue, ringed, like my own, with the second sight. Where was he calling from? Who was he?

I stiffly got to my feet. "Here cousin, let me look at that."

I bent a little, for Bradan, at twelve, was much shorter than I— he had not the benefit of a mysterious father who made him tower above the *tuaha* of the Trabally. He was compact and dark and strong like all the village people. I bent his chin up into the light. A bruise was already forming.

"Sorry, cousin," I said again. "*Granaidh* Aefa will fix something for ye when we get back. Where is everyone?"

"Osheen and Kerr sent me back to say they have killed, and they are coming."

I regarded him wryly. "And who is helping them carry their kill?"

"Dahi and Kira." Too young to make kill this year, they came to help carry.

"That's good." I sat down again. There would be six of us to carry three animals. The two younger children would struggle to help the two young men bring the two harts to me, but from here, things would be much better. I could pair myself with Osheen, and Kerr could carry the other animal with Bradan and Dahi. Kira, only eight years old, could manage our carrypacks and quivers so the rest of us were free to lift.

I began to look about for a sapling thick enough to bear the weight of the hart, but not so thick that we would struggle to shoulder it. Settling upon one, I took my stone axe from my belt and began to cut it down. Bradan was quickly by my side, steadying the thing so that my blade found solid purchase. Soon the timber lay on the ground and I was trimming the ends. We tied the hart to it by the feet and practiced hoisting it. It would do well.

It didn't seem long before we heard the voices of Kerr, Osheen and the younger children. When they broke through the trees, they wasted no time evening up the loads between them so we could all set out down the Ridge Path. Kerr and I were at the front and for a while, when the path was wide enough, traveled in tandem with our animal between us, trading stories of how we each had made our kill.

When Kerr, Osheen and I taunted each other about our prowess, the younger children giggled with delight. I placed Kira in front of us to gauge the pace, and when the little lass began to flag, I stopped the group for water and the last of the food we carried.

It was nigh unto dark when we reached the village. Sending the younger children home to their maams, Kerr, Osheen and I bound the back legs of the deer and hoisted them into the trees. There they would drain of blood before morning, and be out of reach of small predators. Tomorrow we might hunt again, while other villagers butchered today's kill and fired up the drying racks. The Hunter's Moon was plentiful that year.

****

I was tying up the last of my cache of collected nuts one day when Fia burst into Aefa's chambers with the news: "Hefin has come!"

Hefin the hill-walker, the trader in exciting and rare goods from far away, always appeared at this time of year. There was much excitement from the first moment he and his broken down nag were spotted by hunters wending their way home. The news came to the village like lightning, so by the time Hefin arrived, a crowd was gathered on the green and all vied for the chance to host him for the nights he would spent in the Trabally.

I jumped quickly to follow Fia, the two of us chattering excitedly of the purchases we might find.

"A lot has happened since the trip to the shieling when we dreamed of this day, sister," Fia said slyly, casting a meaningful glance in my direction. I blushed, for I knew Fia was teasing me about my interest in Kerr. Was it so evident to everyone?

"I would say so, cousin," I shot back, lowering my head to fix my eyes on Fia's belly. I raised my hands up in exaggerated surprise. Fia threw back her head and laughed, her arms encircling me and squeezing so hard I squealed.

"Don't knock us over!" I yelped. Arm in arm we continued to the green where Hefin's many wares were laid out on blankets, the *tuaha* hovering over them like flies. We two cousins knelt by a blanket covered with hanks of fine-knotted necklaces—tough leather thongs hung with iridescent cowrie and snail shells.

I grasped one and held it up for Fia to see.

"Look at this one, sister," I breathed, "See how the green-blue of the sea so slightly colors it and here, over here, it is white as wave-foam!" It was the shell of a sea snail, the sides battered away by the relentless waves to reveal the inner chambers. The curves that delineated these had been smoothed into two rings. Through one of them a thong was threaded, letting the shell hang at a graceful angle.

"It is beautiful, Ronnat!" Fia said, "See how the blue reflects yer eyes!"

"Oh shush, Fia!" I was embarrassed to hear my cousin's flattery.

"Try this, lass." The voice was soft and deep. I whirled to face Kerr, who had come up behind us unnoticed. He held the mirror provided by Hefin up for me, and with his other hand took the necklace from me and laid it alongside my face so that the shell fell at the little hollow at the base of my throat. Yes, it brought out the blue of my one eye. One eye. How could he admire that thing? But it was admiration in his face that I saw, and I blushed furiously.

"Ye should have it, Ronnat," he said softly. I quickly took the necklace back from him and put it down, shaking my head. My heart was beating as if I was running.

"No, no, it is very dear. I—I have no use for such—pretty things." I ducked my head, remembering that he had done a kindness. "But thank ye, thank ye." I quickly rose to my feet pulling Fia after me into the crowd.

"What are ye about, Ronnat?" Fia's whisper was harsh. She stopped and shook her arm from mine, grabbing my face between her two hands. "Stop being a little fool, sister! He has noticed ye and it is obvious ye have noticed him! Go where the Maam has made the path so easy!"

And easier still the way was made, when the festival of the sea came upon us.

****

Manannan was the sea god of the *tuaha*. Upon his dark stallion, he was the god of both fishermen and horsemen. His festival commemorated the end of the fishing season, when all of us helped the fisherfolk pull their currach boats and nets up to the village for their winter mending and storage. We shrieked with glee as young horsemen, shrouded in black to disguise themselves, stampeded down the beach to honor Manannan and his stallions. They raced up and down the sand, screeching like banshees and amazing the gathered crowd by standing on the backs of their horses as they galloped furiously, some jumping from one horse to another, then back again.

At the end of the grand display, some of the young horsemen would veer into the crowd of villagers to catch the young lasses of their hearts by the arm and swing them up on the mount behind them. As the villagers ululated and the young horsement roared, the village lasses so purloined whooped. Together they would gallop up and down the beach, ending the mad display by the gentle depositing of their sweetheart on the green, where preparations for the night feast were in full swing.

It was at the rites of Manannan that year that I turned my back on the hubbub for a moment as I whispered to Aefa that Fia would never again have to endure the wildness of the beach gallop, she being handfasted and carrying a bairn. With my face pressed close to Aefa's ear I did not see the dark rider split from the cavalcade and make a beeline to where I stood. I turned back towards the spectacle just as he wheeled next to me, reached down and grabbed my right forearm.

A swift kick to his horse's sides, and I found myself flying through the air my momentum turning me nicely and depositing me behind him on the animal's back. Out of reflex I grabbed around his waist as the horse snorted and bolted back to the racing herd.

At the end of the beach the riders and their passengers about-faced and launched back towards the villagers. But my captor's mount continued, unchecked, until he brought it up short just under the overhang of cliff that divided the sand and gravel from the bluffs above our small harbor. He grabbed my arm again, and swung me down, dismounting in one leap before me, never once dropping hold of my hand. With his other hand he pulled off the fine woven black mask that covered his head and eyes.

"Ronnat, will ye ride with me often?" Kerr's hawk-like intensity transfixed me. "Will ye let me come to ye, and will ye join the dance with me tonight?"

I was startled and could only stammer a less than enthusiastic affirmation. This was an anguished request to court me, yet my lukewarm response was enough for the hopes in him. He took off his gloves and from his fingers dangled the blue and white shell necklace from Hefin's bounty. I know my eyes registered surprise.

"Will ye give permission, lass?" Kerr's whisper was deep and low. My skin prickled as I nodded, and he placed it gently around my neck, carefully gathering up my hair and twisting it gently to pull it through the leather thong. The iridescent shell lay framed by the small depression at the base of my throat, just as it had the day I first saw it.

Kerr donned his gloves again as he vaulted up onto his horse, then grabbed my forearm and swung me up behind him. Without a word, we set off at breakneck speed for the village gathering.

****

That night was a time of feasting and dancing and ritual mumming made that much more exciting for me by my wild ride with Kerr that afternoon. The smell of the spitted, roasting lamb was almost too much to bear. Its skin hung over a rock by the fire of sacred rowan, oak, and bramble. Under it, slowly baking in the intense heat, was the special bannock, the harvest cake made from sheep's milk, bird's eggs, butter, and a bit of all the cereals and grains we had so recently brought in. The hearty mix of grains made it hard to knead, though us village folk bent together to the task, jabbering about the strength brought by this year's harvest.

As I joined this struggle I laughed with the others until breathless, and sang the rhythmic kneading chants. The dough changed before our eyes, lightening in color, becoming evenly grained and stretchy.

Softly golden from the eggs and tacky to the touch, it was ready to bake. Onto the flat rock it went. While we sang to the plenty of harvest, next to the hot fire it baked into a fragrant, airy, wonderful delight. As acolyte, I broke off the first piece and tossed it into the fire as a libation to the Great Maam of All.

The savory smell of the roasting lamb and the first fat geese of the season lured all from the villages to the feast. The geese were stuffed with apples, nuts, and herbs, and slow roasted on a spit, making them flavorful and moist. It was now the beginning of the apple-picking season, and the sweet smell of the roasting goose and apples elicited sighs of wellbeing.

In this high holiday season, Aefa and I led double lives of labor—that of our ritual duties, and that of bringing in the bounty for the winter. These festivals were the dividing feasts of the equinox: the grains were in off the land, fishing season was over, fruits and nuts were dried and bagged, the hunting and meat harvest was in process. Not long ago the stock animals were blessed with salt, fire and water, and then turned out to fend for themselves until the dreaded slaughter day came.

The celebration of thanks to the husbandman of the forest, the green leaf man, fell a few days after the rites of the sea god. Aefa and I led the villagers to the great wood, and there we went from one revered tree to another, pouring on a honeymead libation to thank each for its sacred service to the *tuaha* for the year, and for all years back to the time of the Salmon Well. Stacks of firewood were gathered from the forest floor for the coming winter. Before we bound those stacks in bundles that every man, maam and child would haul to the village, our prayers lulled the sacred trees to sleep for the winter.

The high holiday season was long, and soon after the rituals of the green leaf man of the forest was the spinners' and weavers' festival. Great stores of fleece had accumulated over the summer when all hands were needed upon the shieling or in the farm field. These must be spun and then knitted or woven into clothing, bed curtains, wraps, blankets and other useful items during the long winter nights before the fire.

On the night of the weavers festival there was no grand feast, but all the families brought food items to the gatherings in the great rooms of the little stone villages. These great rooms would host the *calanas*, the making of the cloth, and so it was fitting that the festival was held here.

Cloth was a gift from the Great Maam that brought our people out of the time when ice covered the land and nothing but furs covered our bodies. During the *calanas*, the cloth had its birth in the bundled fleeces of spring and early summer. These we sorted, washed, picked, combed and made into rolags, the puffs of cleaned wool prepared for spinning. Then came the spinning itself, knitting, weaving, and the waulking of the cloth—the beating of it to a rousing song that tightened and straightened its weave. There were many chores to bring wool into clothing and the other needs of a household.

Aefa and I joined each household in bringing a handful of fleece to the weavers' rites that opened the *calanas*. All our bits were bound together into a sacred bunch for the making of cloth was a village task over all. The evening began with Aefa's blessing that took over where the spring rooing charm had ended. *Go shorn, come woolly* had been the blessing of the rooers as they released each sheep from its plucking. Now, as the fire was lit, all our hands brought out our hanks of fleece to chant through the grand scheme of the *calanas*.

In the long winter night, all are brought together for the protection of the young and old. First we sorted our handfuls from fine to coarse. *Ye Great Maam, who giveth plenty to each kind, give us wool spun from the green grass and the sheep's belly.* Then we washed the hanks and held them before the blazing fire, where they dried swiftly.

Consecrate the flocks and the little singing lambs that increase the generations of our herds. We teased the lumps and tangles out of the fleece. *Bring from them to us the wool, and the milk to drink.* Our wool was then combed, and each of us made a tiny rolag. *May no dearth be ours of the clothing that warms and protects.*

To mimic the time of dyeing, we dipped each hank in woad and salt water, and held it up to the fire to dry again. *Every color in the bow of the shower has gone through me fingers, blue, and roan, and color of the sheep, and never a particle of cloth was wanting.*

Finally, we braided the little rolags of wool together into one dolly. *Bless me O Great Maam of All. Consecrate the four posts of me loom, thrums and thread of the plies, give yer blessing everywhere, on every shuttle passing under the thread.*

That is when we began to strain upwards as one chanting whole, those who were taller creating a foundation on which to lift those shorter, feet upon shoulders until at last the dolly we had made was hung by the tiniest lass upon the roof beam of the great room. *May the one who wears this clothing never be wounded, may torn they never be, may the shield of the Great Maam be theirs.* In one great whooping cry as we passed the tiny lass down the ladder we had made of our bodies the weaving hall was blessed for the winter.

After the ritual, out came the food and the weaver's mead. I loved its light and frothy texture bringing a feeling of relaxation, yet it was not so strong as to make the head swim or disturb the evenness of the weft of the weavers. Soon after we finished our first cups, the chatter died down. Sated, we sat before the heat of the fire, and the stories started.

Aefa called us to the fire this night, for a story hung heavy upon her tongue. She pulled the little children into her lap, and began.

Long ago a tuaha maam sat up late one night pulling and sorting wool, as her family were all asleep and she had so little peaceful time to herself to do such. In the very dark of the night she heard a voice whining at the door and crying, "Open, Open!"

"Who calls?" asked the good maam, for surely no one

disturbs a family so deep in the night without good cause.
  "I be the one-horned Faerie-Maam," came the cry.

In all, thirteen evil faerie maams burst through her door that night and took their wool picks to the fleece, muttering and chanting in a language so old the maam knew it not. Of course she was terrified of them. They pressed her into service when they commanded her to bring water. She was beyond frightened, and then a sacred salmon in the well instructed her in how to outwit the evil creatures and drive them from her family forever.

Aefa ended her tale in a mournful low voice that stopped suddenly, letting complete silence enfold the room. We, her audience came slowly awake, as if from a trance, and blinked our bleary eyes as we rose. I sat with my two little cousins, Maev and Kira, in my lap. I hugged them to me, and set them on their way towards Fia and Grania. They were little maams, the future of our village, and I smiled across the room to my cousin and aunt.

It was time for each of us to creep through the passageways of Cloch Graig to our own chambers, tired and fulfilled at the ending of the high holiday season of the year. The Hunt Moon would die with the full moon that now shown huge and brilliant in the sky. The food was in for the winter. The shelters were protected from harm.

In this time of year, as the light faded into the dark cold of winter, we would begin to draw into ourselves and spend our time about the hearth fires of our family chambers, or together in the great room, spinning, weaving, mending nets, making garments and repairing boots for the next spring. In the night the little stone village gave up an occasional laugh or murmur, as it was also a time of making bairns, and telling stories. Always making bairns and telling stories.

As the crowd shifted and moved, I reached for Bairnie, and remembered that he was far off in the high pastures with my *daideo*. As always, that little stab of loneliness went into my heart. For once I welcomed the dark time of year that lay before us, for it would finally bring an end to my separation from my beloved companion.

11. WITHER MOON

I turned and gazed at the sun sinking in all its glory, and began to mouth the words I knew so well: *Sun-Maam, the eye of glory, the eye of the hosts, the eye of the living pouring upon us at each time and season, pouring upon us gently and generously: glory to ye, glorious Sun-Maam, face of life.*

My whispered prayers were borne aloft by the gripping hum of all those who stood upon the hilltop with me, mouthing the words in unison on this so important of sunsets. The autumn wind was stiff, bringing with it the smell of frosty hay and dry earth from the remains of the crops that had been turned back into the ground. Our words began to stitch the sky to our being until we rolled as one mass with the wind and the great heaving breaths of the earth we stood on.

It was *Sauin*, summer's end, and the eve that brought the feast of the dying sun. This was the first of the three days that marked the end of the time of growing light and delivered us to growing darkness. The bounty of the harvest had been picked, the stalks were shriveling, and the summer plenty was safely put away for the times of hunger. The land was dry, bare, brown and fading towards the starvation of winter. On some mornings the meadows already sparkled with a scrim of ice crystals.

Tonight in the Great Turning of the Year my people would feast and light fires to the dying sun. Tonight, the veil between our world and the world beyond was so diminished that in places it tore, and the dead and the living passed easily through it. Tonight we would take advantage of the thinning between the worlds to predict the future and speak with the past.

I shaded my eyes from the glare of the sinking sun. Even so, I could barely make out Aefa's shape against the stabbing light. She was shrouded in black, the black that came from the walnut hulls, as were we all. Her robe touched the ground, and over it was a black woolen cape, steeling her against the chill. She stood with both arms raised to the horizon, hands lifted in supplication.

Tonight was the most magical of nights when the dead walked among the living. In the wildness of the snapping bonfires, the separation between past, present, and future was lifted as Seeing and prophecy linking the living to the dead augured the future. Aefa began the ritual words that made a whorl of sky and water to reach those we loved and tie them to us with a thread of life that winnowed down into depths we could not fathom.

Tomorrow, the Day Out of Time, was the day that brought all the days of the thirteen moons of the year to match the total number of the days of the sun-year. The sun and moon years ran neck and neck with each other, and each had its own stone calends—one with thirteen upright stones, one with twelve. But on the Day Out of Time, they became one. This was a holy day above all, a day of shadows and mysteries and secrets.

It was also a time of broken-heartedness. Our maams and children hid in the houses while the men and young lads and lasses in silence gathered up the household beasts to be culled for the winter. They were herded to the shoreline and slaughtered where the waves might wash the blood away. It was a necessity of survival, but a consuming grief also, for these were beasts upon which much love was bestowed.

The third and final day of *Sauin* began the New Year. We called it the Day of the Winter Dead, when the dead time of winter was honored for its power to generate the coming life of spring. In it, we as families and villages of *tuaha* honored our dead and spoke to them. We gathered early and snaked our way among the family tombs, the names of our beloveds uttered aloud in singing sorrow. Chanting and wailing we made our progress from burial chamber to burial chamber in remembrance.

As usual, before leaving our little house in the stone village on this holy day, Aefa blessed and then smothered our house fire—as had everyone in the whole of the Trabally on this day. The hearths would be left cold until rekindled with the burning embers of the *Sauin* bonfires. These new fires would welcome the returning souls of the dead to the sumptuous feast offerings we prepared for them during these three whole days of *Sauin*. Winter was death time, but death brought a renewal of life. And so we would feast with our ancestors in honor of this.

Our villagers gathered at the high place as the sun sank lower, pulling its glory down below the farthest mountains so that only a sliver of its flame could be seen on the horizon. Then, the sky exploded in a fanfare of orange and purple. At this, we uncovered our heads in the wind, bowing low to receive the last of the dying year's light, chanting our farewells as we had learned them from our maams, and they from their maams, all the way back before the time of the Salmon Well.

I am in hope, I am pleading, I am making me supplication in its proper time that the great and gracious Sun-Maam will not put out for me the light, even as she dost leave me this night. The words were a gull's conversation gathering short cries and weaving them into the patter of feet and chortle of gullets until the sound took off as a body unto itself, the *tuaha* merely its many mouths.

As the sun passed below the brow of the hill, there was a lull in our chanting, the world waiting tense and expectant. The wind, sharp on my ears as it whistled at this height, was heavy with spirits. Suddenly the paralysis was broken by a wild cry, picked up by first one masked figure, then another, as torches were kindled, and the torch-bearers leapt to touch the bonfires with their guttering sticks, shrieking and whooping and cavorting in mad glee.

I recognized Osheen and Braden in their midst wearing the horned headdresses I had helped them make. They dove into the gathering dark, tearing down the hill to bless the fields by galloping sunwise around the four corners, touching each with their torches as they passed. When the fire-bearers returned, their cries reached a crescendo as they ran sunwise around the bonfire, spiraling nearer and nearer to the burning coals until they could go no farther lest they be immolated.

The bride of *Sauin*, the maam chosen to represent Bri in all her power to brew winter death, then tame it with spring life, appeared. This year it was Osheen's mother—Arda—for he as her youngest child had reached an age that released her to this task. She carried large three-sided furrowed bannocks in the shape of the sacred opening to the womb; these brought the blessings of this night. The other maams flanked Arda and when they reached the gathering place, spread out and sat in a ring of wisdom around the fire, the circular earthen trench filled with their wraps and furs and woolen blankets. They would preside over this sacred night as the Great Maam fueled the turning season.

As the hours of dark wore on, the music and dancing increased in frenzy as if the inevitability of winter could be shaken off with delirium. When the fires began to die down, we young folks ran through them, sanctifying ourselves for the year to come.

When only the murmuring coals remained in the pitch-black night, the wind died, and we stretched around the quieting fire. This was the time for the telling of the ritual tales for this holy time. It was Kriafann, my uncle known as The Fox, who began the tale this night. His voice rang deep and penetrating against the snapping and popping of the fire.

This lass was a beautiful lass, young and strong and able to heave the ewe at the rooin' same as any lad. She had the habit of runnin' wild up in the fields and pastures past the light of day, and the village tongues wagged that she'd find herself caught in the faerie's web one fine day. And so it was one morning in her frolics she came upon a sea rose growing in the high pasture, far from the foamy shores where it belongs. She stopped and went to the bush and her eyes fell upon a double rose, growing there in the branches. She couldna restrain herself, and her hand went forth to pull the rose no matter the warnings of her own folk to leave a magic rose alone.

And so she grasped it and pulled it, and her tug was felt through the fog between the worlds, for the roots of this fair rose were in the breast of a lad held prisoner in the land of the Faerie. By her insistent tugging he tumbled through the veil and into her arms right there in the high pasture.

The fire popped and spit just then as if it spewed a comment from the dark world we could not see. I gazed into the orange glow. I knew this old story by heart, and I remembered, eyes smarting, the first time I heard it from the sharp tongue of old Mae. The old biddy had looked straight and disapproving into my blue and hazel green eyes, cackling, *Such we think, young Ronnat, is the story of yer maam and how ye came to be so fair and braw and freckled among us dark smallfolk. For she never named yer father, and surely he was not amang the Cloch Graig villagers, and for that ye'll be an outsider all yer life.* All the other children except my cousins moved away from me then, staring at me and voicelessly daring me to follow. I swallowed a hollowness brought up by the memory as Kriafann continued.

Aye, how they looked deep into each other's eyes in that one instant. So she was caught tighter in a faerie trap than if her arms and legs had been wound with ropes. She was drawn into his deep green eyes and they became locked in a lover's gaze.

As my thoughts took wing, I wondered what double rose my maam may have found and planted upon me that I would always to be different among my own kind. I knew the lesson of the story well: it was about staying among folk familiar instead of striking out to a new land. It was about loves strange and foreign. My own maam had chosen the latter, and whether the world she chose was faerie I did not know, but certainly it was foreign, for my own speckled skin and red hair testified to that.

My eyes were nearly closed by the last of the tale, but the leaping shadows of the dying fire still played upon my lids. My differences would always set me apart, just as if I was half faerie. I opened my eyes wide again.

The villagers around the fire were shifting and picking up black cinders, warm, but not hot, and rubbing them across their faces, blackening themselves to hide from the faerie spirits as they went home in the dark.

I rose and began to fold my blankets. A dark figure came into the circle of light and straight to me. It was Kerr. I knew his shape even before I could fully see his face.

"Hello, Ronnat," he whispered softly. "Are ye staying on the hill tonight?" I ducked my head and fussed with the folding of my blanket.

"Nah, Kerr, I'm going down to the stone village with *Granaidh* for the Seeing." With most of the rest of the village folk Aefa and I would retire to our stone chambers for the supper mash of roots and fish, and the making of the ritual cakes. Then we would begin the Seeing to read the future while the door between the worlds was down. For us, as Death Crooner and her acolyte, this was a solemn task.

"Ah, yes," he said softly, nodding his head in understanding. "I'm staying tonight for the Ritual of the White Mare." It was my turn to nod. Kerr was quite a horseman, as he had proved on our wild ride up the beach. He being of age, tonight he would remain at the hill top fire for the secret induction into the Horse Clan. There he would receive his one true word, the one that would call even a wild horse to his hand.

"May ye receive a powerful word," I felt the pull of unbidden longing to stay and see that, but Kerr's commitments tonight could not be shared by the uninitiated, and I had duties with Aefa. I flung the folded blanket over my back and smiled hesitantly. "It's a grand night for it."

Pulling a glowing log from the fire to rekindle the fire in our hearth, I started down the hill. I know Kerr fixed his eyes upon my retreating silhouette as it passed into the cold white light of the moon. I know, because years later he told me that he did, how his eye followed my slender dark shape as it grew smaller and smaller, until all he could see was the capricious dance of the orange torchlight I carried.

****

Aefa was already at the winter chambers snug in the covered stone village when I arrived, she having left the bonfire right away with Kriafann and Arda. She was taking the root mash we cooked yesterday down from the stone shelves. As I kindled the fire, Aefa began to warm the mash and stir in the fish.

"*Granaidh*," I said, pulling a stool up to the fire as the flames caught and glowed. "*Granaidh*, why isn't Grania to be the Death Crooner that follows ye?"

Aefa stopped stirring the fish and roots, and looked sideways at me. Her lips pursed; her eyebrows bunched together.

"Ah, then it is time for that question, love?"

"Yes, *Granaidh*."

Aefa put her arms down, and bowed her head, thinking. She raised her eyes to me then, cocked her head to one side, and sighed. "Surely ye have noticed the special way that Grania has as a maam."

"She likes it fine, 'tis true," I said.

"True enough, she likes it. But do ye see how the little ones come into her arms, no matter who is their maam, and quieten?"

"Yes, *Granaidh*."

"Well, that is the call for Grania. She is called to be a maam, to love life and to make life, to help it grow, to soothe, to sing, to rock, to hold a hand, to tell a small amusing tale, to dry tears."

"But isn't that what ye do too, *Granaidh*?"

Aefa let out a laugh at this, for in truth, she did many of those things.

"But Grania doesn't see beyond," she said to me. "Her eyes are fixed right here, in this world, in the small comforts of it that she can provide for the young ones. Her eyes don't see the future, they don't see the past, they don't see the deep beneath the deep or the spirit or the faerie, or the un-named hurt in the eyes of a lad that spins into a story. She is content.

"But a Death Crooner, that is a different sort of solace. It is the touch that brings souls into the world, and takes them out again when it is their time. It is the sight that sees the future and past as well as the present. It is the ear that hears the wind of the stars in the song of the morning lark, and sees the swing of the heavens on the owl's wing. It is the tongue that tastes spring in winter, and winter in spring; it is the nose that catches the heaven of the lavender flower, or smells the darkness of evil on a stranger. Grania has none of those senses, however lovely and wonderful she is in her own world."

Nodding, I stared into the glowing fire, my gaze frozen by the pulsing embers and caught in their trance. I spread my eyes wide, as if the molten glory might never be enough. Aefa's soft movements as she stirred and warmed the mash became an odd music beside me. I blinked my eyes, but they remained fast on the fire.

And suddenly, he was there again, the lad with the long sunlit hair and the wide blue eyes, calling *Ronnat, me sister, I have found ye, at last I have found ye!* I shook my head to clear the vision, and as it whipped away from me, I could not help but blurt out, "I am here, I am Ronnat, don't leave me!"

"What is it, child?" Aefa dropped her spoon against the side of the wooden bowl and fastened her eyes upon me.

I whipped my head from side to side, shattering the mirage.

"It is the dream, *Granaidh*," I bleated, and sank to the floor with my head in my hands.

"What dream, love?"

"A—vision, of the beautiful lad. His hair is white and his eyes blue like the sky over the sea. He's calling me sister, *Granaidh*, he's calling me again. What does he want? He says he is me brother, but I have no brother."

Aefa put her arm around me and stilled me.

"It is the Sight has got hold of ye, love—ye are of an age for it to come, at last. There is nothing to be done about it until it brings him to ye in this world. We cannot know until then." She smoothed my hair as she had done ever since I was a small lass, and holding my face in her two hands, laid her cheek against mine. "But know that he is coming, love, and look sharp for him."

****

The Day Out of Time dawned dark and dreary, one ray only of the sun piercing the cloud cover, and that gone in a twinkling. A thin cold mist sat in the air, unmoved by breeze. I could smell the raw cold of the winter sea in it, though the waves were nearly still, as if in rebellion against the perverse function they were to have today—carrying the blood of the loyal beasts to the vastness of the sea.

Dark masked figures left our houses in the murky gray, and found their way to field and byre. They lead the marked beasts on cloth-muffled feet to the water front, where they were hobbled, and their bawling cut mercifully short by the swift hands and sharp stone knives of the butchers. Young people of our villages drew lots for this sad work. They were shrouded in their killing garments so they might never imagine they were to blame for the deaths. They worked silently under the heavy burdens of this day.

I knew the cost of this grim task on the souls of the young who must do their duty for the first time. I pulled the door flap aside just enough at dawn to see the shape of Osheen, known to me even in the drape of his dark cloak, stumbling in the mist and dark towards the fields.

How he sobbed for many a day afterwards, the first time he served. So much so Aefa was called to croon his young spirit back from the fear of gore and into his young body again. She returned more than once to Osheen, until he finally passed the experience behind him and accepted his duty as one of the providers for the village. I felt sad that this year he must do his duty once again to the death that had so scarred him. Though the lasses might help with the carrying and salting and washing of blood, it was only a task for the lads to do the killing itself, as they did not carry bairns within.

I let the curtain fall and turned back in with a shudder. There were some benefits to being Death Crooner. Not participating in the year-slaughter was one of them. Aefa's and my primary ritual duty today was to take the bowl of blood from house to house, blessing the four corners and door step of each. Then we moved on to the animal shelters, touching each living beast's forehead with a drop of blood from the slain, whose spirits would keep the living in the coming year.

Some years the wind was off the water and despite our custom of staying in and staying hidden, at times a pathetic bawl or the smell of blood and salt air rose to the stone village. I remembered those times with nausea, even now, even as I stood as a Death Crooner's apprentice who understood how those sacrifices allowed our lives to continue.

This would be a grim day, with only the making of the root stew to break its tedium. No meat would be eaten out of respect for the given lives of the poor dumb beasts. No turning must be done today, for that was contrary to the turning of the year. So there was no spinning of the spindle nor grinding of the quern stone. A dull day, to be sure, locked in quiet agony about its purpose.

But at the end of the day came consolation. Those like Osheen who partook of the slaughter rituals would have straggled back from the beach laden with meat to be stacked in the smoke houses or salting bins. At long last, the bloody work done, they would return to the sea, strip themselves of their clothing in the freezing air and burn it in a fire at the water's edge. When its work was done, the fire would drown in the flood of the incoming tide. When the water returned to the depths of the sea again, it would carry blood and the year's sorrow with it into the unfathomable depths.

From where they dropped their tainted clothing, the laborers of death proceeded naked to the brook that coursed across sand to the ocean. Following it up to its first pool, they washed off the day's blood, ridding themselves of its heavy burdens in the shockingly cold, clear water. In its turn the rill carried the sullied water back to the Maam Ocean. Silently their families stood by with warm wool blankets and cloaks, and once they were wrapped, returned them to their chambers in the stone village.

At sunset, my aunts gathered their children and their foodstuffs and left their own homes to come to Aefa's—something that all aunts and children were doing with their own grandmothers now. This gave the slaughterers privacy in which to pray and ritually leave their bloody work behind. When they emerged from their prayers, they stepped into clean, new clothing and walked with a settled soul to join their families for the night's festivities.

I traversed the tunnels to the outer cold evening air with Aefa as the old maam took the bowl of blood to bless the animal byres. I wasn't needed by her, I just wanted the chance to come back into the warmth of our house, to be assaulted by the fruity smell of the rich cream mash of ground roots, cole, and wild onions. My head swam with the deliciousness of tonight's spread. I, like those whose day's work robbed them of a taste for beast, would not miss the roasted meat. I basked in the heady fragrance and warm comfort that oozed from the fragrance of the root soups and holiday bannocks.

As Aidan and Kriafann and the older children drifted in from their ritual cleansing, and Aefa returned from the byres, the pall of the day was cast off, and the joy of another harvest feast and a close family time around the hearth prevailed for us. When we all were sated, the fire was a seething bed of hot embers, lighting and warming the stone house with a golden glow.

Aefa removed her shoes and headwear, and stood with her back to the stone dressers that stored our food. She held her arms wide to take in her family. Her eyes were closed, her chin lifted towards the smoke hole. All quieted, and she began the chant of the Seer Clan. *Maam before me, Maam behind me, Maam over me, Maam below me, I on her path. Ye, O Maam, in me steps.*

She walked three times, sun-wise, around the hearth, continuing her prayer. *Great Maam of All, stay ye behind me to give me eyes to see all.*

I, like Aefa, was one of the Clan of the Seers, and this, above all, allowed us to fulfill the duties of the Death Crooner. The gift of the Seers was always inherited, and mine came from my maam, who got it from her maam, Aefa. It was through the maams that it was said to be traced all the way back to the Salmon Well and beyond, to the days of ice. As a Seer I must follow closely behind Aefa parroting her words, that I might learn them for the day I would walk the boundaries on my own.

I see me daughter by the Salmon Well, seeing all that is, assuredly I set the Seeing towards the Salmon Well, and that was true work. The Great Maam of All teaching the tuaha, that I see assuredly. Our spells quoted the winds of time, pulling the rush of the world in toward us, and with our sounds, releasing a declaration that we, Death Crooners of the Trabally, could move mountains.

I rose, closed my eyes, and walked to the door whispering a repetition of everything Aefa said. *I am going without to the doorstep of me house in the name of the Great Maam of All, stronger of sight than all. I go out in the name of the Maam, I come in, in the name of the Maam. I walking in yer path O Maam, ye, O Maam, upon me doorstep.*

Aefa reached the doorway of our chamber house and put a hand to each side, leaning upon the jambs. *Maam before me, behind me, over me, beneath me, within me, without me, the Maam of marvels leading me.*

Now she opened her eyes, and crossing the threshold, went out through the passageways to the western doorway. She fixed her gaze before her and chanted, oblivious of me, her shadow.

As we stepped from the dark tunnel out into the open air at the west entrance, Aefa's ululation split the dark and she began to chant again. *We come to renew to ye The Day Out of Time, as it has been since the far ages. Ascending the wall of the house, descending at the door, me prayer to say modestly, as becomes me.*

Mouthing it together, Aefa aloud, me in near silent echo of her, we began the sunwise trip around the village. At the north we stopped. *The Death Crooner will go sunwise around her children. She it is who wears the hand without meanness, the hand that distributes the Day Out of Time.*

At the east we paused again and put our open palms upon the outer wall of the village. *May the Great Maam of All bless the dwelling, each stone, beam, stave, all food, drink, and clothing; may health be always here.*

At the south, we turned our backs to the wall, and wailed our chants to the south wind. *The hand of the Great Maam be on those who wish this household harm. And on the curses of plaintive buzzard, drooling boar, snarling badger, foul woodcat.*

When we finished, we progressed sunwise the remainder of the way to the western tunnel from which we had emerged. There we entered the passage and continued until we ducked under the lintel stone into the warmth of our house chamber once again. It was time for the Seeing to begin.

Aefa formed the three fingers of her left hand into a hollow log. She blew through the tube for Lass, Maam, and Crone, then began to rune the hymn of the dying sun. *The roar of the hunt on the hillock of Sauin above me. The weeping of the maams on the mud-plain of the river at the entrance of this plain. Maams bereft, fierce the contest that will come after it, that will come heavily on them, fierce the contest.*

I chanted my part close upon Aefa's. *Message of truth without message of falsehood, that I meself may see the semblance, joyous and mild, of all that is amissing to me.* Suddenly the room began to shift and spin, the gold of the firelight exploding into a blinding glare and the sound of my family's voices as they joined along with the sacred words dissolving suddenly into the cries of seabirds that dove from their nests high on the towers of stone that stood just offshore. Behind the eerie cries of gulls plummeting from skellig to sea, the steady tick of the chant like a musician's tapping foot tried to tie my spirit to earth while the magic flung me aerie with the sea birds.

Out of the shining light emerged the lad with the ice blue eyes, his white hair suffused with the sunlight so that I could not see his face clearly in the glare. He was crouched in a skin currach boat, pitching and rocking in the waves, his ice blue eyes boring steadily into me.

Sister, he pleaded, *Find me. Find me. Find me.* His voice was not pitiful or lost, but firm. I could discern his strength in its tenor. He came closer to me through the blinding light, but just as I was to see his face clearly, the world tipped sideways as something dark with sorrow crushed the white gold of the image.

I hit the matted floor with a heavy, hollow thud, a feeling of dread suffusing my being. I let out with a long wail of sorrow, deeper than the sea, wider than the horizon, farther away than the stars behind the moon.

Aefa darted to my side, wiping my brow and talking softly, grasping my face in her hands, and coaxing my spirit back into my body. It was the way of my visions that they came over me, possessed me, and though I was not lost to the memory of them, I was nevertheless unable to halt their flooding of my life-spark until they had run their course. After some moments, my head cleared and I sat up, tears streaming down my face.

The startled faces of my family met me, their bodies frozen in place. I wept openly then, as *Granaidh* Aefa soothed me. Soon Arda and Grania moved gently to put their hands on me, then the little children, and the men. Surrounded by their warmth, my sobbing quieted.

"Aye so," Kriafann muttered softly, "She is of the Clan of Seers. And her Seeing is strong. She will be Death Crooner in her time."

****

I woke groggy the next morning, my head stuffy and slow, as if I had drunk too freely of the mid-winter ale. I lay curled on my furs, where I had been moved to sleep off the aftermath of my vision while the family continued the feast of the Day Out of Time with stories and soft songs until they, too, crept off to their own houses and bed chambers.

The third day of *Sauin* was still before me to get through, and I was exhausted. It was the Day of the Winter Dead. Not only did it signify the true entry into the winter, the shortening of the days and the dying of the light, but also that the veil to the otherworld was closed again. We must pay homage to our dead, now out of our easy reach for another year.

In the early morning mist my whole village came to the gathering place. Green in the summer, now it was brown with the death of winter. We stamped our feet to stay warm, waiting for all to assemble, our breath coming out in clouds. I felt tired and unsteady on my feet.

Aefa took me under one arm, pulling my cloak more tightly about me. The old maam beckoned across the green to Fia, who stood still, her eyes riveted on me while Grania whispered in her ear. Fia had come back from her home with Bran in Clochbeg to process to the tombs of the dead with her own family and village. She dropped her maam's arm and ran to me, taking my other arm, standing close so her body's warmth reached me as well.

Aefa moved away then, and stood by Kriafann as he motioned the musicians to begin the hymns of the drums and bones. They launched the flutes high above the percussive beat, trilling out the Great Music that gathered spirit and sorrow, weaving it into a longing for the dead and celebration of the living.

As one body, our group began to traverse the intricate path that took all the family tombs into its course, however scattered over the plains and slopes surrounding Cloch Graig they were. Betimes our voices rose to carry the tunes emanating from the throng of musicians, repeating the old laments, first one lass's sorrow ringing out high above the rest, and an answering chorus from the men, the maams moving it forward, the children's clear, soft voices in their time as well.

Our ancestors were buried in stone chambers under mounds of earth, resting in the safety of the Great Maam of All. The stone door lintels to these tombs opened into tunnels leading to their bones. As we went from tomb to tomb, my head began to clear. Shortly, I joined the voices in the chants, my words ragged as if I leaned against the warm flank of a cow in a darkened stone barn, straining for sleep whilst my hands pulled hard at udders, straining for milk. At long last I was fully awake, enough to join in the songs as well.

This was a long day's pilgrimage. It took us up byways and across meadows and upon hillsides and into areas that were shrouded in woodland. Slowly I regained my wits. In the past this pilgrimage was always one I held dear to my heart. These were the songs to the Dead, to those we loved who had passed through the veil to the otherworld. It was from those who were now dead that we had learned all we knew and treasured, it being passed down from maam to daughter and da to son all the way back to the

Salmon Well.

It was late in the day when we came to the tomb of my own family, the ancestors of Aefa, She Who Walks Alone, Death Crooner of the Trabally. Nestled at the bottom of a low rise, its doorway was blocked by a huge flat stone that could be pushed sideways into the wall to allow entry. I had visited this place every year since I could remember.

The dank moss that clung to the sides of the stone doorway was beautiful to me. The aged stone sill, scribed with the crackling of time, bore a scattering of carved sun disks beginning on its front and continuing up the stone jamb on one side, across the lintel, and down the stone jamb on the other side. The door to my family's tomb was an old friend to me. It promised lightness to my being. It comforted me in the darkness of death.

The other villagers stayed outside the tomb, sitting and resting, pouring themselves ale from the skin bags and gnawing on bannocks and sweet meats brought for the march. Aefa, Grania, Aidan, Kriafann, Arda and I slipped into the narrow doorway and down the tunnel into the depths of the dark. My younger cousins waited outside with those my own age. I went in under the title of my apprenticeship. After our sacred words to open our time with the ancestors, the children would, in turn, enter.

The faintly moldering smell of the dark passage prickled my nose. I stumbled, caught myself, and groped for Aefa's cloak before me. My *granaidh* lit the small torch she carried, and began to chant softly as she walked farther into the tomb. *A perfect calm is on sea and on land, peace is on moor and on meadow. The Maam's joyful glance and smile are to the feeble one and the ocean. Be it a day of peace and joy when the bright day of me death dawns, may the Maam's hand seek me on the white sunny day of me death.*

A shadow flitted across the very edge of my vision. I turned my head sharply. I could feel by the deadening of the air that we were in the tomb proper. The little torch, so bright in the tunnel, seemed small, dwarfed by the huge central room from which three other caverns radiated out under the hillside.

Aefa was to my right, and to my left, I sensed a presence deep in the sorrow of bairns dead in their maams' arms. I caught my breath in a sob, and felt Aefa's hand clutch at mine and hold it tight. She continued squeezing my hand to give me strength as we faced my maam Ayveen's grave, a small depression in the floor covered with rounded stones from the brook.

O Maam, give me of yer wisdom, yer mercy, yer fullness, yer guidance, yer holiness, yer shielding. O Maam, give me of yer surrounding and of yer peace in the knot of me death. O give me of yer surrounding, and of yer peace at the hour of me death!

Out of the dank of the stillness a cloak darker than death whirled around me, entombing me in a foul-smelling wave of terror and loss. I struggled and gasped, my sorrow bursting from me in the chilling scream of a maam dying in childbirth. I fell to the floor, twisting and turning in the coils of a great viper whose poisonous breath I could not escape.

Aefa called in alarm for another torch, and pushing the one she carried into Grania's hands she knelt by me, cushioning my head with her own cloak, as Grania threw hers over me too. The two maams of my heart bound my flailing arms and legs in their cloaks, and swiftly my uncles Aidan and Kriafann followed suit with their own.

In all the years after that night, I would only remember that I struggled with a dark beast of death, there in that cavernous tomb. I would remember its nauseating breath, and its green, clinging limbs that wrapped around me, tearing the wind from me and shoving its claws into my mouth to rip screams from the back of my throat.

I fought mightily and from nowhere there came into my hand a sharpened wooden spear with which I parried and lunged at the monster and its gyrating, vine-like arms. Wherever I punctured, green blood spurted, lighting the tomb with its fiery essence. In that light I could see the horrified faces of my family, and Aefa's lips moving calmly in a strong prayer of healing.

I swung around yet again to strike the beast through its most vulnerable spot, its eye, and then, I could see that the great spider carried the head of Darmid, my beloved *daideo*, in its mouth. His face was wracked with pain, his mouth wide with his suffering, his eyes turned back to show the whites. My own bloodcurdling scream ended my struggle in a collapse of limb and body, as blackness swallowed me.

12. DEATH MOON

I wakened after my horrific vision feeling shattered and weak.
I kept to my bed for so many days, ministered to by Aefa and
Grania's soups and medicinal gruels that the village began to
whisper that I could not endure the responsibilities of a Death
Crooner, that I was too weak in constitution.

Aefa snapped angrily when this possibility was brought to her.

"She is just young," she growled, "Let me not hear that it is
said that in her innocence she should have the skills and strength of
a seasoned Death Crooner. Does the fisherman, and the farmer,
and the maam not have the necessity for training and hardening in
the fire of experience? Then why not a Death Crooner? By the
Great Maam, she is little more than a child. She has the gifts, now
give her time that she might hone them."

My *granaidh*'s sharp wisdom was always received with
respect, and the nagging tongues quieted. When I could sit up,
Aefa and Grania brought Ohran to tell me stories. When I could
stand, they walked me through the dark passageways out into the
white winter sunlight, nesting around me warm furs and woolen
robes so I might feel the light upon me and take in its healing rays.
When I walked unassisted, Aefa began to bring me to the byres so
I could breathe in the strength of the beasts, run my hands through
their soft fur, and receive their rubbings and lickings.

I myself felt in a fog, unable to shake off the heaviness of that
day in the tombs. At night I cried out as I lashed against the arms
of the beast, flinging my robes and bruising my hands and feet as I
kicked and hit the stone sides of my bedchamber. Aefa always ran

to me, woke me, sat me up, smoothed my brow, and made me drink the bitter potion that drew me back into sleep again.

On the fifth day I began to speak, but Aefa kept me in our home chamber, feeling it was better to protect me from the waning moon and the full dark before the start of the Death Moon. After the unrelenting ritual duties of the Wither Moon, the Death Moon brought a respite, for it had no sacral demands save those of the new and full moons, and for this, Aefa could be at my side constantly. On the seventh day, I began to be angry, and Aefa knew my healing would soon complete its course.

"What happened, *Granaidh*?" I asked, grumbling at the weakness of my legs and the strict regimen of healing broths and gruels that Aefa persisted in giving me. I tried to stand to give myself more room to spin out yarn, but the standing soon wearied me and I had to sit.

I asked her if we could roast some of the winter's meat so that I might gain strength. She refused, saying the meat was too heavy, too rich for me still.

"Am I so injured that I cannot take of the meat?" I growled. "Even the roots? Ye act as if I lost me teeth, not me senses!"

Aefa laughed and set her spindle down. Her days were now spent before the hearth, spinning and weaving in the winter moontides.

"What happened, me lass, was that ye wrestled with a spirit. That is what the Day of the Winter Dead is for. That is what we Death Crooners do. There was a spirit wanting to tell us something before it went back through the veil, and it found ye."

"Ye make it sound like it didn't nearly take me with it to the otherworld, *Granaidh*! Why did I go down, foaming like a mad animal? Can't yer potions keep that at bay?" I scowled, furious that underneath my anger was my fear that Kerr might have seen me in such a state.

Why did I even think of him, when what was at stake was my calling? I did not like the fact that my heart beat faster when I thought of him, or when he was near. I hated that the loss of concentration brought on by his gaze on that fateful day in the womb chamber drew me off the ritual. His image now had grown to such strength that when I longed for him, I began to question the mantle of the Death Crooner that should be mine.

Always before I had accepted the developments that came upon me in preparation for my life work. Now, I bridled. I found them—even unfair. I was disgusted with myself, and I was disgusted with my—duty. Sometimes I was furious with Aefa, and that frightened me and made me angrier still.

Aefa lifted her eyebrows at the vehemence in my voice. She was not surprised, I know that now. To her it was past time for her granddaughter to begin the petulence that descends upon the young just before they come of age, no longer really children, but not yet fully adults.

"No potion can stop the power of the dark, me love. But ye with yer powers as a Seer can take it in and shape it and use it, and help us understand it." She drew her thin hands across her forehead, grasping errant gray locks and securing them behind her ears.

"And since the time of the Salmon Well the Clan of the Seer has been passed from parent to child. It is the way of all in our clan to be overcome by visions. It is the way of these visions to be mysterious—it is a mystery from whence they come beyond the veil, it is a mystery sometimes, to discern what it is they mean, it is a mystery why most *tuaha* are unable to See, but some, in every generation can do so—like I can, like ye can.

"What is not a mystery, me love, is that the Great Maam of All provides us with this gift that we might bring some help and peace to the losses of time, and find for ourselves the meaning of those losses. When a lad or lass has been found to possess the Second Sight, it is their responsibility to be committed to service by it, for the good of their village and in gratitude to the Great Maam."

Her voice dropped to a harsh whisper. "Think, Ronnat, think on it! What did ye see? What came at ye in the dark?" She fixed her gaze on me, and waited quietly for my answer.

I looked down at my hands. I clasped and unclasped them in my lap. My heart raced and the shaking began deep within me, spreading to my arms and legs, until no amount of hand-wringing could control it.

"I don't know, *Granaidh*," my voice squeezed tight in my throat, "When I seek the memory, I find only fear."

"That fear ye must conquer, me love. Ye must give it a face, and that face will tell ye what is required of ye. That is yer place;

that is yer quest and call. Ye must overcome the fear, and provide knowledge from the spirit world to yer family and village."

I shut my eyes then, and drew in a deep, slow breath, as Aefa had taught me. I willed my muscles to relax, willed my eyes to stay shut, willed my breath to quiet, to sink to that deepest place within me wherein dwelt my own bright kernel of life.

Aefa whispered the prayer of the Seers to me, encouraging me to breathe deep with it, providing the pathway for my memory to traverse the path back to the tomb. *Great Maam of All, stay behind me to give me eyes to see all me quest with yer love before me, with yer grace which shall never be darkened, holding yer life in me vision ever.* Her whispering seeped into the fog of my memory, pulling me through the passageway towards the inner chamber, willing me, leading me, to clash again with my memory of the darkness blacker than death.

I felt the prick of mould on my nose again. I could touch the rough stone side of the chamber, could feel the compact dirt beneath my feet and the contrasting smoothness of clay slip formed from the moisture oozing in a sheen across the stones and running down the walls deep underground. I caught the shadow that brought the darkness, and my eyes flew open. The black receded. My mind cleared. The tomb was gone. I would not visit that blackness today.

I turned to Aefa angrily. "If this is a gift, *Granaidh*, why does it go from me?"

Granaidh shook her head.

"It does not go from ye, love, ye go from it. Something in it frightened ye, and ye will not let yerself find it again. *Try to remember, Ronnat, try to bring the vision. Life may depend on it!*"

I threw my spindle down upon my sleeping furs and staggered from our home, gripped in the strong passions of my youth. I didn't want to recall that horrific vision. What Aefa said made me feel desperate, and a failure. What if life did depend upon me? How was it fair that I must embrace the darkness of that terror again, that someone else might not die? Was I a sacrifice?

I came to the end of the passageway where it emptied into the community room and stopped short. Several of the village maams were inside, their looms set so they faced each other in a circle while they wove. They chattered happily, and as I lingered in the shadows, still out of sight, they broke into song, the haunting melody punctuated by the sounds of their looms.

I would make the fair cloth for ye, thread stout as the thatch-rope. I would make the feathered boot for ye, ye beloved of men. I would give ye the precious anchor, and the family tools which me daideo had. Me love is the hunter of the bird who earliest comes over misty sea. Me love the sailor of the waves, great the cheer his brow will show.

My heart caught in my throat. I could see Fia and other lasses our age in there, easy amongst the maams, singing and laughing of their love for the lads, weaving upon their looms, some of them already as proficient as their maams. I could weave. It was something I resisted as a young lass, but I was now good at it nevertheless. But weaving was not my purpose in life. I had another purpose, as *Granaidh* Aefa was ever wont to tell me.

I ducked my head. Why couldn't I have a life like these other lasses, whose greatest expectation was the weaving of cloth and the tending of bairns? Why did I, Ronnat Rua, have to fail at my purpose, a purpose I did not choose, and at this time, did not want? Why did I have to bear so much responsibility for the wellbeing of others, while being provided with so little provision for my own?

I hated this purpose that both required I celebrate my longing for Kerr, and yet made me reject the thought of him coming near, because he pulled me away from it. I had given permission for him to court, but how I ran and dove and hid to prevent any chance of meeting him in a place where courting might happen.

I turned from the happy hum of the maams, and went a different way through the passages. Situated at the far end of the village, in a tiny chamber lost in the darkness of the tunnels, was a secret place. Once it may have been for storage, but over time, it was forgotten. I discovered it when I was just a little lass, and it was here that I went in the winter moontides when things did not go my way, when I needed to simply be, to be alone, to be quiet.

I squatted low, felt for the door in the dark, and carefully slid through the small opening. I could just fit, tall as I was now, if I curled up like a wee bairn in the womb. It was a long time since I crept into this place, but it still held peace for me. I pushed my fists into my eyes and let the hot salt tears flow as they would. When the sobs came, I held my breath, unwilling to unleash any clue of where I was.

As my frustration and anger blew its maelstrom out, the sadness set in. I mourned for Bairnie, I mourned for my beloved *daideo*, Darmid. My eyes snapped open in the dark. That was it. I missed them. Bairnie was my comfort, and *Daideo* was wise. He would be able to advise me. I missed his rough hands, chapped from the cold in the winter, but soon smoothed by the lanolin in the wool he worked. I would go to him. I would go to him now.

I crept out of my tiny cave and walked quietly through the passageways back to our home chamber. My eyes were so used to the darkness the very vaguest bleed of light from open doorways was enough to find my way clearly.

I slipped back into the house and went and knelt at Aefa's feet. My *granaidh* lowered her spindle to the ground slowly. She steadied the yarn with one hand in her lap, and used the other to tip my chin up to her.

My eyes filled with tears again. Aefa clucked and whispered, "Nothing to cry over, love, nothing to cry over."

"*Granaidh*, I am so angry. I don't want these gifts. I'm not strong enough. I just want to live!"

"This is living, me love. This is a way of living that does not become tedious with time. There is always something new. There is a lifetime of pleasure and adventure for the Death Crooner. There is work, aye, there is hard work. But with it comes the steady rhythm of the year, the miracles of birth and the consolations of death. Ye're young. Ye don't have to do it all now."

I shook my head from side to side. "But I don't want to do any of it now. I want to go to me *daideo* Darmid. I want to fetch me Bairnie. It is too long to be without them. I want to travel to the shieling, and I will be back before the deep snows. I can do it, *Granaidh*."

"Aye, lass, ye can do it. 'Tis a fair request. Ye need not take on the duties of the Death Crooner now. Ye have been sent a message. It will come clear with time. But to come clear, ye must be at peace. Darmid will bring ye that." Aefa wound the length of yarn onto the shaft of the spindle, gave it a whirl and dropped it, setting it spinning again. I watched its tight circle, hypnotized with its steadiness until it began to slow and wobble a bit. One little twist from Aefa's fingers, and it sped up again, tightening its orbit.

"But lass, can I persuade ye to stay with yer old *granaidh* until the new moon rites, to be with me for that, love, before ye leave? Just for that?"

"I'll think on it, *Granaidh*, I'll think on it. 'Tis likely." I rose to my feet and gathering my thick woolen cloak, wrapped it around my shoulders and headed back into the passageways. I needed to get out into the clear, cold early winter air. I needed to think on Aefa's proposal, and consider what I should bring with me for the trip back to the shieling. For the first time since the horrid vision in the family tomb, I felt energy in my feet.

I cut across the gathering place to the rocks on the bluff overlooking the beach and made my way slowly down to the strand. The beach pebbles were slick with the newly receded tide and a misting of snow. The water was choppy and a stiff wind blew icy crystals. I tightened the hood of my cloak and began to walk up the waterfront in the direction of Clochbeg.

My eyes were focused downward, as the footing was treacherous. The steady crash of waves deafened me to other noises. When a cough startled me, I looked up. Kerr was coming towards me across the sand. I stopped, regarding him soberly.

"Ronnat," he said simply. He walked up to me and stopped. He gently touched my arm. "I have not laid eyes on ye for a very long time." He looked away up the beach, as if he had something difficult to say. Then he turned back, and locked his eyes to mine. Something warm stirred within me. "The villages are talking of yer day in the tomb—are ye hurt? Were ye hurt, Ronnat? What happened?"

I ducked my head, embarrassed. Why should I be ashamed of the life that until now had been my quest and calling? What was happening to me? What was happening all around me? I mumbled, and Kerr put his fingers under my chin, grasping my face lightly to keep it focused on him. Reluctantly, my eyes met his.

"What do ye say, lass?" he asked softly.

"I had a vision in the tomb. It was frightening. It was— something is wrong. Something, or someone, I don't know--I can't put words to it, I can't even think—it hurt me, I fell and I struggled and I woke in *Granaidh* Aefa's house in the care of the maams. I know not what happened to me. And my spirit will not let me remember." I stopped, and sighed. "It doesn't make any sense to ye."

"Nah, lass. I am not unacquainted with the life of the Death Crooner. In me family beyond Clochbeg, that is me maam's sister. Things ... happen. The power is great."

I looked at him intently. "Then ye know of it?"

Kerr nodded. That nod brought a relief that flooded me with resolve. I knew what to do now, and with that knowing came a calm.

"I will be going away, Kerr, I will be returning to the highlands. It is a thing I must do."

"Aye, lass," he said, "If it is a thing ye must do, then it is to be done." He touched my shoulder lightly, and when I did not turn away, he slipped his arm around me and pulled me gently to him. His arm was warm in the brisk wind, but not tight. He was a horseman, and he already knew me to be like a young foal that seeks closeness but will buck and bound away if it comes too sudden or too strong. "It is a thing ye must do, but must ye do it alone?"

"Aye, I must do it alone." I closed my eyes and let myself for one moment relax into the strength of his embrace. The strong feelings that tore through me at the closeness of his body, the warmth of his arm, made me want to forget all that the vision had thrust upon me. I lifted my head up then, looked straight into the liquid night of his eyes and repeated: "Aye, I must do it alone."

****

I waxed more anxious as the new moon rites approached. Berating myself for being convinced to stay for them, I was short with my speech and preoccupied in my work. Aefa urged me to calm, to will myself to pull back from the distress of my imaginings, to prepare for my trip and pack with good, steady sense, thinking on the practicalities of weather that might challenge my journey.

At last, upon the dark night of the new moon, all was ready for my departure. I stood with Aefa and the villagers on the high place, murmuring the words of prayer to the absent moon. *Hail unto ye, black jewel of the night! Beauty of the heavens, maam of the stars, fosterling of the sun, majesty of the stars, black jewel of the night!*

The words caught at my mind and whirled it away from me, up into the moonless night sky, speckled with stars. My vision was penetrated by their burning. They erupted from the sky and spilled down around me in a cascade of falling torches. I felt myself slipping to the ground again, hitting the cold snow as blackness descended upon me.

I knew *Granaidh* Aefa would come, I could hear the far-off exclamations of the villagers around me. Where were they? Why were they so far away? I heard them calling to each other to catch me up and cover me with warm furs. But only one came near. I recognized his bent shape and my heart swelled in love.

My *daideo* shuffled to me through the snow. He appeared hunched, and he moved in slow motion, as if a greater weight than all the world and the night sky stood upon his shoulders, crushing him down. At last his face, gaunt, white, with dark circles under his eyes, hovered above me.

Ronnat, he said quietly. I tried to answer, but my tongue was tied.

Ronnat, he said again. I stared up at his hovering figure, bent with age, huddled with sorrow and sickness above me, but I was paralyzed with cold that seeped up through my cloaks and took hold of my limbs and my tongue so that I could not move.

Ronnat, he said a third time, and this time, it was begging. His eyes held the sorrow of all time. *Do not let me die upon the mountain,* he begged, *Find me, Ronnat, find me, find me beasts. Do not let us die upon the mountain.*

He faded as he reached for me. I could see the night stars right through him as he disappeared. My scream finally took wing from my mouth in a helpless anguish. The arms were about me then, picking me up and swirling the warm robes over me. Before the deep sleep of the visions came upon me, I felt myself lifted and strong arms began the descent to the stone village with my exhausted body in their grasp.

****

When the weighted sleep of the vision left me the pre-dawn dark poured hardness and sorrow into my soul. I opened my eyes and sat up, the plea of Darmid still echoing in my aching head. Aefa lay covered by robes in her bed.

I quietly stepped over the stone sides of my own bedbox and gathered the pack I put together for my trip. I pulled on my thick woolen leggings, and strapped on snow-proofed, oiled leather ones. In no time, about my shoulders were my sweater and cloak, my thick woolen socks and oiled leather boots upon my feet. In one hand was the pack, and in the other the carry-bag of food.

I gazed at Aefa's sleeping face. Surely my *granaidh* was showing her age now. When I was a little lass, she would have jumped up the moment my eyes opened. She must be losing her hearing, I thought wryly.

I sent my love silently to her in my short prayer of leaving: *I am weary, and forlorn. Lead ye me to the land I seek. I go for to journey. Be to me as a star, be to me as a helm, from me lying down in peace to me rising anew in strength.*

I ducked out the door of our chamber, taking care to tread quietly through the outer passageways until I slid the outside door stone aside and stepped into the pregnant dawnlight. My breath frosted the air and settled upon my outer garments wet with the warmth of me. Sliding the door stone back in place, I hoisted my pack higher on my back, and began a measured tread along the trail I knew so well in the summer. But now it was a different land—a land of faerie covered with the sparkle of new snow.

Across the gathering place and down the hill I went. When I skirted the beach and finally struck back inland I felt a newfound excitement stir. The smell of ice crystals was upon my nose, and I stopped briefly to take up a fluffy handful of snow in my mitten and cram it into my mouth. That reminded me that I had left so quickly I had not thought to break my night fast. I might come to regret that, but I was desperate to strike out before anyone knew I was gone.

The faint winter sun pulled itself above the horizon, veiled by the cover of morning mist ever-rising from the snow. The air was perfectly still and for this I was grateful. No ice crystals cut my cheeks or blew across my eyes to blind me. I made good time for the whole of the morning—but began to understand how even the summer trip must now challenge my *granaidh*'s strength. I was making this trek so much faster alone, even with the winter snows on the ground.

By the midday height of the sun I was past the foothills and drawing near the oak savannah. I paused on the ridge to survey the valley stretching out below me. The stark shapes of bare trunks marched across the swales of white, their intricate black fingers reaching upwards to the pale blue winter sky. Beyond them, rising, I could see the beginning of the moorland, which would lead me to the mountains.

Spreading a thick fur over the soft pack of snow, I nestled myself in it and brought out bannocks and dried meat from my carry-bag. I munched one, then the other, and in between, filled my mouth with the clean snow, letting it melt and slake my thirst.

The savannah looked so different in the winter. During our spring and fall trips to the highlands I would be fascinated by the rippling run of leaves whistling before the wind, spreading like pools of minnows below me. Now, in the winter, the trunks were laid bare, each a unique spidery figure in outline.

As I contemplated them and ate, far off down the valley I saw a grey shape depart from the thick of the forested foothills and begin its way up through the savannah. My eyes fixed upon the figure, first a pulsing dot, then, I could make out its form. A wolf. It was a lone wolf. It seemed to have purpose, picking its way carefully through the snow, stopping to sniff a tree trunk, or raise its head and sniff the wind. A beautiful creature, I could see even from this distance. I had no fear.

I picked up my food and stored what was left away in my carry-bag, slinging it over my shoulder. I shook the snow from the fur, which I wrapped about myself again. I began to walk downhill, planting my feet carefully, fearful of taking a headlong tumble on ice hidden beneath the snow. But the white stuff had begun to warm in the sun, and pack under my weight. My footing became surer, and I was able to pick up speed despite my burdens.

Slowly, what had been a dot, then an animal, came closer. Our paths would cross eventually. I shook my head and stared hard. There was something familiar about this creature. My eyes returned to it often. The closer I got, the more the sight disturbed me.

Then, the animal reared up its head and fixed its gaze on me. All that distance away I could not see its eyes, but clearly, it was alerted by me, too. Something fell into place—the tip of the head, the gait. I suddenly recognized them in all their familiarity.

"Bairnie!" I shrieked the word, and began to stumble and run. "Bairn—here lad! Bairnie, come to heel!" Across the distance still between us, I could hear him whimper. He leapt, and began a headlong rush at me, as I in turn sprinted as fast as the snow would allow towards the gray beast.

And then, we were together, me squatting, Bairnie leaping and licking, whining and yelping and me crying in a joy without words or measure. I fell to the ground, and the soft thing was upon me, rubbing his head against me. I grabbed the ruff of fur around his neck hugging him hard. All the pent-up longing of the past moontides was released in an outburst of joy. I sat with my arms around him, and he stopped his frenzied, breathless panting long enough only to lick my face.

"Bairnie! What are ye doing here, lad, why have ye come back? What is it, lad?" I ruffled his head, and sunk my fingers into his beautiful coat, turning his face to mine, and shaking him a little. "What is it?"

The dog leapt to his feet and whined at me, pawing the snow, charging off in the direction from which he had come. He stopped, glanced back at me, lowered his head, and then made a dive in that direction again. He wanted me to come. I knew this game of his, it was his invitation for me to run with him.

"Now, now, lad, come to," I said. He streaked towards me, then lunged back again as if to invite me to chase him. "Nah, nah, come to me Bairnie." I dropped on one knee and held out my hands. He stopped his prance and came to me. I had shed my pack and was opening it, taking out a stout hide rope. I tied it around his neck.

Something was not right, I knew this now as a certainty. The dreams were telling me something was amiss with Darmid, and here was Bairnie to bring testament to it. He pulled a bit, wanting to go back in the direction he had come, but I sternly called him to heel. I began to pat his head and grabbed it again, looking into the blue and hazel green and brown eyes that matched my own.

"Tis *Granaidh* Aefa we need, lad," I whispered. "We need to go back to the village and get *Granaidh* Aefa. Then we'll go find Darmid." The dog made no more resistance to me, and we struck

off towards the top of the bluff to pick up the trail back to the
Trabally and Cloch Graig.

****

When we reached the village the outer doors were shut against
the night already, but not secured. The villagers knew one of theirs
own was still out. I pushed the stone aside and loosed Bairn from
his tether. He ran ahead of me through the passageways to find
Aefa, while I rolled the stone shut and secured it. Curious heads
poked out of doorways at the sound of our passing. A small group
followed us, Grania and Kriafann coming right behind Bairnie and
me into Aefa's chamber.

Aefa knelt by the hearth, spinning, and Bairnie ran to her,
snuffling into her hands, so that she dropped the spindle with a cry.
With another, she jumped up and threw her arms around me. Her
hands then fell to Bairnie's ears, and she rubbed them.

"What became of ye, me heart, what is it?" she moved quickly
to the larder and brought down a bowl of gruel, setting it in the
warm cinders to heat. "Ye're freezing, me love! Come, take off the
wet things and hang them here." She moved her blankets, warming
for the night on the firescreen, and one by one took my things and
hung them to dry.

Grania was ladling a bowl of the warming broth for Bairnie,
and tearing up bannocks to put in it. She set it on the floor, and he
wolfed it hungrily.

I took off my skin boots and outer woolens and hung them on
the rack before the fire. Grania fell to rubbing my feet until blood
and sensation came back into them. Aefa helped me pull a dry
sweater over my head, then shoved a steaming bowl of broth into
my hands.

"*Granaidh*, something is amiss," I cried breathlessly.

"Aye, child, tis so, tis true. When did ye come upon the pup?"

I recounted my journey, step by step, and the meeting of
Bairnie in the savannah. "*Granaidh*, the last vision—it was me
daideo. Darmid is hurt, or sick, I know it. Bairnie would not have
left otherwise. I think he was coming back to get us." I stroked his
silver-gray head then.

"I came back to get ye, *Granaidh*, for ye to bring yer

medicines. Ye have to come with me, *Granaidh*, I need ye to go to the mountains with me, and find Darmid, and cure him, and bring him back here if needed."

Aefa dropped her head. "It cannot happen in the winter, me love. I fear I be not strong enough for the walking of it in this cold."

"But *Granaidh*, we cannot leave Darmid to himself. He'll die. I know what the dreams were about now, he'll die! He begged me to bring him and his flocks down off the mountain." Aefa looked soberly at Kriafann and Grania as if to beg their assistance.

They shook their heads.

"Nah, Ronnat," Kriafann said, "*Granaidh* is too old for this trip. She'll make ye the medicines for bonebreak and for fever, for chilblains, and the flux, and ye must take them yerself."

"But uncle!" I pleaded, "I cannot bring him back by myself! What if I must carry him?"

Kriafann looked long and hard at me, and putting up his hand to caution me to wait, he disappeared out the door. Grania was rubbing my hair, wet with sweat and frost and snow, on a soft woolen cloth. She began to brush and braid it then.

"Someone should go with ye, dove," she said, "But not Aefa. Ye know the medicines yerself, and ye'll have to trust yerself to use them."

I turned to Aefa again, just as Kriafann came in the door; with him was Osheen. Osheen stared worriedly at me, and punched my arm lightly by way of greeting. He and his father stood back, looking to Aefa and me to finish our conversation, but I turned to Osheen instead.

"Will ye be coming with me, then?"

"Aye, cousin," he nodded. "I'll come with ye." He turned to Kriafann, "And Da, will ye come with us as well?"

Kriafann looked grim. For Aefa to admit she was beyond a trip in the winter meant that he was needed here, too. It would be to him that the villagers would look for direction should Aefa fall sick.

"The Great Maam save all here." The traditional greeting was deep and comforting as the creak of an ancient oak in the wind as Kerr ducked through the doorway. His eyes went straight to mine, and then circled the room, looking expectantly into the faces of all.

"What have I stepped into?" he said. "I heard that Ronnat had returned with the silver dog, and I...."

Osheen stepped towards Kerr and thumped his friend in greeting on the left shoulder. "Get yer things, Kerr," he said, "We're going on a winter journey with me cousin."

Kerr's eyes lit wide at the prospect, but before he could reply, Osheen strode past him out the door, to get his own pack together. He shouted back over his shoulder, "And make sure they're warm and that yer own back is as strong as an ox, for we've a task ahead of us."

13. COLD MOON

For the second day in a row I rose in the pitch dark and mouthed journey prayers desperately. *Aid me in distress of sea and of land. Watch me by day and by night. Be shielding me, possessing me, aiding me, clearing me path and going before me soul. In hollow, on hill, on plain, on sea and land. By me knee, by me back, by me side, each step of the stormy world.*

Osheen and Kerr arrived at our door soon after. *Granaidh* Aefa was already up and moving about in the light of the hearthfire, newly stoked and burning brightly. The old maam served us a hearty drink of oatmeal, honey and mead, and a rich venison stew. She placed a bowl on the floor for Bairnie as well, for his work would be as strenuous as ours.

I ate eagerly, the first real substantial meal I had had in many a day. The needs rising from the exertions of the day before, and the trip to come, called for it.

Our eating was hurried. Soon we hoisted our packs and stood for Aefa's blessing. She first touched my forehead, as the leader of the expedition, and crooned, *Protect this one from suffering on land or sea, from grief or wound or weeping. Lead her to a house of peace this night.*

Turning to Kerr and Osheen, she placed one hand on each of their foreheads and recited *Bless these ones, the earth beneath their feet, the path whereon they go, the thing of their desire. Be shielding them, be aiding them on sea and on land.* Then she bent and covered Bairnie's soft head with her hand. *Bless this one, ancient friend, true-hearted protector; make not his path diverge from theirs; keep injury from his loyalty.*

Our little group ducked out the low doorway into the pitch dark. Dawn was not even a thought on the horizon, but we knew our way and struck out across the gathering place. For a long time we walked in the still of darkness. The early morning was near silent, for the birds of winter did not venture out until the sun was higher in the sky. The muffled movement of fur-bound feet—both canine and *tuaha*—moving through soft snow was all that broke the quiet.

When we stopped to rest, some hours and a good distance later, the sky had brightened considerably. One word of prayer put its foot from my mouth out into the day with tentative longing. As the light increased it met such a chorus of birdsong that it ran back to its mother and pulled her to bright sunlight and the promise of windblown hair. Our dawn prayers rose together, and when they were completed, we began to talk, now that we could see each other's faces.

"Ronnat," Osheen shoved a bannock into his mouth as we rose from our resting place. He stooped to catch up the good clean snow to melt in his mouth along with the bread. Both Kerr and I were looking in his direction.

"What, Osheen?" I asked, and when he continued to chew noisily rather than finish what he had started to say, I continued, "Is it that ye're so proud of finally being able to feed yerself that we must watch ye do it?" Kerr chuckled and Osheen waved his hand to shush me, furrowing his brow in annoyance.

"Ah, go on with ye," he said, wiping his mouth on the back of his mittened hand. "I only wanted to ask ye..." he paused, tossing the last bit of his bannock to Bairnie. The dog caught it deftly, swallowing the thin tidbit down with great relish, as if it were the size of a large roast.

"I only wanted to ask ye what ye saw in the tomb, and what ye saw at the new moon rites. Everyone's been talking about it and no one seems to know what happened. It's tedious not to know, cousin. What happened to ye?" His voice was strained with concern, his eyebrows crunched together in the middle of his forehead. He glanced sideways at me, trying to discern the impact of his prying on my mood.

I let my breath out in resignation. I looked at Kerr. He, too, waited. I began.

"It only started in the tombs, Osheen." Stumbling to put experiences that had no substance into words, I spoke, finally, of the day in the tombs, the visions that followed, the suffocating agony of an evil that had no name, an urgency that had only the language of dreams. Kerr and Osheen listening silently as they walked, occasionally breaking in for clarification, or to expel their breath in a rush of concern.

By the end of my tale I was walking a few paces ahead of them. I turned suddenly, and stopped. "And so, I know it is our *daideo* now; it is Darmid who lies dead or wounded or sick, at the end of our journey. Bairnie would never leave him or Crag upon the mountain for any other reason."

Osheen and Kerr stopped abruptly when I turned around and faced them. Osheen looked down into the snow, his face frozen in a concerned scowl. "But Bairnie is untried—he's a young dog. Maybe he just—missed ye."

Kerr shook his head. "Nah, Osheen that is no ordinary pup. I watched him at the shieling, Ronnat is right. He would never run." He looked straight at me. "Bairnie came back for a reason, Ronnat. This is yer test. It is the test of yer strength and resolve as a Death Crooner and Seer."

"Aye, I think that, too, Kerr," I said, "I *know* that." I turned and began to trudge again.

The sun was not yet at its zenith when we came to the ridge above the sweep of oak savannah where I met with Bairnie the day before. Two days in a row of journeying that taxed the feet and the back and the soul made my muscles cry out for mercy. But we could only pause to rest briefly, eat, and consume snow.

Pushing on without sleep, we hoped to reach the high shieling in time to keep Darmid from embarking on a journey of his own— to the next world. I blinked at the thought: if, indeed, he had not already departed.

As we left the savannah and started up the steep slopes, we struggled, slipped down repeatedly, and held onto each other for support as it grew dark. The sun on this side of the mountain had melted the thin layer of snow just enough to make the path slippery. As darkness fell and the temperature with it, the moisture froze into a sheen of ice that made our climb treacherous. Bairnie lost his footing and scrambled as well. The moon rose late, and in the pitch dark before it did, we groped, stumbled, and fell exhausted many times before reaching the high pastures.

Then the moon was all the way up. New and small as it was, it cast little light, but the vast expanse of highland snow-cover magnified that light to illuminate the familiar landmarks and rock cairns. We were coming close to Darmid's dwelling place. I recognized the small mounds of snow that dotted the pasture as the crouch of stone huts that stored hay for the winter feedings of the stock that remained on the mountain. Bairnie began to whimper, run ahead and doubled back as if to lure us on. Off he ran again, and returned just as quickly.

"Come to heel, Bairnie!" I commanded hoarsely, my voice harsh with cold and exhaustion.

"Why not let him go, Ronnat," said Kerr, "He knows where he is going, and so do we." The dog's urgency spurred our tired limbs and we picked up our pace. Soon, our shuffle had turned into a brisk walk on the relative evenness of the high ground, then an intense march, and finally, when the silhouette of Darmid's hut broke the horizon, a clumsy run. The hovel was dark. No smoke rose from the thatched roof, no sound came across the snow except our own labored breathing. No light save the thin new moon.

Bairnie bounded ahead and began scratching violently at the door, whimpering and barking. I heard no bark from within, and my heart froze in fear. Where was Crag? I pricked up my ears for the sounds of sheep, but noted none. Where was the stock?

Kerr and Osheen took off at a run, Kerr's longer legs outstripping Osheen and reaching the hut door first. He pulled Bairnie back and began to move the heavy wood door. It was inadequately closed, a sure sign of the weakness of the one who tried to shut it. Kerr heaved his shoulder into it. As it budged Bairnie pushed his head and shoulders through and with a whine disappeared into the dark. We could hear his pacing and whining inside.

A deep chill gripped my chest, deeper than the black silence of the hut. Then I heard it, a low guttural sigh I knew came from my *daideo*. I followed the sound to his bedchamber and found him piled deep under robes of wool and fleeced sheep skins.

"*Daideo! Daideo!*" I sobbed, throwing myself to my knees.

He moved his hand in the dark and I put mine upon it gently.

"*Daideo,*" my voice softened, for now I knew only the thinnest thread held him to life. But still, he lived. "Where is Crag?" The words were out before I could stop myself.

"Ahhhhh..." the noise that came from his tired mouth seemed to speak his sorrow. His hand thumped helplessly at his covers.

I called to Kerr and Osheen, but they were right behind me. With ready strong arms we lifted the old man to sit upright. He winced and sucked in his breath desperately.

Osheen kindled a torch, and with it the haggard, grey face I had seen in the vision leapt from the darkness. Darmid's eyes were closed. His lips were parched, dry, broken in spots and bleeding.

"Water!" I hissed at my cousin. Osheen grabbed a bowl and ran outside to pack it full of snow. Returning to us he put the torch under it, and began to melt it while Kerr built a fire on the hearth.

Quietly and quickly we worked. Osheen held the bowl, Kerr held Darmid, and I, spoonful by spoonful, dripped water between his lips. Inside, I prayed fervently: *I ask from me mouth, I ask from me heart, I ask through me hands, O Great Maam of All, deliver this one from death, deliver this one unto me,* but aloud I only said, "Not too much at once, cover him again, and we will wait."

By now the fire was going well. With the door shut properly, it began to warm the hut. Osheen slipped out to bring in more wood, peat, and dried dung. Kerr took the torch and whistled for Bairnie.

"I'm going looking for the stock, Ronnat," he said, and ducked out the door too.

I squatted by the fire and pounded a bit of dried meat in the quern. When it was powdered, I began to stir it into the slowly warming water. Soon, a broth simmered, filling the hut with its robust fragrance. I went back to the bedchamber and began to spoon water between Darmid's lips again. When he sucked in and licked his lips on his own, I switched to the broth.

Osheen returned with an armload of fuel. Kerr followed, a worried look on his face. He held Bairn on a short tether, but the dog kept pulling towards the door. When Kerr had secured the stone, Bairnie pawed it and whimpered. I cocked my head quizzically at him, but he shook his head slightly, and put a finger to his lips, so I did not ask aloud.

The lads began to melt another bowl of snow and prepare more broth, which they thickened into a gruel with oats. This was for the three of us to slake our hunger and restore our strength. Slowly, tenderly, we took shifts for the rest of the night, one awake to feed Darmid tiny spoonfuls of broth every little while, the other two sleeping.

By the dawn light Darmid seemed just a bit stronger and could respond to my directions. *"Daideo,"* I said softly. "What happened?"

Darmid opened his eyes just a little. "The ram," he said weakly.

I shuddered. Somewhere on Darmid's body there must be a gore from the ram's horns or sharp hooves. My mind raced at the possibilities, and I silently asked the Great Maam of All to spare him, this old man who was father and grandfather and most beloved to me.

"And Crag?" I asked, "Could he not ..." Darmid gave a slow shake to his head, the effort of it almost beyond him.

"Killed," he whispered weakly.

Ah, so *Daideo* well knew what Kerr found the night before. Looking for the stock, Kerr surmised Darmid turned all of them loose before he struggled to bring his wounded body into the hut. He found the chickens frozen, unable to fend for themselves in the cold—they would at least be of use in making nourishing broth.

He came upon a place where mud, snow, and blood together told the story of a terrible struggle. There he found Crag's mangled and lifeless form. A tear pushed out from my lid and ran down my cheek for what I could not change. I turned to the task ahead.

"Daideo," I soothed, "I have to find where ye are hurt." I slipped softly into the healer's request, a prayer, a pleading, and a ritual. *Give yerself over to these the hands placed upon me arms by the Great Maam of All for the ministration of her healing. Placed upon yer body to bring her milk of healing.*

Kerr and Osheen were both awake, and stood over me ready to bring what I needed. They moved as one to peel back the tumbled bedclothes a few at a time so I could find the damage to Darmid's old frame.

Upon his arms were flesh wounds, scrapes, the blood dried and crusted but no danger to him. A bump rose from his skull. His breath caught when I touched it. We moved to his lower body and I felt his abdomen. Kerr and Osheen turned him slightly so I could run my eyes over his old backside, but aside from bruises, nothing was broken there. We replaced the covers to keep him warm, and began to move the blankets up from the bottom.

One foot bore a deep gash from sharp hooves, something that would require poulticing and cleaning and binding to heal shut. Farther up on one thigh I found the source of his calamity. On his right leg above the knee, towards the inside of the thigh, a wound that still seeped blood was beginning to fester. I recoiled from the odor, then gathered my courage and pressed on with my examination.

By some miracle the horn that tore him there did not finish the job by slicing through the large blood vessel. That would have been a swift, sure death for him alone here on the mountain. He would have gone to the other side in good company with old Crag. That would have been a merciful death.

The blood vessel was nicked just enough to add a seeping blood loss to the tear of muscle and sinew that he sustained. The wound was deep, his weakness from bleeding now being fed by the appearance of fester.

I closed my eyes and begged the Great Maam of All for her hands and her mercy. A fast death on the mountain alone might yet prove to have been better than what lay ahead for him. The wound could still kill him if the festering took hold. I hoped that the slow leak of blood had kept it clean enough to respond to my medicinals.

I stood then, and gave Kerr and Osheen their directions. "Cover him well except for the wounds. Pull away the coverings and cut away the clothing that is stained and remove it from this place. Make me a quantity of water heated to the boiling in two pots." I left them to their duties and went to the carry-bag of herbs, poultices and teas.

First I removed the packets of dried masterwort, bluebell, borage, aspen, bay and briar. Taking a goodly amount of each, excepting the masterwort— too much of it could prove dangerous so I added it with great care—I mixed all in a small clay bowl, then added two bits of the bark of the blackthorn.

All of the herbs went into the bowl of melted snow steaming

slowly among the coals. These would slowly warm and infuse the water with a tonic tea to ply Darmid with. I knew the fever would come as I tended his wounds, and so into the balms for healing I mixed the herbs that treated fevers.

When Kerr brought me the boiling water I gently shook in dried and powdered serpent tongue fern, a bit of ground barley, and oil from the beech tree's seeds; this I would use to cleanse the wounds. Then, I took alder, beech, woundwort and brownwort leaves and laid them side by side in yet another bowl of warmed water. Upon it I laid a fine-woven cloth that it might absorb the herb-infusion. This I would use to poultice the wounds.

Finally, out came salves of serpent tongue fern, good for drawing the evil out of old wounds that would not heal, and bryony with a touch of nightshade that would dull the pain of it. These I mixed together into a soft greenish paste and spread it upon a cloth to be impregnated with their essence. I set it aside. All was ready.

I motioned to the lads, and they came to my side again. I pulled away the cloth that lightly covered Darmid's thigh wound. The odor of death rose and all three of us flinched. I knew what it meant.

"Hold him," I whispered.

Kerr took Darmid's head and shoulders gently, his hands cradled around the old man to keep him from lurching should the pain become too much. Osheen settled at his feet, to hold them as well if the need arose. I knelt and prayed as I had never before, begging in agony for the intervention of the Great Maam. *Be at me breast, be at me back, be at me hand, be upon me forehead, ye to me as a star, ye to me as a guide, what harm soever might it leave these wounds through me hands.*

Wetting the fine-spun cloth in the hot infusion, I began to carefully wipe around the wound, working from the outside to the inside, from the crusts of dried blood into the tears of flesh. I worked quickly to take advantage of the heat in the water, for when it cooled, it would not clean as before.

The herbs did their work to dull the pain and my fine, deft fingers cleared aside the detritus of the old wound. When it was clean, I took the razor-sharp wound-stone from its pouch. Signaling the lads to hold the old man tight, I slipped it across the ragged skin that bounded the gash, and the infected flesh fell away.

Darmid moaned and tightened his body in pain, but remained as still as he could. He understood the enormity and challenge of what I did. I allowed him to settle, rubbed a pure salve of the bryony and nightshade onto the jagged, dead area, and cut away again. As the outside layer came back, I found the black flesh beneath.

The wound had begun to putrefy. Darmid's life would be forfeit if my ministrations fell short. Why fever had not erupted yet I did not know, but surely, I must try to avert the inevitability. I was glad I had included the herbs to treat fever in his tea right away.

Flushing his ragged injury with the infusion once more, I cut away every bit of the blackened flesh and poured the healing water over it again, until all that was already dead was gone. Darmid moaned, and when the tears of pain ran down his face, they ran down my own and Osheen's as well. This was our beloved *daideo*. Kerr touched our shoulders but did not need to say anything. We nodded and took his heart-comfort in.

When the rotting skin and underlying flesh had been removed and the full wound flushed again, I laid the poultice over the gash, covered it with the wetted cloth and bound it firmly to the wound. After he rested, I slowly massaged his hands and feet to dull the memory of pain. I asked Kerr for the tea, and spooned it into Darmid's mouth.

Just as we had the night before, we took shifts spooning the liquid between his lips every little while. At the moonrise, I removed the poultice, spread the wound thickly with the salve I prepared, laid a cloth upon it and bound it again.

Darmid opened his eyes then.

"Lassie," he whispered, "Yer *granaidh* speaks through ye." He closed his eyes again, and fell into a sleep so deep we covered him thickly and all slept until the morning.

****

I woke early. Darmid still slumbered, so I left him to benefit from my ministrations of the day before. Kerr and Osheen, also exhausted, were burrowed beneath wool and fur. Bairnie was curled up tight next to me, buried under my coverings, but as soon as I moved, he sat up.

I pulled on my heaviest sweater, my skin boots with the felted lining. Signaling Bairnie to follow, I quietly stepped out into the icy morning air. A silvery sheen of mist rose from the thin covering of snow as the morning sun began to touch it. *Ye maam of the moon and sun, of stars beloved. Great Maam ye knowest our need. Maam of life and love be with us through this day, this night. Be with us in all yer healing glory.*

My breath came out in sharp round clouds. I struck out across the dooryard and up the path towards the pasture. A faraway bleat cut through the cold air, bringing a smile to my face. Though the chickens might be dead, and there was little chance that the cow had managed to feed itself without Darmid to do it, at least some of Darmid's flock might yet be salvaged. Bairnie pricked up his ears, then looked at me.

"Go out, lad," I said. He took off like a shot in the direction of the cry.

Leaving him to his work I found the small stock barn of stone. Kneeling sadly at the tangle of fur that had been Crag, I placed my hand upon the still form. When he found him the night we arrived, Kerr brought him here from the high pasture. *To yer sleep, gentle friend, ye have protected us with yer loyalty. Ye have protected us with yer valor. To the Great Maam, valorous friend, go to her gentle breast.*

Crag had been as loyal a dog as any *tuaha* had ever had as a friend. I wanted to make a bonfire, immolate his body, and bring the ashes home to our family tomb. But that couldn't happen now, in our desperate plight. Our first priority was to make Darmid strong enough to bring down off the mountain and as far as Cloch Graig.

I gathered Crag's frozen body in my arms and ducked out of the barn, carrying him around behind it where the winds crossed and deposited a drift of snow in the eddy. I scraped away a square of the stuff, laid Crag's body in it, and covered it again with the snow. This would keep him for the while. We would build a cairn over what was left when we next returned.

Walking to the front of the stock barn again I peered across the white expanse. Bairnie had not returned. He would work silently to round up whatever sheep he had heard across the pastures. I looked out over the high ground, wondering where the bleat had come from, and where the rest of Darmid's flock would hide itself—if there was anything else left of his flock.

Last night we had spoken of our need to take Darmid back to the stone village. If any of Darmid's animals still lived, we could not leave them here. Some might survive the winter in the highlands, for they were a tough, sturdy little breed. But for many generations these little sheep had lived with the *tuaha*, and the loss of the wintering fodders might be devastating to them. The loss of the entire herd would be devastating to our village as well.

Kerr and Osheen had already trekked all the little stone huts that stored food and fodder for the beasts and spread it out across the pastures for whatever livestock might still survive and wander in. I searched for every bit of food stored in every nook and cranny in Darmid's hut, above every rafter in the stock barn and the stone huts for food storage around his dooryard.

We met in the hut for hot tea and to compare our findings.

"One thing is certain," Osheen said, "We cannot surive a winter in the highlands, for Darmid's supplies will support only himself, and altogether we are four."

Kerr turned to me, the question in his eyes. I shook my head.

"Darmid will need long healing and many moontides of care," I said by way of reply to his silent question. "So, were we to stay until Darmid is healed, his winter stores will never last and all of us will starve."

"What if I went back to the stone village for more supplies—" Osheen began, but Kerr cut him off with a shake of his head.

"The heavy snows that start after winter solstice might keep ye from ever returning, friend, sure death for whoever stays on the mountain waiting for ye."

I took one last sip of my fragrant tea and set the cup down.

"The best chance of preserving life of both us and herd will come with bringing all down to the stone village as soon as we can move Darmid." We sat in silence for a few moments then. There was only one path that lay before us. Darmid must be strengthened and a sledge constructed to carry him. Bairnie must bring in any of the flock that remained, and herd them down the mountain.

I left the hut then, and closing my eyes, lifted my arms to the rising sun, surrendering my body to the Great Maam of All. *Each day that we move, each time that we awaken, be with us through these days, be with us through these nights.*

I turned in place, facing the south. *Ye hast raised us freely from the darkness of last night to the kindly light of this day, to the rising of this life itself. With the aiding of yer mercy, cover ye us with the shadow of yer wings.*

I turned again to the west. *Ye Maam of all, bring me this day each thing me eye sees, each sound, each odor, each taste, each ray that guides me way. Ye, that me heart seeks, ye that me living thirsts for.*

I turned then to the north. *Do ye bless me on this day in me wild thought, in me desperate need, in me rough prayer, in me inadequate spell. Ward off from me the bane of faerie as ye did from before the beginning of me life, as ye will after the end of me life.*

As I finished my prayer I faced east again, towards the sun that shone clear and white gold above the horizon now. *Grateful to ye for the gifts upon me each day and night, on sea and land, each weather fair or foul, each calm, each wild. I give ye me thought, me deed, me word, me will, me understanding, me wisdom. I beseech ye to keep us in the gentleness of yer heart, the nearness of yer love, in the specter of yer healing, Great Maam of All, giver of life.*

Lowering my arms I breathed in deeply and opened my eyes into the bright morning light. Far across the high pasture I watched Bairnie break into my range of vision with a clutch of sheep. His silver form darted back and forth behind the small clot of animals, their mottled brown, black and white coats setting them off from the stark white of the snow under them. He drove them expertly across the pasture and down to me.

Moving quickly to the stock barn I opened the gated doorway wide. I sent a piercing whistle out across the last distance and Bairnie's head shot up, eyes burning in my direction. He changed course slightly, easing the sheep off towards his right to drive them to me.

I stood with my hands upon the wood and wicker gate, chirping him in. The final long, low sound told him to tighten his circling so he could drive them hard right into the shelter, stopping just short of going after them himself.

I lifted the long gate and swiftly marched it closed. The beasts stood with their legs spread, panting into the cold air, puffs of breath rising like smoke off a fire. The heavy winter wool hung on them in shaggy coats tinged with ice.

"Good lad, Bairnie." I ruffled the fur on the top of his head. "Come to heel." Bairnie attached himself to my side and we headed back to Darmid's hut. Kerr was stepping out the door as we came across the dooryard. He ducked his head by way of greeting.

"Ronnat, good day." he said.

"And ye, Kerr." I replied.

"What have ye been doing so early?" he asked.

I smiled at him by way of reply as we stepped back inside. Kerr pulled the door closed behind us. Osheen was by the hearth adding turf to it and stirring a slowly bubbling gruel.

"I've been counting sheep," I announced happily. "Five are in the stock barn now."

Osheen tasted the gruel and smacked his lips noisily, as if it was the heartiest mutton stew ever to be had. He made me laugh. My cousin's command of the ridiculous always entertained me. Waggling his eyebrows at me he took a dollop of the gruel and adding more water, handed me the bowl.

"Darmid is awake and hungry, as ye can see for yerself."

I turned, and my eyes widened with pleased surprise. Kerr and Osheen had propped Darmid up in his bed chamber, piling robes behind him and under his leg to ease the swelling.

"*Daideo!*" I crowed. Darmid's wrinkled face, yellowed with the tinge of sickness and great effort, broke into a wan smile.

"Aye, lass," he whispered. "Aye, lass." I carried the bowl of gruel to him and fed him gently while I told him of my morning—the burying of Crag in the snow, the sound of the bleating, the expert work of Bairnie bringing the ewes in.

Darmid nodded his head as I spoke. When I stopped he said softly, "Aye, lassie. He's a fine sheep dog."

I put the bowl of gruel and spoon down and grabbed Darmid's hand. I held it against my cheek, then kissed it as if I would never let it go again.

"Ye frightened me, *Daideo*," I whispered, my voice catching.

"Aye, lass," Darmid replied, "An' I frightened meself." He was silent for a long moment, gathering his breath. "Yer *Granaidh* has done her work well with ye, and I am here still, though." His breathing was labored with the effort of speaking.

"Lads," he continued faintly. Kerr and Osheen bent close to hear him. "Would ye take Bairnie over the pastures today while Ronnat tends her old *daideo*?" Both of them nodded vigorously. "Mayhap," he continued, "There are more ewes wandering that ye can gather." He sank back on the pillowed robes exhausted from the effort he had expended.

Kerr, Osheen and I looked at each other in awe. He was well enough to give direction. There was hope, here.

I continued to spoon feed him the watery gruel and more of the healing tea from the day before. Then I ate my own gruel while he rested, fed Bairnie, and discussed the plan for gathering the flocks and the necessity of going down the mountain with Kerr and Osheen. We were in agreement that we must leave at the very earliest moment we were able to move Darmid without fear for his life.

The two lads bundled warm then and left with Bairnie to gather what ewes they could find. Both had been coming to the shieling since they were infants, and knew the byways they must traverse to seek out all the secret hiding places where the sheep might be.

Rams we would leave upon the mountain, for they had the greatest chance of surviving and they would be too difficult to move. They were dangerous beasts, as Darmid's accident proved. There were rams in the village, anyway, and very few were needed to continue the flock.

After the lads left, Darmid stirred from his nap. I unbound his wound for inspection. The drawing salve was doing its work, pulling the pus out of the wound. No more black flesh was visible, no more blood flowed from it. I gently cleansed it again, but since no more cutting was necessary, I soon had it poulticed and bound.

"Sleep more, *Daideo*," I said to him. "I will leave this on until the sun is over its zenith and coming down. Then it is the salves again." Darmid nodded wearily and closed his eyes once more.

When I was sure he rested comfortably, I added more turf to the fire, cleaned up the morning's meal and ducked out of the hut. I wanted to scavenge wood to make a sledge upon which to haul Darmid. The highland pastures had no forest, so wood was scarce upon them. I circled the outbuildings, and in each looked above into the eaves to see if anything was stored there.

In the stock barn resting upon the rafters above the sheep was a small bundle of cured saplings, each a little less than a hand's breadth in diameter. They had probably been prepared by Darmid in the event of needing new gates. I pulled them down and brought them to the dooryard, where I laid out the shape of a forked sledge upon the ground.

Slipping back inside the hut, I paced out Darmid's height, then went out and adjusted the frame. It would need to be long enough for him to lie full flat out on it. Then, there would have to be enough room at the front for me, or Kerr or Osheen, to harness it to ourselves. We would pull it and also use our bodies to block it, to keep it from racing out of control downhill as we came off the mountain.

We could take shifts hauling. Bairnie would drive the sheep. One of us could carry food for the trip itself, one of us could pull the sledge, and one of us could carry other sundries on his or her back while directing Bairnie and holding the shepherd's crook. At last, I added a bit to the length so that we might tie Darmid's winter food stores onto it, saving much from going to waste.

After binding one end of each side together with its mate, I lashed cross-slats split down from the saplings, each wider than the last by a hand-span, until the back end of the sledge was sufficiently broad to give it stability. Placing the slats at regular intervals, upon them I laced skins with hide strips. As I worked, I stopped and lifted the thing to be sure I kept it as light as possible.

The sun was high in the sky; I went back into the hut to attend to Darmid, easing as much more tea and gruel into him that I could. The poultice was renewed, and then the salves and bindings. At the end of my ministrations Darmid was exhausted and took his refuge in sleep again. I put more peat on the fire and returned to my sledge-making.

When Kerr and Osheen came back from the pastures they reported with glee that they had found fifteen ewes in one place, and eleven in another, bringing the re-collected herd up to thirty-one animals. They discussed their adventures as they made a stew for dinner. I used a bit more of the powdered dried meat to make a broth for Darmid, and Osheen spooned it into his mouth, preserving his strength enough so he might comment on our conversation.

"That is a goodly part of the herd," he said faintly. "More beasts than that ye will have to struggle to get, and perhaps make yourselves more danger than good." We nodded at that wisdom, for indeed, this was a sizeable group of animals to bring down the mountain with one dog, a severely wounded old man, as much of his winter stores as we could manage to haul, and just the three of us.

I changed Darmid's dressings again and fed him a bit of gruel and tea before I banked the fire for the night. He was stronger, but I reminded him to call to me if anything was needed in the night. Osheen and Kerr were already wrapped tightly in their robes upon the floor, taking long regular breaths.

When I pulled my own robes over my head I mumbled the night prayer, exhausted, grateful beyond my wildest hopes. *Great Maam of All, as I put off me clothing, grant me to put off me struggling as easy as the haze rises from off the crest of the mountain. Shield our bodies in yer mantle. Help our hands to issue yer healing. Bless O Great Maam the journey, the way, the hearth we seek. Be thyself our staying.*

The last of the prayer had barely trickled off my lips when I, too, was sound asleep.

****

With the morning's light Darmid was awake and managed to push himself into a sitting position before we young folk stirred. I rose gratefully to my tasks. He was alive, he was getting stronger.

Kerr soon joined me at the hearth, stirring the oats for our breakfast as I made more cleansing herbs and healing tea for Darmid. When Osheen finally pulled himself from beneath his robes and stumbled out the door to relieve himself, Darmid was spooning his own gruel and tipping a mug of the strengthening tea to his lips.

"*Daideo*," I said, "It is time."

The old man took another sip of his tea, and put another spoon of gruel into his mouth. "Tell me, lass, how is it to be done?"

Osheen was back now, and the four of us began to converse

about the sledge, the herd, and our preparations to leave the mountain.

Darmid told us of the wintering supplies that must come with us or be lost, and the ones that might stay upon the mountain until we returned to the shieling in spring. We argued back and forth about whether Darmid should be able to stand before we left—and then decided that his sitting up was the most we could hope for. If we were to wait longer, we might miss our chance to get off the mountain before the big snows came.

We cooked porridge to pack for food along the way. That, along with the dried berries and nuts from Darmid's stores should keep us well-fed for the trip.

The lads and I bound the supplies Darmid suggested we take into bundles as tight and compact as we could, and lashed them to the sledge. It seemed our preparations took far less time than we imagined. The sun was not yet directly overhead when we were ready to leave.

"*Daideo*," I asked, "Is it better to leave today and leave sooner, or leave upon the early morning and walk in the light?" Darmid paused little before agreeing that we should leave as early in the predawn as possible, enabling us to take as much advantage of journeying in the light as we could. By traveling all the day without sleep and far into the night, we would be able to reserve the dark time for when we had already entered the Trabally, a land so familiar to us as to make the struggle easier despite the dead of night and winter.

"Besides," I concluded, "Should we need to, one of us can break off and make time ahead and bring some villagers back to ease our final steps."

It was decided, then. We spent the remains of the day resting and eating and drinking to stoke ourselves for the long haul ahead. I prepared a sleeping tea and we retired as soon as the sun went behind the hill in the afternoon.

In no time, we were up in the pitch dark reciting our journey prayers in earnest. *A rock ye art at sea, a home ye art on land. The Great Maam's shield about us, o'er us, against the screech of vulture, the gnawing of the night creatures, against snow and ice, against fall of foot or twist of ankle or fever of wound, against injury or foul weather, against all these, Great Maam protect us.*

We set out then in silence through the cold windless air. I felt I was still asleep, perhaps dreaming as we trudged, unstoppable, through the dark before dawn. We were silent, and Darmid, though he must be suffering from the movement despite all our attempts to cushion him with wraps and robes and furs, put his face beneath the coverings and went back to sleep.

Kerr took the lead with Bairnie, driving the ewes before us. The dog worked tirelessly, for the creatures were skittish and afraid. They did not make this trip each year as the village beasts did. They only knew that they were being driven, and this made them bleat piteously and attempt to bolt away even in the dark. It was everything Kerr and Bairnie could do to keep them together and prevent them from flinging themselves off steep grades.

Osheen was the first to drag the sledge, for I wanted to walk beside it, studying Darmid and checking him often to see if the strain was too much. I had packed his wound with salve as late as possible the night before, an extra layering of it and a thick, loose binding to keep it in place.

I wanted to make the entire trip without opening his wound to the air, so I need not have a fire nor water to cleanse or re-pack it again. My supplies of salve were running low. I would welcome any measure of speed with which we might attain the Trabally and Cloch Graig.

Often I had to rush to Osheen's side and help him drag the heavy sledge upslope or downslope on slippery ice. Twice we nearly went over, and once Osheen fell and caught his hand beneath the staves, howling in pain. But what better for pain than cold, and we had plenty of that, so we soon picked up and continued our journeying.

As the light came into the new morning, just the same as on our trip up the mountain, our tongues were loosed and our hopes heightened. The coming down was hazardous and hard on our knees and balance, young as we were, but in some sense it still felt easier than the climbing up. We stopped before descending to the oak savannah, and at that, pulled out packages of food and ate our fill.

I hand-fed Darmid again, for we all agreed it was best for him to stay snugly covered, putting as little stress upon his healing as possible. Osheen was exhausted from dragging the sledge, despite the amount of time that I had assisted him. He readily traded with Kerr, and took his post at the front with the sheep and Bairnie.

Kerr was bigger and stronger than Osheen, and did not need my assistance as much as my cousin had. Still, by the time the sun was high overhead, we were a weary crew, and beginning to wonder if the trip would ever end. How were we to know that a bitter end was to threaten our quest as the afternoon light was dying down?

We had just started up after our final resting place before we began the last leg of our journey. We had left the relatively flat expanse of the peat bog, and pulled through the bottomland forest that would bring us to the bluffs overlooking the beach. That bluff would be our last challenge, as the beach beyond it was long, flat, and led straight to the edge of Cloch Graig.

I was at last taking a shift with the herd. Swiftly, our excitement rising as we entered our home territory, we negotiated a wide expanse of switchbacks down the sea-bluff to the strand that would lead home. The flock had lost its skittishness and settled into the long march. Bairnie was weary, yet attentive to my directions and did a fine job of keeping the herd close together and moving forward down the trail. He did not once let them stray over the edge of the steep slopes or go too fast or balk and refuse to budge. That took some doing, as he must leap down and up again to keep the herd together for the descent.

Kerr and Osheen had the sledge. Perhaps it was exhaustion, or just the capricious danger of a trip in winter over snow and hidden ice, or perhaps our eagerness to reach home made us careless. As we came over the crest of the bluff we saw we would have to turn the sledge at a sharp angle to stay on the path. Osheen, the lighter of the two lads, was in the front. Kerr helped steer from behind and dug in his feet to hold the sledge back from picking up speed and careening to the bottom.

As Osheen gave a sharp pull to negotiate the turn, Kerr gave a shove to the back end, pushing it towards the bluff. But the staves of the sledge and Kerr's foot hit a smooth patch of thick ice, somehow untouched by the hooves of the flock that had gone before. Kerr could feel the sledge swing wide, and the enormity of the potential disaster leapt to his mind. He yelled ferociously, "Osheen!" but too late.

Osheen felt the frame of the sledge hit. He began to scream as sledge, harness, Darmid, and he went over the steep embankment at the edge of the first switchback. Kerr grabbed helplessly at the sledge, serving only to change, not stop, its trajectory before it whipped away from his hands altogether. The heavier back end swung around, pivoting from the pointed front, with Osheen dangling helplessly in the harness.

With its front pointed uphill and the heavier back end down, it slid backwards, hitting the path below hard, shaking Osheen and loosing a scream from him so blood-curdling I heard it far up the beach even over the din of the flock I drove. I turned towards the noise in time to see the sledge appearing to go end over end. My heart skipped a beat, and then I bolted back toward the lads.

As the back end of the sledge hit the ground, the front end toppled over to the side. Osheen was slammed to the ground, his leg crushed at a crazy angle beneath him. The path stopped the sledge's fall, and it was still. Osheen lay unconscious.

Kerr, in his efforts to stop the careening vehicle at the top of the switchback had also lost his balance. He tumbled over the edge, mercifully free of the sledge but hollering as he fell over the side, slid across the path, and continued down the second riser until he came to rest on the beach. The wind was knocked out of him. He strained to draw a breath, his urgency to go to Osheen and Darmid not enough to undo the impact of his fall.

I reached Kerr and quickly guessed his relatively harmless condition. "Help me when ye can stand!" I said, and ran up the ramp of the first switchback, where the vehicle, its passengers, and cargo lay.

"*Daideo*! *Daideo*!" I screamed as I came to the sledge. Darmid was shaken, but still bound tightly into his litter, and since the sledge did not turn all the way upside down, he was unhurt.

"Ronnat, help the lad!" his voice came out thin and weak, but firm. I ran to Osheen. His face was white as a cloud, blue tinged his lips.

Panic gripped my arms. Though many years of training by Aefa had bid me meet the disasters of life calmly, the endangered before me now were Osheen, my beloved cousin as close as a brother to me, Darmid, my revered grandfather, and Kerr, for whom I made honey in the heart of me.

I pulled out my knife and began to slit the leather of the harness. Osheen slumped to the side, ashen, still. In a rush of strength I pulled the pointed front of the sledge right up over Osheen's head, and set it down straight on the path, the thing now resting fully in the position in which it was meant to be used.

Quickly I removed one of the coverings from behind Darmid and laid it out upon the ground. I felt Osheen's neck and back—all seemed well. But I thought the leg twisted beneath him must be broken. I supported him under the shoulders and pulled him backwards, and when I laid him down upon the skin robe he cried out in pain even in his unconsciousness. The leg would not straighten. It was bent out at the top of the knee in such a position as might guarantee a deadly break above that joint.

I leaned back upon my heels, breathlessly assessing what I must do next. My medicines were still bound to the sledge. Jumping up, I began to cut them loose with my knife. Taking them in hand, I moved another robe from Darmid and placed it on top of Osheen. He must have warmth, or the life would surely go from him before I could help him.

Kerr rose, finally, and begun to stumble up the hill.

"Go back down, Kerr," I cried. "Whistle for Bairnie. Call him to heel, and then command him to drive the flock back to Cloch Graig! I need ye here, but if he can get the herd to the village, there will be help!"

Kerr stopped his clumsy climb and stumbled out on the beach, leaned over at the waist to draw breath. He rose suddenly, and his piercing shepherd's whistle cut through the cold air. Bairnie, keeping the flock encircled far down the beach as I had directed him to, shot to Kerr. I could hear Kerr talking to the dog, then came his sharp command, "Go out!" His arm swept the horizon, a silhouette against the darkening sky and the cold orange of the winter sunset.

As Bairnie ran for the flock, Kerr's whistle reached my ears. It said, *back to the barn. Drive them home.* Bairnie came abreast of the ewes and began to move them up the beach at a fast clip. It was a straight, wide expanse from here to the beach below the stone village. I had hope that even if he no longer remembered his Cloch Graig home, at least he would be seen and the village alerted to look for us.

When Kerr came to me this time, his breath was fully back in his lungs, though he panted still with the shock of what happened.

"Help me!" I cried, and we pulled the load off the sledge in the dimming light and sorted through it for the items we needed for Osheen. I muttered a prayer to bring the villagers to me, as much for my own morale as my need for assistance.

Ye to me, ye to me, by the water, by the air, by the forest, by the Great Maam who knowest me very heart. I launched those words into a sky made live with orange, blue, and burning gold of sunset, taking no more than the briefest pause to empty my whole being of fear, and call in the Maam to fill its place with my people.

Then I cut away Osheen's leggings and to my surprise found a badly dislocated knee, but no bone break. It was swelling rapidly.

We moved the robe out from under him and piled snow upon his leg on the bare ground. I found the potion Aefa gave me to reserve for the worst of times. I dropped it between Osheen's lips, sending him from the unconsciousness of deep pain into a deep and painless sleep.

"Kerr," I commanded hoarsely, "Take yer axe to the top of the bluff and find two stout sticks."

When he brought these to me it took both of us to steady Osheen. Kerr restrained him tightly while with one sharp pull on his leg, I straightened the dislocation and brought it back into position. Even in his deep stupor Osheen moaned piteously, and his face crumpled with pain.

"Help me bind the two sticks the length of the leg," I instructed Kerr and then we packed it with cold snow again. Under my breath I chanted the healing charm: *Bone to bone, vein to vein, balm to balm, sap to sap, skin to skin, tissue to tissue, blood to blood, flesh to flesh, sinew to sinew, marrow to marrow, pith to pith, fat to fat, to this foot, this knee, this thigh.*

When Osheen began to stir and cry, I gave him more drops of the sleeping draught, praying fervently to bring the villagers to us. Osheen needed to be moved much more carefully than we could do with Darmid in the sledge—and Darmid, unable to stand, must stay in the sledge. I shuddered to think what could have happened if this had occurred farther from Cloch Graig.

Darmid seemed to know what I was thinking, and reached his arm to me as I crouched near him, holding food for him to take.

His big hand rested upon my shoulder.

"Ye have done well, lass," he said gravely, "There should never be question again in yer own mind, or any other, that ye are well suited to the mantle of yer *granaidh*."

"Aye, so, tis truth in that," echoed Kerr. He was sitting by Osheen, grasping his hand in his own, waiting with words of comfort should he stir. "'Tis much we have to thank the Maam for, and yer cousin will be thanking ye most of all, Ronnat."

My wan smile was overshadowed by the dark knit of my brow. I was exhausted by the grueling demands of the last week at the shieling, the physical exertions of our travel, and my new fears for Osheen. I wanted Aefa and the comforts of our chambers in the stone village. I wanted to crawl beneath my wool coverlet and sleep until—maybe forever, if that meant I never had to think about the duties of a Death Crooner again.

But a new feeling stirred in my young heart, too. A feeling that I would get up and do all those things necessary to meet the needs of those around me, not because I was resigned to it, but because I was called to it.

And here were the things that called me to it: the crumpled body of dear Osheen, deeply unconscious beside me; Darmid in his litter, old, wrinkled, but strong in the love he had always shown me and an eddy of swirling comfort to me now, just by his very presence. And finally, Kerr, beautiful of shape and face, gentle of spirit, the strength of a mountain in his arms. He knelt beside me, looking to me with an admiration that made something within me stir and think of homefires.

The shadow left my brow and I smiled gratefully at the world the Great Maam had made for me.

****

The light of the rising sun stole across the white expanses of snow and penetrated the Brú—the womb chamber beneath the sacred hill—where it spilled its bright seed into the inner sanctum. The spirals and lozenges carved upon the stones quivered and undulated with the breath of the Great Maam. I caught my own breath in wonder, as I had first remembered doing when I was barely walking. The Womb Chamber was coming to life with the low, persistent tones of the most sacred wooden flutes.

Our musicians stood at the door of the passageway, extending their long wooden horns into the tunnel to provide the ritual magic of their music to those who consecrated the turning of the light. Underdin was provided by the rumbling of the thunder drums. The pattering of Kerr's smaller drum started soft like raindrops and built into a sharp clatter.

As the sun illuminated the back chamber, marking the much-desired winter solstice, the music swelled to crescendo, and the ululations of the Death Crooner and her people filled the chamber with an intensity that was painful to me, so gripped was I by its fervor. From this day forth, the days would lengthen and the winter nights shorten until spring arrived in full.

Suddenly, all was quiet. The musicians quickly withdrew their instruments, and Aefa, her sons and daughters and grandchildren around her, squatted on the floor, chanting the prayers of the new-found sun. As her apprentice, I started the prayer with a high keening that relinquished itself into words so ancient each generation had to be taught them anew. *Hail to ye as ye traversest the skies above the winging heavens. From darkness to light, sowing yer father's seed in earth's womb. Ye bringest light, ye bringest life.*

As we chanted, we turned slowly until all faced the passageway that led to the outside. In the short time that the sun lit the chamber this year before it lanced skyward, the moon could also be seen, sinking from its journey of the night before to pass beside the sun before it buried itself in the horizon. This was a year of great import, when sun and moon greeted each other between day and night. Our words drew those radiant orbs to one another, stitching the sky back together with our magic. *We lift to ye our hands. We bow to ye our heads. We give ye of our love. We raise to ye our eyes.*

This was an auspicious time for The Calling of the next Death Crooner. Our ritual group crouched, muttering the sacred words of this holy time, undaunted, unstopping, unstoppable for the brief moments that sun and moon would stand together at the mouth of the Great Maam's womb.

I, after all my years of Aefa's tutelage, in the face of the not-knowing of my origins, in gratitude for the lore and craft that had

saved the lives of my *daideo* and cousin, I whose breath caught at
the beauty of a tender lad with curling black hair; I was ready to
accept the call to the Great Maam's work. I called my oath to the
two great circles of light that bounded our lives as they briefly
shimmered next to each other: *I bend to ye me head. I offer to ye
me love. Ye moon of all the ages, sister eyes of the sun in this holy
time. Ye torch of the sky, sister eyes of the moon in this holy time.*

As the two lights passed each other, one disappearing below
the horizon, the other rising out of sight above the passageway,
darkness settled quickly in the chamber. Aefa grasped my hand,
and we stood slowly, carefully, in the dark. The chantings of the
tuaha had receded to a harsh whisper as we all shuffled to face
each other and complete a circle that began with Aefa and ended
with me. As our eyes adjusted to the growing dimness, shapes
appearing even as time melted away.

I stepped out of my robes, letting them fall to the ground,
naked as the moment I came from my own maam's womb, I now
went naked to the Great Maam that I loved. Aefa raised my hand.
*To ye, O Great Maam, I give this child. I bathe her face in the nine
rays of the sun. I wash her brow in the nine lights of the moon. I
steer her boat o'er the nine waves of the sea.*

I closed my eyes and felt the darkness of the chamber, so
recently alive with sun's fire and moon's silver, press in around me
like a soft shawl as Aefa continued her chant. *I bathe her for ye, O
Great Maam. I wash her for ye, O Great Maam. I steer her for ye,
O Great Maam.*

I inhaled slowly. My place in this ritual was as recipient. In
receiving the call of the Great Maam I would reach to the
ancestors—the past—with one hand and with the other, beckon
bairns from the womb, inviting the future.

My senses were open for the entry of the Maam: my ears to
hear the ancient words Aefa cast on my behalf; my eyes to register
the powerful darkness of the womb that gives all life; my skin to
tingle with energy, bathed in the vibrations of the sacred flutes and
drums and invisible chorus of spirals carved upon the stones of the
chamber; my nostrils to flare with the scents of lavender, flea-bane
and maam's-balm that had been strewed deep under the hill here in
anticipation of the rites; my tongue sweetened with the honey and
garlic that was placed there to ready me for my consecration.

I bathe yer palms in showers of sun, in lustral fire, in the seven elements, in the milk of honey. Aefa pressed the lavender oil onto my body and continued to voice the words of the Great Maam to me.

I place the nine waves of the Great Maam upon ye. Darkness flees before ye. Ye are the brown swan, going in among us. Our hearts are under yer control, our tongues are beneath yer foot. A shade are ye in the heat, a shelter are ye in the cold, eyes are ye to the blind, staff are ye to the wanderer, an island are ye at sea, a well are ye to the thirsty, health are ye to the ailing.

She rubbed the oil well into my skin, sprinkling more on me as she massaged it up my arms, across my breasts, down my naked thighs and onto my bare feet before the knee maams raised my robes and wrapped me in them once more.

Thus I was consecrated to my call on the longest night of the year. Time would turn with the fertility of the sun's light in the Maam's great womb, quickening her with the growing life of spring and lead all the world and its *tuaha* once again from winter's deep. A time of feasting would follow, a time of bonfires and cozy hearthfires that would drive the cold winter away. Ritual burning of oak and the strewing of mistletoe and holly would banish the stale airs of homes closed to the cold and kindle the lights of lovers.

On this greatest of nights we marked the sacred turn of sky where daylight would now increase and the dark of night recede as the ever-turning spindle of the year brought us towards the light again. On this, the darkest of nights, the Great Maam became every maam, shielding in her belly the new life to be born at spring.

And I, a lass, stepped to the threshold of her womb, and took her blessing upon me.

From the Saga of the Heroine...

In this auspicious time,
before she found her brother the sea-battler,
before she built her house upon the isle of the Sunt Kelda,
before she came to be known as the Heroine,
before she came to be known as the Red-haired Daughter of the
Sea-farer,
In this auspicious time
the young lass Ronnat Rua, the Dogmaiden, the Tamer of the
Silver Dog,
accepted the call of the Death Crooner into her heart
and as a gift to the tuaha, set herself upon the path
to carry the wisdom of the Great Maam of All
and the bones of their ancestors
for them.

BOBBIE GROTH

GLOSSARY

DEATH CROONER OF THE TRABALLY'S FAMILY

Aefa from the gaelic Aoife (Ee-fah), meaning "beautiful, radiant, joyful" and associated with the greates warrior in the world. Aefa is the Death Crooner of the Trabally.

Darmid from the gaelic Diarmuid, meaning "without enemy" Aefa's lover and father of her children, a shepherd. Aoife and Diarmuid were demigods and great lovers in the ancient tales.

Kriafann from the gaelic "Crimthan" (Kree-ah-fann) "The Fox" Aefa and Darmid's eldest surviving son.

Arda from the gaelic "Ardagh" (Arr-dah) meaning "from the high field". Kriafann's wife.

Ohran from the gaelic Odhran (or-rahn) "dark haired" Kriafann and Arda's eldest son.

Osheen from from the gaelic Oisin (uh-sheen) "little deer;" Kriafann and Arda's younger son; Ronnat's beloved cousin-brother.

Grania from the gaelic Gráinne (Grahn-ya) meaning "sun" or "grain" Aefa and Darmid's elder surviving daughter; Ronnat's breast mother.

Aidan from the gaelic (Ā-den) meaning "little fire" Grania's handfasted lover.

Fia from the gaelic (Fee-ah) meaning "wild" or "weaver" Grania and Aidan's eldest daughter; Ronnat's breast sister.

Bran from Irish gaelic (Brahn) meaning "raven" lives in the next village, Fia's handfasted lover.

Bradan from the gaelic (Bray-din) "a salmon" Grania and Aidan's eldest son.

Dahi from the gaelic Daithi (dah-hee) "swift and nimble;" (Dah-hee) Grania and Aidan's second son.

Kira (Kee-ruh) from the gaelic "Ciar" meaning "dark" twin sister of Maev; Grania and Aidan's daughter.

Maev from the gaelic Maeve or Madb (Mave) meaning "she who intoxicates." One of Grania and Aidan's girl twins.

Dag from the ancient (Dahg) "good" Grania and Aidan's youngest son.

Ayveen from the gaelic Aoibhinn (Ā-veen) "beautiful" Aefa and Darmid's youngest daughter, Ronnat's mother.

Ronnat from the gaelic Rőnnat (row-not) "little seal" protagonist, and next Death Crooner of the Trabally.

Kerr from the gaelic "Ceri" from "ceru" "to love," Ronnat's love interest, Bran's brother, a resident of the next village.

THE MONTHS OF THE OLD LUNAR CALENDS

1. Hunger Moon: winter month of the old 13-month lunar calendar corresponding roughly to late mid-December through late January.

2. Snow Moon: winter month of the old 13-month lunar calendar corresponding roughly to late January through late February.

3. Sap Moon: very early spring month of the old 13-month lunar calendar corresponding roughly to late February through late March.

4. Rain Moon: spring month of the old 13-month lunar calendar corresponding roughly to late March through late April.

5. Blossom Moon: spring month of the old 13-month lunar calendar corresponding roughly to late April through late May.

6. Berry Moon: early summer month of the old 13-month lunar calendar corresponding roughly to late May through late June.

7. Antler Moon: summer month of the old 13-month lunar calendar corresponding roughly to late June through late July.

8. Salmon Moon: summer month of the old 13-month lunar calendar corresponding roughly to late July through late August.

9.Harvest Moon: late summer month of the old 13-month lunar calendar corresponding roughly to mid-August through mid-September.

10. Hunt Moon: autumn month of the old 13-month lunar calendar corresponding roughly to mid-September to mid-October.

11. Wither Moon: autumn month of the old 13-month lunar calendar corresponding roughly to mid-October through early-mid November. Samhain, the New Year, occurs in the Wither moon, so the Wither Moon is the last month of the "old" year.

12. Death Moon: Early winter month of the old 13-month lunar calendar corresponding roughly to mid-November through mid-December.

13. Cold Moon: Winter month of the old 13-month lunar calendar corresponding roughly to late November through late December.

GENERAL GLOSSARY OF WORDS AND CONCEPTS

Ancient New Year: The new year of the old calends, called "Samhain" or "Sauin" or (now Halloween) consists of 3 days in all (think of the current celebration of Halloween and Dia de los Muertos and All Saints Day). The first day of the celebration is the last day of the old year, called Shogh ta'n Oie (show-tan-Oh-ah), meaning "This is the Night" similar to Hop-tu-Naa a festival from the Isle of Man which is the celebration of the original New Year's Eve (Oie Houney), which, on the Christian calendar is October 31. 'Hop-tu-naa' is believed by some to have evolved from the Manx "Shogh ta'n Oie", which means "this is the night," a phrase chanted repeatedly to honor the night. The second day of the festival is called Amach Lá D'am (Aw-mach Law Dam) which means "The Day Out of Time." In the early calendar, each year had an "extra" day that would be added to the total of the 27 days of each month of the 13-month moon calendar, to make it coincide with the 365 day sun calendar. Traditionally on this day the stock were butchered and preserved for the winter. The third day of the festival was called Lá Na Marbh Gheimhridh, (Luh Nuh Marv Ye-vree) "The Day of the Winter Dead", when the dead time before winter was honored for its immense power to generate the coming life of spring. Traditionally, which is still practiced in the Celtic cultures of Spain and their diaspora in North and South America, the tombs of loved ones were visited all day and night, offering food and blessings and prayers, and talking to the dead.

Bairn: or Bairnie from the gaelic for "baby".

Bri: Brigh (bĭree') pre-Celtic goddess of generative power and childbirth who became Bride to the Celts and St. Bridgit to the Christians; daughter of the Great Maam, and also the Great Maam herself.

Brits: "the freckled ones" ancient name for a common appearance of the people who later became Britons.

Calanas: (cah-lah-nahs) the whole process of procuring and processing wool to the finished product, yarn.

Calends: "calendars;" a circle of thirteen upright stones is a moon calendar; a circle of twelve upright stones is a sun calendar.

Clochbeg: "small stone" Bran and Kerr's stone village.

Cloch Graig: (kluhk-grehg) "stone village" Ronnat and Aefa's stone village.

Creel: a basket designed to serve as an evaporative cooler when lined with mosses.

Da: (dah) informal address to father, "daddy".

Daideo: (dye-dee-oh) fond name for grandfather; "grampy".

Equinox: An equinox occurs twice a year, around March 20th and September 22nd in the modern calendar. The equinox occurs when daytime and nighttime are the same length in the movement of the earth through the solar year, whether moving towards winter or summer.

Frithing: divination, prophesy.

Granaidh: (gry-knee) affectionate term for grandmother, i.e., "granny"

Knee-women: midwives, the women who assist birth, catch the baby and bless it.

Láir Bhán: (lah-er vahn) "white mare;" the induction ceremony for a secret society of horseme.

Maam: (mahm) ancient cognate for "mother", the "Great Maam" is the goddess of Ronnat's people.

Manannán: ancient sea God whose celebrations have been absorbed by Michaelmas when the Christians took over the British isles.

Mea'n fo'mhair: (min-fah-vehr) old Mabon, the autumnal equinox, when the Greenman of the Forest was celebrated.

Nalbinding: (nahl-bine-ding) an ancient one-needle knitting technique similar to crochet.

Oimelc: (EE-mulk) also Imbolc: celebration of birth of new lambs and coming in of ewe's milk. Later Christianized as Candlemas.

Rolag: (row-lahg) long whorl of cleaned fleece from which spinning is done.

Rooing: the plucking of wool from ancient sheep, whose fleece drops itself one or twice a year, without shearing.

Runing: (roon-ing) a chanting song style.

Sauin: Samhain: (saw-in) the new year in the 13-month lunar calendar; harvest of the meat, celebration of the dead; Halloween and Day of the Dead are modern remnants of this event.

Second Sight: the ability to see beyond the veil into the next world; prophesy. Ronnat is a member of the SEER clan, (clann an fhrìtheir) (klan an fri-hair) "the children of the seer;" the traditional prophetic families with the Second Sight.

Shieling: summer pastures and the temporary living shelters in the uplands.

Si: sidhe (shee) the faeries. Faeries in the tales of this part of the world are not little tiny things, but often the size of full human beings, capable of great support, or evil.

Skein: (skayn) spun yarn wound upon a niddynoddy to desired length then pulled off and knotted loosely to prevent tangling, prior to winding into a ball.

Skelligs: sea rocks; particularly stark pointed rocky islands where seabirds nest.

Solstice: the point in the solar year when the sun is present most or least. The winter solstice marks the shortest day and longest night; the summer solstice marks the longest day and shortest night.

Tonntabán: (tawn-tah-bahn) means "whitecap" or "white wave;" Bairnie's mother.

Trabally: from the gaelic Trabaile (Truh-balley) meaning a village located on the beach.

Tuaha: from the gaelic tuatha (TOO-uh-huh) meaning "the folk" or "the people."

Waulking: (waw-king) a process of beating hand-woven cloth to even out the tension and tighten up a home-weave, accompanied by an ancient singing tradition that makes the work less tedious.

ABOUT THE AUTHOR

Bobbie Groth has had a life-long devotion to the study of history, archeology, ancient art, folklore, and religion, which included a year at Oxford University, trips to Ireland, Scotland, Greece, and Rome, among other countries, and some on-site archeological experiences. As ordained clergy she made a professional life providing spiritual care, guidance, and education to persons recovering from violence. Now she divides her time between writing, her dogs, and playing traditional Celtic music.